# Christian JACQ
## the son of enlightenment

**SIMON & SCHUSTER**

London · New York · Sydney · Toronto

A CBS COMPANY

First published in France by XO Editions under the title
*Le Fils de la Lumière*, 2006
First published in Great Britain by Simon & Schuster UK Ltd, 2010
A CBS Company

This paperback edition first published, 2011

1 3 5 7 9 10 8 6 4 2

Simon & Schuster UK Ltd
1st Floor
222 Gray's Inn Road
London WC1X 8HB

www.simonandschuster.co.uk

Simon & Schuster Australia
Sydney

A CIP catalogue record for this book is available
from the British Library

ISBN: 978-1-41652-662-9

Typeset by Hewer Text UK Ltd, Edinburgh
Printed and bound by CPI Group (UK) Ltd, Croydon, CR0 4YY

# To the Ferryman

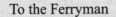

In order to create, one must continue to be inspired.
*Mozart*


The initiate is dressed in radiant garments. All that was disordered within him becomes ordered.
*Denys the Areopagite*

# 1

*Salzburg, 16 January 1779*

Miss Pimperl, the fox-terrier bitch, bounded towards the door of the Mozart family's large apartment and started barking in a way Leopold had never heard before.

A carriage had just halted outside the fine middle-class residence where the family of musicians had been living since 1773.

'Wolfgang is back!' shouted his sister Nannerl, an austere young woman of twenty-seven who was devoted to her father.

Leopold opened the door. Miss Pimperl hurtled down the staircase and ran to meet Wolfgang Mozart, a small man with light-coloured hair and lively, slightly protruding eyes.

She licked his cheeks for ages, delighted to be once more with her favourite, who had been away so long.

A few hundred caresses later, the young musician was finally able to embrace his father and his sister, who were on the verge of tears.

For Wolfgang, who was soon to celebrate his twenty-third birthday, this return to the loathed city of his birth signified failure and imprisonment. His father had demanded that he spend time in Paris, which had turned out to be as hateful as Salzburg and much dirtier. The whole experience had brought him bitter disillusionment, exacerbated by two unhappy events: the death of his mother, who had been buried far from home, and the loss of his first great love, the singer Aloysia Weber, whom he had hoped to marry. Using his over-long exile as an excuse, she had dismissed him from her life in a humiliating way.

Now he was back where he'd started, once again a servant under the thumb of the Prince-Archbishop of Salzburg, Count Hieronymus Colloredo, a heartless tyrant whom he called 'the Grand Mufti'.

Was Wolfgang now reduced to being a second-rate manufacturer of light music, designed to amuse His Eminence and high society?

No, for his journeys and ordeals had matured him. He still had entire confidence in his own creative abilities, after so many hours spent mastering every style and, as he put it, 'stuffing himself with music'. Although battered and bruised, he would not surrender and he was determined to prove his valour.

And then there was his clever, cheeky little cousin, die Bäsle, who would bring some gaiety to the Mozart residence, where Anna Maria's absence weighed so heavily. A great lover of rude word games and scatological jokes, like Anna Maria and Wolfgang, she had accompanied him during the last part of his journey and planned to dispel the sadness which inevitably surrounded this reunion.

'Come along, let's have a shit and then something to eat and drink,' she proposed. 'And then we'll start all over again! What has your cook Theresel prepared for us?'

'A capon, one of my son's favourite dishes,' replied the master of the house.

Miss Pimperl licked her lips at the prospect.

'I have had an old harpsichord and a brand-new wardrobe taken up to your room,' Leopold informed his son. 'You will feel at home there, I hope, and you can work at your ease. First thing tomorrow, the prince-archbishop will officially appoint you organist to the court and cathedral of Salzburg, with an annual salary of four hundred and fifty florins.'*

'And the servant's livery . . .'

'It is the rule, my son.'

'I'm thirsty,' die Bäsle reminded them, determined to avoid boring subjects. 'Would you like me to describe that fat man in Augsburg who farted like an elephant after he'd had too much cold meat?'

Even straight-laced Nannerl could not suppress a half-smile.

As they shared the capon and a full-bodied red wine, they all enjoyed the warmth of a united family, facing the future together. Thanks to father and son's salaries

---

* One florin = a little less than twenty euros.

and the fees brought in by Nannerl's piano teaching, the Mozart family would lack for nothing.

Wolfgang must simply forget his dreams of glory and fall at the feet of the Grand Mufti, without a word of protest.

Despite his cheerful appearance, Wolfgang's thoughts were wandering. He thought about his strange protector, Thamos the Egyptian, who had promised not to abandon him, and about his plan to compose an opera devoted to the mysteries of the sun-priests. But he lacked solid information, and he was not going to obtain it in Salzburg. And yet, he wished to see through the darkness and gaze upon the Light he had briefly glimpsed with Doctor Mesmer, the high priest of magnetism, or Baron Otto von Gemmingen, the author of *Semiramis*, a drama about initiation which had been stillborn because of the war of succession which had broken out over the throne of Bavaria.

Through *Thamos, King of Egypt*, a work dealing with the brotherhood of initiates, Wolfgang had come close to the great secret. And he would never give up his quest to discover it.


*Salzburg, 27 January 1779*

On the 20th, Wolfgang had finished a sonata for piano and violin,* in order to celebrate the family reunion

---

*K378. K is the abbreviation of Köchel. The knight Ludwig von Köchel (1800–1877) was the first to attempt to draw up a chronological catalogue of Mozart's works. The first edition appeared in 1862. Musicological research has made it possible to correct several errors, without which we can precisely date all of the known compositions.

with music. The sweet, nostalgic andantino, a modest evocation of recent sufferings, was followed by a finale filled with good humour. And five days later, he and his sister Nannerl played a dazzling concerto for two pianos,* whose third movement, which was extraordinarily dynamic, touched upon tragedy without becoming maudlin. While preparing a series of eight minuets for piano with trios,† the young man joyfully celebrated his twenty-third birthday in the company of his father, his sister, his little cousin and his Salzburg friends, among them Anton Stadler, who possessed an innate sense of celebration.

'What about girls?' he whispered into Wolfgang's ear. 'Surely you're not going to be content with that naughty little girl die Bäsle?'

'All we do is joke.'

'Well, that's not enough!'

'I was very much in love, Anton.'

'And don't I know it! What was her name?'

'Aloysia Weber, a wonderful singer who will make a fine career for herself. Her voice is capable of expressing every kind of feeling.'

'Her voice, her voice . . . What about the rest?'

'She's a very beautiful young woman, serious and determined.'

'So why did you abandon her?'

---

* K365, a work which Mozart himself did not consider negligible.
† K315a.

'On my return from Paris, I determined to ask for her hand in marriage. She rejected me.'

'What an idiot! She doesn't know what she's lost.'

'Don't talk about Aloysia like that. A woman must retain freedom of choice, even if that choice profoundly wounded me.'

'In other words, you are still in love! You must lay siege to the fortress again!'

'No, her decision is final. Doubtless she loves another man.'

'Too bad for her! Salzburg has no shortage of pretty girls. I shall introduce you to a few young persons who are most agreeable and not at all shy.'

'That is not what I want, Anton.'

'Come, Wolfgang, come! Surely you are not planning to spend your days composing religious music and entertainments for Colloredo?'

'I shall have to do exactly that.'

'Salzburg must not become a prison! Fulfil your obligations, and then enjoy yourself.'

'Aren't you thinking of marrying, Anton?'

'There's no hurry, I still lack experience. What if I marry the wrong girl and miss out on the right one?'

Die Bäsle raised her glass in honour of her cousin, and the assembled guests wished him a very happy birthday.

# 2

Before the destruction of his monastery by the Muslims, Abbot Hermes, heir to the tradition of initiation, entrusted his disciple Thamos with the task of preserving that tradition. He was to do so by passing it on to the Great Magician, who had been born somewhere in the West.

With death in his soul, Thamos had left his country to seek out this exceptional person and to prepare an environment favourable for his initiation into the Great Mysteries which he, in his turn, would pass on.

Wolfgang Mozart was the Great Magician, and Freemasonry was the sole framework capable of raising him up towards the Light.

And yet Thamos the Egyptian, who had become Count

* Tallinn (Baltic states).

7

of Thebes and produced the necessary wealth through alchemy, was experiencing doubt.

Mozart was also a young man of twenty-three, whose genius was still locked away beneath an outer shell of feelings, ambitions and disappointments. Would his purity, his willpower and his desire for knowledge be sufficient to shatter it?

As for Freemasonry, which was divided into several branches more or less hostile to each other, could it really succeed in overcoming the conventions, folklore and vanities of its leaders in order to form a true receptacle for initiation?

Thamos had several options under consideration and was travelling all over Europe, in search of Brothers or lodges worthy of training the Great Magician.

At Reval, near the Baltic Sea, the Egyptian attended the creation of the Isis Lodge, under the aegis of a curious thirty-six-year-old, Count Alexander de Cagliostro, the pseudonym of Joseph Balsamo. Initiated in London in 1777 in a lodge comprising cobblers, stone-cutters and wig-makers, he had stated that 'all light came from the East and all initiation from Egypt'.

Carrying on the teachings of the alchemist Paracelsus, Cagliostro claimed to know the secrets of herbs, stones and magic words, and to possess an elixir of good health.

The man had a certain presence. At the sight of Thamos, he tensed.

'Whence do you come, my Brother?'

'From the monastery of Abbot Hermes.'

'Where is that?'

'In southern Egypt. Today, it lies in ruins, but its radiance endures.'

'I am a nobleman and a traveller. When I act, peace returns to hearts, health to bodies, and hope and courage to souls. All men are my brothers; all countries are dear to me. I travel through them so that, everywhere, the Spirit may descend and find its way to us.'

'Forgive this impudence, but how did you receive initiation?'

'Like Moses, I had the grace to be admitted before the Eternal One. Unable to keep this treasure to myself, I decided to share it. Today, my country is the one where, at a given moment, I walk. In reality, I am from no time or place. My spiritual being lives its own eternal existence, outside time and space.'

'What are your plans?'

'To put into practice a new Rite, which all Freemasons who seek truth will follow. I must leave; other towns await me.'

Thamos remained doubtful. The man's extravagance and his outrageous remarks seemed characteristic of a charlatan, unless Cagliostro was using them to hide an authentic search.

His actions would provide the answer.

# Christian Jacq

*Salzburg, April 1779*

As he composed a Mass for the coronation of the Virgin*
of the church of Maria-Plain, Wolfgang turned once
again towards the figure of Our Lady and asked her to
help him one day to escape from his Salzburg prison.
The work was a powerful one, giving an important
place to the orchestra, and it was played at Salzburg
Cathedral, where it did not attract criticism from the
prince-archbishop.

As for Thamos, he was struck by the beginning of the
soprano solo in the *Agnus Dei*. It heralded a future vision
which the Great Magician would bring to perfection.†

The Virgin was not indifferent to the musician's
prayer, for she granted him a period of equilibrium,
vitality and pleasure in living, as testified by his *Sunday
Vespers*,‡ written in the tonic key of C major.

This return to religious works did not meet with much
enthusiasm from Anton Stadler, who preferred the vigour
of an Overture in G major§ intended for an *opera buffa*
performed by a visiting troupe. Despite his efforts, he
could not persuade his friend to behave like a young man
of his age and forget for a while this music to which he
devoted every second of his life. Even while they were

---

\* K317, *Coronation Mass*.
† I.e. the aria *'Dove sono'* sung by the countess in the *Marriage of Figaro*, whose sacred character is undeniable.
‡ K321.
§ K318.

10

playing skittles or darts, Wolfgang was present only in appearance, for his thoughts were wandering elsewhere, in search of a new idea.

Leopold's fears were dispelled. At the end of the day, his son was readapting extremely well to life in Salzburg and behaving like a good servant of the prince-archbishop. Matured by his ordeals, Wolfgang had accepted his fate which, after all, was hardly unbearable.

*Brunswick, May 1779*

'My Brother,' said Charles of Hesse to the Grand Master of Strict Templar Observance, 'I have an extraordinary guest at the castle of Göttorp! His name is the Count of Saint-Germain, and he claims to be several hundred years old, and to have never known death because of an alchemical elixir which he alone can manufacture. So I have opened the doors of my laboratory to him. Where previous experimenters have failed; perhaps this fellow will succeed.'

'Let us hope so,' replied Ferdinand of Brunswick, leader of the Templar Order, who was still dreaming of bringing together as many Freemasons as possible, but suffering many spiritual and material difficulties. 'Charles, do you believe in the esoteric message of John the Evangelist?'

'Of course!' exclaimed Hesse, assistant to the Grand Master of Strict Observance.

'Do you also believe in the importance of the Jewish Kabbalah?'

'Who could doubt it?'

'And yet, Christians and Jews remain separated, and Jews are not admitted into our lodges.'

'A regrettable error!'

'Perhaps we can correct it. Two exceptional men are asking to talk to us about a remarkable plan.'

# 3

Josef Anton, Count of Pergen, was a faithful servant of Empress Maria Theresa, sworn enemy of Freemasonry. At her command, he had created a secret service fighting against this tentacled beast, which he regarded as attacking the fundamentals of society, morality and religion, as well as having as its undeclared aim the conquest of power.

Anton had to be extremely careful, for he acted without reference to the Minister of the Interior. A man wedded to his files, the count had followed every stage in the evolution of the Orders and lodges, thanks to a network of informants supervised by his right-hand man, Geytrand, a former Freemason. After betraying his oath and his Brothers because he had not been promoted swiftly enough, Geytrand now dreamt only of destroying them.

Josef Anton detested the summer, light and warmth. He closed the shutters on his office windows, drew the curtains and worked day and night by lamplight.

Geytrand was pouring with sweat, and had swollen ankles. He, too, hated this time of year and could not wait for the cold weather to return.

'Herr Count, I am quite certain that the Duke of Brunswick, Grand Master of Strict Templar Observance, and his assistant Charles of Hesse are leading a new offensive.'

'Against the Duke of Sudermania, the Swede who has seized control of the seventh province of this Masonic Order?'

'No, hostilities seem to have ended. This concerns a new Masonic Order, the Brothers of Asia, whose subversive nature seems undeniable to me.'

'Who is in charge?'

'Two of Brunswick's protégés.'

'Who are therefore untouchable,' lamented Josef Anton, who had already experienced one uncomfortable failure by directly attacking highly placed Freemasons.

Among their ranks were many nobles and eminent citizens, capable of destroying him by demanding that his investigations cease. True, Maria Theresa was protecting him, but would the real master of the empire, Josef II, prove equally hostile to Freemasonry?

'One of the founders of the Initiated Brothers of Asia,*

---

\* Von Ecker-und-Eckoffen, dismissed from the Order of the Rose-Cross for insubordination.

an adviser to the King of Poland, is very attached to John the Evangelist. The other will surprise you. His name is Hirschfeld.'

'A Jew?'

'A specialist in the Talmud and in an enormous esoteric work, the *Zohar* or *Book of Splendour*, which reveals the secrets of the Jewish Kabbalah.'

'Reliable information?'

'Very reliable, Herr Count.'

'What are your sources?'

Geytrand would have preferred not to mention them, but could not avoid doing so.

'One of the Duke of Brunswick's man-servants, who is particularly gifted in the art of listening at doors and excessively well paid, and one of the Brothers of this new Masonic Order. He does not look favourably upon its true goal: the reconciliation of Jews and Christians within the same religion.'

'What madness! These Freemasons are even more pernicious than I thought.'

'A lodge of the Brothers of Asia will probably be created in Vienna.'

'All its members must be placed on file and watched. We shall not let them destroy our society, my dear Geytrand.'

*Salzburg, 3 August 1779*

The peaceful symphony in B flat major,* with its reduced orchestra, had reassured Leopold. No tension, nothing dramatic, a pleasant fluidity. On the other hand, a new serenade† surprised him, because of several unexpected, even shocking details.

A little too solemn, the work opened on a slow movement and included an andantino in D minor, which was sombre and full of pathos, never before heard in such a context. As for the other surprise, right in the middle of the second trio a posthorn played the fanfare heard on mail coaches!

'Why these flights of fancy?' Leopold asked his son.

'Because I aspire to take one of those coaches and leave Salzburg. My first movement rejects Colloredo's yoke, and I depict him as he is while, during the allegro, I declare my will to fight.'

'My son, do not confide that to anyone but me! If the prince-archbishop realized . . .'

The situation scarcely improved with the divertimento‡ written for a wealthy middle-class woman in Salzburg, Frau Robinig, a friend of the Mozart family. Into the andante with variations, Wolfgang slipped grating, almost aggressive passages, by way of a rebellion against this facile genre which he could no longer bear.

---

*K319.
† *Posthorn-Serenade* in D major, K320.
‡ Divertimento *Robinig*, K334.

'I do not like that woman, neither do I like this music,' he said to his father. 'While I continue to be locked away in Salzburg, I shall compose it no longer.'

Thanks to its charm, Frau Robinig was pleased with the little work.

*Vienna, 10 August 1779*

In a discreet apartment in the suburbs of Vienna, unknown to the police, Thamos, Count of Thebes, received two notable visitors.

The first was a thirty-seven-year-old mineralogist who worked at Vienna University, Ignaz von Born, a man with a long face, a wide forehead and dark eyes. He was also an alchemist and Freemason, on whom Thamos was relying to inspire one or several lodges with a true spirit of initiation according to the tradition which the Egyptian was revealing to him little by little.

His second guest was Baron Gottfried van Swieten. Aged forty-six, born in Holland and the son of Empress Maria Theresa's personal physician, this brilliant diplomat had held posts in Paris and London, and then in Berlin. In 1777 he had been appointed director of the Imperial and Royal Library, where he occupied an official apartment.

A sworn enemy of Freemasonry, he was playing a dangerous game. Initiated in Berlin, he avoided frequenting Viennese lodges in order to keep the ear of the powers that be and warn his Brothers in the event of serious threats. A supporter of the reforms advocated by Josef II, he hoped that the regime would become more liberal.

Between Ignaz von Born, who was austere, deep and silent, and Gottfried van Swieten, a talkative man who enjoyed high living, the current of brotherhood flowed with difficulty. However, Thamos was anxious to link them together in order for them to build the temple and each take part, according to his particular genius, in the Great Magician's initiation.

Von Born knew everything about van Swieten, and vice versa. The three men shared one major preoccupation: was there a mastermind lurking somewhere in Vienna, charged with the task of hunting down Freemasons?

'I have not obtained any reliable information,' declared von Born. 'All the lodges in Vienna are more or less closely watched, but nobody has heard that anyone is directing the surveillance, other than the Minister of the Interior.'

'I had occasion to meet the chief of police,' said Gottfried van Swieten, 'and we shared our mutual dislike of Freemasonry. According to him, Empress Maria Theresa herself is dealing with this matter. Has she delegated it to a man she trusts, and if so, how are we to identify him? Asking too many questions would arouse suspicion.'

'Do not take any risks, Baron.'

'And what about you, Thamos? How do you escape the empress's police?'

'I travel a great deal and have a variety of residences. As soon as a Masonic movement appears which might be useful to initiation, I owe it to myself to gauge its importance. Despite the difficulties we are coming up against, we must continue to build the temple right here, in Vienna.'

'When will the Great Magician cross its threshold?' asked the mineralogist.

'Neither the man nor the musician is yet ready,' answered the Egyptian. 'There is still a great deal of work for him – and for us – to do.'

# 4

Treatises on mathematics, comedies, tragedies, novels ancient and modern, poetry . . . Wolfgang read a great deal and very swiftly, not to mention his regular visits to the Salzburg theatre, where travelling players acted out a great variety of plays, notably those of William Shakespeare, which the musician liked very much.

As he was watching a performance of *Hamlet*, Thamos sat down beside him.

'The actors are not too good,' whispered Wolfgang, 'but the text is gripping. For a few hours, I escape from Salzburg!'

'I should like to introduce you to Böhm, the troupe's manager. He has a surprise for you.'

Intrigued, the young man accompanied the Egyptian to the manager's office, where he was warmly greeted.

'Ah, Herr Mozart, what a pleasure to meet you! One of

my friends, Baron Tobias von Gebler, has told me about a drama which no longer interests him, *Thamos, King of Egypt*. He gives you complete freedom to develop it and set it to music. For my part, I should like to stage this play. Are you interested?'

'I shall set to work immediately.'

Contacted by his Brother Thamos, who had seen von Gebler again and persuaded him, the Freemason Böhm was delighted to include a German musical drama in his repertoire.

As for Wolfgang, he felt driven by a formidable energy and saw the possibility of bringing his great project to fruition. As an overture to the work, he would use his symphony in E flat major*. Then he would rework the orchestration, reorganize the choruses he had already written and add at least one new one, in place of the instrumental finale, in order to give the work more amplitude and majesty.

'Shall we study the libretto together?' asked Thamos.

'Whenever you choose.'

*Thamos, King of Egypt: Act One*

From the library at his private town house, Thamos took a novel by Abbot Jean Terrasson, entitled *Sethos*. Wolfgang devoured it in a night and in doing so experienced the atmosphere of ancient Egypt.

---

* K184 (No. 26), dating from 1773.

Then, along with his mentor, he journeyed to the holy city of Heliopolis, where the priests and priestesses of the sun officiated. The High Priest, Sethos, was preparing to crown young Thamos as pharaoh.

'That name is yours, too,' said Wolfgang. 'What does it signify?'

'Thamos is a transposition of Tuthmosis, "He who is born of Thoth", the god of sages and scribes. He wrote a book revealing the lore of initiation, whose last custodian was the head of my monastery, Abbot Hermes.'

'Did he pass it on to you?'

'If the cycle of transmission had been interrupted, would the sun still rise? Let us return to your work, in which the number Three must feature in several different forms.'

'For what reason?'

'Oneness, the number of God, is incomprehensible to us. At the birth of duality, which is both marriage and separation, creation develops. The first perceptible form is the triangle formed by the great goddess Isis, her husband Osiris and their son Horus. When a creator acts according to the rule of Three, assimilating it into the very heart of his thoughts, he carries on the primordial work.'

'Three flats, three chords, progressive thirds, vocal trios . . . There are ten ways I can make this number live!'

'On no account must you use either convention or artifice.'

'Sometimes, it is not I who creates the music, but the music that creates me. When that happens, the tide flows and nothing can stop it.'

'May the gods guide you towards the light, Wolfgang!'

'The light of Heliopolis?'

'The sacred city is in grave danger because of a revolution fomented by cruel Ramses. He has dethroned the wise Pharaoh Menes, whom everyone believes is dead. In reality, he is hiding behind the name of Sethos, the High Priest, and he must crown Thamos, the son of Ramses.

'That young man is pure, upstanding and generous, the exact opposite of his ignoble father! He wishes to marry a wonderful young woman, Saïs, who is in love with him. Now, Saïs is not whom people think she is, either! During the revolution, according to the official version, Tharsis, the daughter of Pharaoh Menes, perished in the flames. In reality, she survived and took the name Saïs, unknown to her father.

'Missing wise Menes, the people begin to grumble against the tyranny and do not endorse Thamos's coronation. If beautiful Tharsis were still alive, she would become queen. The situation seems even further compromised because Mirza, High Priestess of the temple, is revealed to be perverse and malevolent. Finding out Saïs's real identity, she confides this secret to the unworthy Pheron, a traitor who pretends to be Thamos's best friend while engineering his downfall. Mirza wants at all costs to prevent the marriage of Thamos and Saïs, who would form a royal couple wedded to justice, and she devises a terrible plan: to throw Saïs into the arms of the traitor, so that he may be crowned in Thamos's place.'

*Thamos, King of Egypt: Act Two*

Wolfgang explored the gallery of the residence set aside for the virgins of the sun. There, he gazed upon wondrous Saïs and experienced the profound love Thamos felt for her. The young woman's feelings were just as intense, but she wanted to devote herself to initiation, to the cult of the Light and the practice of the Mysteries.

'This way of thinking serves the designs of High Priestess Mirza,' observed the Egyptian. 'If she remains with her Sisters, Saïs will not meet Thamos and the marriage will not take place.'

'Mirza dares to tell Thamos that Saïs loves the traitor Pheron!' exclaimed Wolfgang indignantly. 'In despair, the prince displays rare nobility by agreeing to give up the woman he so wanted to marry. It is Saïs's prerogative – as it is every woman's – to choose her own destiny.'

'Despite his pain, Thamos even agrees to consecrate this union,' said the Egyptian. 'All that matters is his beloved's happiness.'

# The Son of Enlightenment

*Thamos, King of Egypt: Act Three*

Wolfgang entered the temple of the sun-worshippers, where the traitor Pheron had sullied his promise, daring to swear on the gods, before his 'great friend' Thamos, that he would for ever be faithful to him.

'Traitors, liars and perjurers always end up making a fatal mistake,' said the Egyptian. 'Pheron's consists of boasting about his success to the High Priest Sethos, unaware of his true identity. In this way, he informs Menes that his daughter Tharsis, whom he believed had perished in the flames, is very much alive and now bears the name of Saïs. "And at my own coronation," adds Pheron, already imagining himself as Pharaoh, "I shall reveal the truth."

'High Priestess Mirza announces to Saïs that she will soon reign. The young woman refrains from expressing her opinion until the right moment: power has little attraction for her. But the traitor Pheron won't hear of it. If, by chance, Saïs refuses to marry him, he will seize the throne by force.'

'Will violence triumph again?'

'Saïs calls upon the soul of her father, whom she believes dead, to guide her. Having spoken her prayer, she decides not to reign in place of Thamos and to remain in the temple with her Sisters.'

*Thamos, King of Egypt: Act Four*

'Thamos has heard the young woman's deliberations. Immediately, he reveals his love to her. Overwhelmed, Saïs explains to him that Mirza the High Priestess is attempting to drive them apart.'

'The time of revelations continues,' said Wolfgang. 'The High Priest Sethos, alias Menes, informs Thamos that Saïs is his daughter!'

'The forces of darkness have not given up. Mirza and Pheron plan to murder Thamos during the ceremony.'

*Thamos, King of Egypt: Act Five*

The entire body of priests and priestesses assembles in the temple of the sun.

'A mixed choir very solemnly celebrates the omnipotence of the sun-god,' decided the musician.

'Then comes the magical sound of flutes,' said Thamos.

'Magic flutes . . . Yes, they announce the coronation of the young pharaoh! Sethos-Menes lights the flame and pours incense on to it. Who would oppose this enthronement?'

'Mirza declares that Saïs, the daughter of Menes, is alive.'

'Thamos kneels before her and swears obedience to her. Pheron asks the future sovereign the decisive question: whom do you intend to marry?'

' "No one," she replies. "I am sworn to the cult of the sun. And if I were to be married, it would be to Thamos." '

'Pheron the traitor rages about treason!' exclaimed Wolfgang, 'and he gives his allies the signal to attack.'

'At that moment, Sethos takes off his High Priest's cloak and appears as Pharaoh Menes. Everyone bows, even the rebels. Mirza stabs herself, and Pheron is arrested. The king allows his daughter to marry Thamos.'

'Thunder and lightning are unleashed,' declared the musician. 'They kill Pheron, who was continuing to blaspheme. At the end of the drama, Pharaoh's bass solo proclaims, in harmony with the choir: "Children of the dust, tremble and shiver!" And the sound of the magic flutes brings back peace and joy.'

# 5

*Vienna, 10 September 1779*

At last it was raining and the morning was very cool. As summer died, Geytrand was reborn, with all the greater strength since the latest reports from his informants had brought him joyful news.

'Strict Templar Observance is in a bad position,' he told his chief, Josef Anton. 'As you supposed, the fierce struggle between the Duke of Brunswick and the Duke of Sudermania is harming the entire Order. The Brother Knights are complaining and criticize the Grand Master for not keeping his promises. The last attempt at conciliation ended in failure. They are all maintaining their positions, and there is no contact between the Swedes and the Germans.'

'Is Ferdinand of Brunswick in danger of being overthrown?'

'Not impossible, Herr Count, but he will fight to the end. He is a cautious man, and for three years has frozen initiations at the top level so as not to let too many wolves into the sheepfold. So he remains surrounded by men faithful to him and will be able to control the senior officials. Better still, he is no longer planning to create lodges in Germany, and no more Knights in Vienna will be armed.'

'We must remain wary. This could be just a bad patch, or a ruse. The Grand Master and his colleague are obstinate men. They will neither give up their powers nor the expansion of the Order. Ensure that our informants do not allow their attention to wander.'

*Brunswick, 11 September 1779*

The Duke of Brunswick was feeling the weight of his fifty-eight years, so heavy compared to the vigorous thirty-five springs of his right-hand man and confidant, Charles of Hesse.

'We are threatened with a split, but I refuse to give up! Our ideal must not disappear because of the ambitions of one Swedish prince.'

'I agree with you wholeheartedly, Grand Master, and I may perhaps have an idea. Lyons, the headquarters of our second Templar province, seems very active. Brother Willermoz has carried out long and patient research which has apparently enabled him to obtain the Philosopher's Stone and knowledge of certain mysteries. Let us forget Austria and Germany, and turn towards the capital of the Gauls.'

Why, wondered Ferdinand of Brunswick, has the Unknown Superior, that clear-sighted Egyptian, not returned to counsel me?

*Venice, 13 September 1779*

Armed with a properly constituted arrest warrant, the police officers presented themselves at the residence of Abbot Lorenzo Da Ponte, who had already been banned from teaching since December 1776, and judged guilty of airing dangerous revolutionary ideas, maintaining that Man would be happier in the state of nature than within social institutions which were too constraining. In short, the abbot had preached the destruction of the Church and of society.

Wisely, the bird had flown the nest before it was captured.

Indeed, that same day Lorenzo Da Ponte, a Jew by origin whose real name was Emanuele Conegliano, crossed the Austrian border to reach safety. A great liar before the Eternal One, a tireless pursuer of women who unhesitatingly abandoned any unwelcome children, he had resolved to leave Venice where, because of his repeated indiscretions, he no longer felt safe. Moreover, the authorities wanted to sentence him to exile 'for public adultery and concubinage', activities which had already caused him to be dismissed from the seminary in Treviso.

All of this did not prevent the priest from possessing cultivated tastes in literature, assiduously reading Dante, Petrarch and Tasso, and priding himself on his abilities as a poet, putting together verses which were rather hollow but correctly constructed. In the high-society salons, he enjoyed considerable success by improvising sonnets or short odes on any subject.

After which he would seduce a lady charmed by his talent and live at her expense, before moving on to another.

And now this gilded existence had come to an end. At the age of thirty, Da Ponte had little fondness for the forced exile which obliged him to wander the roads in search of paid employment. So he would visit the Viennese court where, rumour had it, a good librettist had every chance of success. And the abbot believed in his own talent as an author. Swiftly, and on demand, he would write the texts demanded by opera composers. As for the competition, he would completely suppress it.

Determined to forget Venice, Lorenzo Da Ponte proudly headed for the capital of the Austrian Empire.

*Salzburg, October 1779*

'Have you heard the news?' Anton Stadler asked Wolfgang.

'Good or bad?'

31

'Excellent, for your former beloved! Fräulein Aloysia Weber has just been engaged by the German Opera in Vienna, where her family has settled.'

'Good for her, she deserves it.'

'Anyone would think you don't feel any resentment towards her!'

'Aloysia is a wonderful singer. She lives her life as she sees fit, and I wish her great success and happiness.'

'You still love her, don't you?'

'Perhaps I shall love her for a long time, even for ever. She is the first woman who awakened this feeling in me – gentle and powerful, tender and violent, calm and burning. Thanks to her, my soul opened itself to this mysterious reality.'

'Then try to understand it better by spending time with other girls! Unless, of course, you are hoping to reconquer Aloysia . . .'

'No, Anton, she left me no hope.'

'In that case, stop moping and learn how to enjoy yourself. Don't tell me that *Thamos, King of Egypt* is taking up all of your time!'

'But that is the truth. I am fulfilling my obligations as a musician-servant as best as I can, so that I can devote myself to this work, whose libretto really excites me. I am a long way from understanding every aspect of it, but I am convinced that music will open many of the doors to me and lead me to the heart of the sun-priests' thoughts.'

'Is that so important?'

'It is vital, Anton! Aren't you interested in the great mystery of our life?'

'For the time being, I am content to live and I am never bored, not for one second!'

'Don't you ever ask yourself questions about the meaning of your existence?'

'Yours are quite sufficient for me! When you have the answers, you can tell them to me. Isn't that the privilege of friendship?'

# 6

*Brunswick, 8 October 1779*

The Grand Master of Strict Observance had sent an emissary to Florence where, according to certain Brothers, an Unknown Superior lived.

At last, Waechter had returned!

Short, fat and voluble, he wore a triumphant expression.

'Total success, Highness! I met an exceptional individual who initiated me into a lodge of the Rose-Cross. He conjures up spirits and makes them appear upon Earth.'

'What is his name?'

Waechter looked embarrassed.

'I swore to keep it secret.'

'What did he advise you, with regard to us?'

'That you must continue, but become closer to the spirits and to the Rosicrucians. The Templar way leads nowhere.'

A long silence followed this declaration.

'You have fulfilled your mission,' said the Grand Master. 'Leave for Denmark, where you will become a minister and chamberlain.'

Waechter bowed very low. He had not expected such a promotion.

Ferdinand of Brunswick picked up a pen.

'I am sending a circular to all the chapters of Strict Observance,' he decreed, 'in order to remind them that I, the Grand Master, am the possessor of secret knowledge. In order to raise themselves to this knowledge, Brothers must show themselves to be virtuous and have more respect for morals. Henceforth, the hierarchic rank occupied by a Freemason will depend upon his degree of initiation into this esoteric knowledge.'

'What about our Templar affiliation?' asked Charles of Hesse worriedly.

'We must listen to the Unknown Superiors, whose wisdom directs us. I therefore officially reject this affiliation and all historical links with the Templars. I renounce the plan to materially restore the Order of the Temple. Each Brother must accept this decision and make my ideas his own. If not, I will dismiss him.'

This time Baron de Hund, founder of Strict Templar Observance, really was dead.

*Vienna, 15 October 1779*

Josef Anton slowly read the 'Brunswick circular', which Geytrand had just handed him.

'Astounding! Why is the Duke undermining himself like this?'

'Because an emissary, Waechter, delivered orders to him from a secret thinker.'

'And the Grand Master allowed himself to be taken in by such nonsense?'

'For many Freemasons, there is no doubt at all about the existence of the Unknown Superiors. The Duke of Brunswick and Charles of Hesse have an iron-clad belief in them.'

'While others believe in Christ, Mohammed or who knows what gods,' murmured Anton. 'Is this Waechter one of the Superiors?'

'Merely a charlatan, to whom the Grand Master naively grants his trust! As a reward, he has been given a fine post at the Danish court.'

'So the Templar ideal is finished?'

'According to Ferdinand of Brunswick, certainly. But rumour has it that this circular has been rather badly received. Many Brothers were hoping for the resurrection of the chivalric Order, from which they would derive material benefits. As the Duke threatened to dismiss anyone who did not listen to him, the dignitaries are supporting him. But faced with criticisms and negative reactions, the Grand Master is already beginning to draw back.'

'In other words,' concluded Josef Anton, 'we are heading off into endless discussions!'

'With a little luck, the Order will collapse like an old ruined castle buffeted by evil winds.'

'Do not rely too much upon that, Geytrand. Even assuming that Brunswick has really been destabilized, he will soon recover his equilibrium and retake command of the boat with his usual firm grip.'


*Salzburg, 30 October 1779*


As he stroked Miss Pimperl, who was lying in his lap, Wolfgang thought about the death of Fridolin Weber, who had passed away on 23rd October. How he would have loved to have had him as a father-in-law, and to have made his daughter happy! Despite Aloysia's success, the good fellow had been unable to bear another move to Vienna.

'We're ready,' declared Anton Stadler.

With great reluctance, the fox terrier was obliged to move and Wolfgang joined his group of musician friends. They played a symphonia concertante,* in which the violin and viola took the leading parts. While he waited for *Thamos, King of Egypt* to be staged, this work had come into his mind.

Its splendour surprised the first musicians who played it. Disconcerted by so much amplitude and expressive

*K364.

audacity, they felt transported into another world, filled with incessant dialogues between soloists, and between the soloists and the orchestra, without interrupting the unity of the conversation. Despite the pain expressed in the first movement, the many themes proclaimed hope and a thirst for life.

The skilful use of silences highlighted the melodic surges, which overwhelmed Anton Stadler.

'Whatever have you composed there, Wolfgang . . . I am completely overcome by it! Are you really a normal man?'

'Shall we go and have a game of skittles?'


*Berlin, 20 December 1779*


In view of the grave difficulties encountered by Grand Master Ferdinand of Brunswick, the two most active members of the Golden Rose-Cross, Wöllner and Bischoffswerder, decided to strike a great blow.

During a meeting of the Mother Lodge* of the Prussian States, attended by Thamos, Count of Thebes, and several notable visitors, the venerable Wöllner spoke up in an extremely serious tone.

'Honoured Brothers, Freemasonry is experiencing decisive times. Our current rite, the rite of the Templar Order, no longer mirrors our profound aspirations.

---

* The Three Globes.

We must now attach ourselves to another tradition, the tradition of the Rose-Cross. The King of Poland, Stanislas II, is one of its illustrious representatives, and Count Dietrichstein has been instructed to create several Rosicrucian chapters in Austria, Hungary and Bavaria.'

This information surprised several dignitaries, who had not suspected the degree to which this underground Masonic movement was expanding.

'Will this lodge nevertheless continue to belong to the Strict Observance movement?' asked Thamos.

'Impossible,' replied Wöllner. 'Our Mother-Lodge and all its daughters are leaving the Templar Order and rallying to the Golden Rose-Cross.'

The defection of the Prussian Freemasons had dealt a severe blow to Strict Observance. Thamos saw a faint smile on the lips of the Jesuits who were hiding behind their Masonic aprons.


*Vienna, 31 December 1779*


Josef Anton was celebrating alone, with just a glass of red wine and a little cold turkey. The festive season exasperated him. Believing neither in God nor in the Devil and still less in human goodness, he could not bear this excess of religiosity and the forced rejoicing, during which the worst of enemies pretended to get along with each other for as long as the banquet lasted.

He continued to work to preserve the Austrian model: social harmony and respect for the ruling power. All anarchic and disorderly elements must be mercilessly hunted down, beginning with this many-headed beast of Freemasonry, whose destruction would take a great deal of time.

Strict Templar Observance had been the cause of many sleepless nights, for its political plans appeared extremely dangerous to him. Creating a militia of Knights greedy for reconquest: did that not mean they wanted to overturn the imperial throne?

By facilitating the entry into lodges of Jesuits, who were very careful not to reveal their membership of that Order, Anton intended both to gather as much information as possible and to pervert the Masonic spirit, by directing the Brothers towards a Catholicism which was tainted with mysticism and secret ceremonies, in other words the Golden Rose-Cross, which had triumphed today in Berlin.

This represented a fine victory for the Count of Pergen, whose strategy consisted of dividing the different Masonic movements, then pitting them against each other, in order to prevent any possibility of a union which would generate formidable power.

The war was far from won for, despite his successes, he could not make an appearance centre-stage. Although robustly encouraged by Empress Maria Theresa, he worried about Josef II's liberal tendencies. Would he be able to recognize Anton's merits, and understand the importance of his mission?

The twelve strokes of midnight rang out, and a new year began. While the revellers embraced, wishing each other good health and happiness, Anton filed his paperwork. No Freemason would escape him, above all in Vienna.

# 7

*Salzburg, 15 January 1780*

Böhm's troupe, which would be spending a few more months in the principality, was rehearsing Shakespeare's *King Lear*.

Wolfgang intercepted the director as he emerged from the theatre.

'Weren't you supposed to be staging *Thamos, King of Egypt* this month?'

'Indeed, Herr Mozart, indeed! But the project is more complex than we had foreseen, and . . .'

'Do not mock me! You have the words and music at your disposal, I am ready to direct it, and your actors are accustomed to learning longer and more difficult works.'

'True, but the technical conditions . . .'

'Tell me the truth, I beg you!'

Böhm dared not look Mozart in the face.

'We are only temporary guests in Salzburg and must have the authorities' approval in order to stage any play.'

'Has this approval been refused?'

'I did not obtain it, and was advised not to persevere.'

'For what reason?'

'Apparently this drama has already been staged, at least in part, and without any success, and the prince-archbishop disliked your music. So it would be inconvenient to persevere.'

'So you are giving up the chance to perform *Thamos, King of Egypt*?'

'I am left with no choice,' lamented Böhm sadly. 'I would so have liked to please you and achieve a great success!'

Wolfgang did not question the man's sincerity.

Colloredo . . . It was always Colloredo! The Grand Mufti was forever interfering, judging, forbidding.

Sickened and tired, Wolfgang walked slowly back home, not feeling the bite of the icy wind. He no longer had any desire to compose. What was the good of creating new and original works, since they would never be played? As for producing a host of little works designed to cheer up the prince-archbishop, he no longer had the heart for it. All that remained for him was to carry out his duties as organist at the cathedral.

*Lyons, 20 January 1780*

Learning of the problems encountered by Strict Templar Observance, Jean-Baptiste Willermoz wrote to

Ferdinand of Brunswick and Charles of Hesse, two great lords whom he admired on account of their titles and their social position.

Thanks to his occult knowledge, the mystic from Lyons declared to Charles of Hesse that a protecting angel remained with him permanently and that it uttered supernatural sounds when it approved of his conduct.

Then he stated: 'Freemasonry essentially has no other goal than the knowledge of man and nature; since it is founded upon the Temple of Solomon, it cannot be a stranger to the science of man, for all the Sages who have existed since its foundation have recognized that this famous temple itself existed in the universe only to become the universal type of the general man in his past, present and future states.'

After emphasizing these truths, Jean-Baptiste Willermoz opened his operational Circle, where he would practise divine magic for three consecutive nights after ensuring that his followers observed a regime of fasting and abstinence. He would pass on to them the alphabetical table of the twenty-four thousand names of the Patriarchs, Apostles and Prophets, the table of the twenty-eight lunar dwellings, a summary of the hiero-glyphs designating the angel-planets and the recipe for manufacturing oil for anointing.

Soon, the disciples of the trader from Lyons would rule Freemasonry and bring it back to Christ the Saviour.

## The Son of Enlightenment

*Salzburg, 27 January 1780*

Anton Stadler attempted in vain to bring cheer to Wolfgang's twenty-fourth birthday meal. Nannerl was as grim-faced as ever, and Leopold himself lamented the sadness of his son, who was unable to compose. Even Miss Pimperl was no longer able to distract him.

'Forgive me, I feel the need of a walk.'

Neglecting a succulent apple strudel, Wolfgang walked aimlessly through the snowy, deserted streets, forming the corridors of a prison from which he would never emerge.

The tall silhouette of Thamos the Egyptian barred his way.

'Why such despair, Wolfgang?'

'Haven't you heard about the disaster?'

'Of course I have.'

'I shall never compose again.'

'Will you bow before the Grand Mufti?'

The young man straightened up.

'Never!'

'Doesn't that cancel out what you've just said?'

'*Thamos, King of Egypt* was so important to me!'

'That work is not dead. By giving it more depth, you have taken another step in the direction of the temple which your music has begun to conjure up. None of your perceptions will be futile.'

'Colloredo has muzzled me!'

'Breaking his power will not be easy, I admit that.

Since he does not like the Egyptian mysteries, let us change our strategy for the time being.'

A glimmer of interest returned to Wolfgang's eyes.

'Another project?'

'A hymn to freedom, in the form of a fable which will once again take up fashionable themes and will not shock Colloredo.'

'As it is not a commission from him, he will ban the work!'

'Possibly. Would you prefer to give up?'

'Freedom . . . I dream of it every night!'

'Then make up your mind.'

It did not take him long.

'I want so much to write! What do you suggest?'

'The story of a young woman unjustly imprisoned, who wants to regain her freedom.'

The smile returned to Wolfgang's face.

# 8

*Salzburg, 1 February 1780*

Wolfgang was hoping to work with Thamos again, but it was Johann Andreas Schachtner, a forty-nine-year-old writer and trumpet player, who arrived on his doorstep, with an opera libretto under his arm.

'A wealthy man commissioned me to adapt a text on condition that I entrusted it to you.'

Schachtner had already pored over *Bastien and Bastienne* and had translated *La finta giardiniera* into German. He did not know that *The Seraglio** derived from a tale by the Freemason Lessing, *Nathan the Sage*, in which he had developed ideas dealt with during lodge work.

'A glass of punch?' ventured Wolfgang.

'With pleasure! It will help me to forget the winter and transport us to the East, to the realm of the sultan

---

* *Zaïde or The Seraglio*, K344.

Soliman, a merciless tyrant. His slaves break stones as they bemoan their fate. Among them is a Christian, Gomatz. Desperate and exhausted, he falls asleep watched by the beautiful and shy Zaïde, a Christian and future favourite in the seraglio. The young woman lays her portrait beside the sleeping man.'

'The moment he wakes,' cut in Wolfgang, 'he gazes upon it and falls in love with her! Together, they sing of their desire to escape and share their love in freedom. But how can they escape?'

'With the aid of Allazim, a servant of the sultan who does not approve of his master's conduct. Moved by their courage, he helps them to get out of the prison and to get to the river bank. Dawn breaks, and the two young people and their saviour say farewell.'

'The storm threatens,' went on the composer, 'and the sultan's soldiers recapture our heroes.'

'Indeed,' nodded the trumpet player. 'Osmin, a slave merchant, brings them back, bound hand and foot, to Soliman, who decides to put all three fugitives to death.'

'Zaïde attempts to arouse tenderness in the monster, but to no avail. Faced with such cruelty, she declares her thirst for freedom and her love for Gomatz. They will die with their heads held high.'

'Impossible to end on such a tragedy,' said Schachtner. 'Allazim reminds Soliman that he once saved his life. In gratitude, the sultan spares his life.'

'Allazim will not abandon the two young people to their sad fate. But how will he save them?'

'By revealing that they are his son and daughter. The sultan grants them life and freedom.'

'I like this theme!'

'Does it not celebrate the magnanimity of a great lord whose cruelty seemed unshakeable? By giving his pardon, he proves his wisdom.'

If only the Grand Mufti could take his inspiration from Soliman, thought Wolfgang.

*Frankfurt, 25 February 1780*

At last thirty-two-year-old teacher Adam Weishaupt was seeing his dream becoming reality! The secret Order of the Illuminati of Bavaria was no longer just a dream, since it now boasted seventy members of great quality, whose intellectual authority was sure to carry weight in the development both of society and of people's ways of thinking.

The majority of the Illuminati were also Brothers of Strict Observance and were beginning to convert many Freemasons to their vision of the world, which up to now had been dominated by Catholicism.

The powerful ideological impulse transmitted by Weishaupt seemed destined to be irresistible but it had encountered a major obstacle: the content of the rituals. Freemasons were not content with theories, however novel and appealing they might be. Some wished to experience ceremonies, work with symbols and gain access to knowledge of the mysteries, beyond mere philosophy.

In this field, Adam Weishaupt was lamentably lacking in skill. That was why he had approached a renowned specialist in Masonic rituals, Imperial Baron Adolph von Knigge. A native of Hanover, with no lands or wealth despite his imposing title, this twenty-eight-year-old liberal Protestant was a playwright, poet and businessman.

Initiated in Cassel,* he belonged to the higher levels of Strict Observance,† but had not been admitted to the ranks of the Berlin Rose-Cross. This humiliating experience had left him with a profound aversion to Christian mystics, whom he considered incapable of true initiation.

Adam Weishaupt introduced himself and thanked Baron Adolph von Knigge for agreeing to meet him in great secrecy.

'Why so much discretion?' asked von Knigge.

'Because I am the head of a Masonic Order, the Illuminati of Bavaria, which is unknown to the authorities and the police.'

'A dangerous course of action, Professor!'

'If one wishes to change the world and serve humanity, one must be willing to take risks.'

'Change the world . . . I say!'

---

* Into the Crowned Lion Lodge.
† As a Knight *a Cygno*.

'Do you consider our society free, just and harmonious?'

Von Knigge was under no illusions.

'That would be stupid.'

'Does our dear Freemasonry seem to you to be equal to the circumstances?'

'Not always, dear Brother. However, it is the sole path which seems to me to be worthy of interest, since ordinary philosophical systems do not satisfy me. In matters of religion, I float between faith and incredulity, for the different doctrines are devoid of meaning. Nevertheless, any sudden revolution would be worthy of condemnation. It could not bring about any progress if human beings, because of their passions, remain what they are today. Only the intellectual and moral improvement of humanity can alter the situation.'

'Jesuits have infiltrated the lodges and are attempting to pervert Freemasons by bringing them back to the Church in an insidious way.'

'That is correct,' agreed Baron von Knigge, 'particularly the Golden Rose-Cross circles.'

'The Illuminati of Bavaria want to stop this drift without coming into conflict with their Brothers, but by offering them a new path.'

'How will you do so?'

'By offering them new rituals which are richer and more profound than those of Strict Observance.'

'Have they been written?'

'Only in draft form,' admitted Weishaupt. 'Alone, I shall not succeed in carrying this task to a successful

51

conclusion. I should like to have your help and your counsels.'

'Speak clearly, my Brother: do you wish me to write the rituals for the Order of Illuminati of Bavaria?'

'If you were agreeable, Baron, we could bring significant progress to Freemasonry.'

'I accept.'

# 9

*Salzburg, March 1780*

Wolfgang's new short Mass* held up well within the time limits imposed. However, his *Benedictus*, which constituted a not-very-religious declaration of rebellion, was not at all to the prince-archbishop's liking. Fortunately, the *Agnus Dei*, although close to opera in style,† possessed such charming sweetness that the master of Salzburg's anger abated.

'All the same, you should be wary,' Anton Stadler advised Wolfgang. 'Colloredo is not completely stupid, and in the end he will notice that your music displays your hostile feelings. And certain of our dear colleagues will be sure to inform him.'

At the start of a radiant spring, Wolfgang forgot the

---

* K337.
† Experts see in it the genesis of the aria '*Porgi amor*' sung by the countess in *The Marriage of Figaro*.

Grand Mufti and put the final touches to his *Solemn Vespers of a Confessor,*\* the jewel of which was an exceptional piece, the *Laudate Dominum* for soprano and choir.

Never before had Thamos the Egyptian heard such a pure melody, capable of expressing the soul's aspiration to the divine and the dialogue between the individual and the community of the stars.

The Great Magician was growing stronger with each day that passed, and this time, he had touched the sublime. On listening to this passage, one's entire being was transported into another world. And this act of praise to the Saviour was raised to the heights of a ritual.

*Weimar, 23 June 1780*

Johann Joachim Christoph Bode, deputy Venerable of the Amalia Lodge in Weimar, was congratulating himself on the initiation of a famous thirty-year-old writer, Johann Wolfgang von Goethe. Author of the *Sufferings of Young Werther*, he was also a playwright, poet, lawyer, chemist and, since 1775, he had also been a political and economic adviser to the Grand Duke of Weimar.

In the absence of the Venerable for life, von Fritsch, Bode carried out his duties with gusto. Goethe enjoyed the ceremony and did not regret having set out on the

\*K339.

path of Freemasonry. He thanked Bode for having interested him in this school of thought, the heir to ancient initiations and the basis of a new philosophy which the world needed.

Like Bode, Goethe feared grave political and social upheavals which would ruin Europe and plunge it into horrible conflicts. So mindsets must be altered and vital reforms carried out if such a disaster was to be averted.

Surely Freemasonry was one of the forces capable of conducting this just war and bringing about the victory of light over darkness?

*Vienna, 1 July 1780*

'So Goethe has become a Freemason,' noted Josef Anton as he read an informant's report. 'Annoying, most annoying . . . If renowned intellectuals begin to join this accursed brotherhood, its weight will become considerable.'

'Intellectuals do not act,' Geytrand disagreed. 'They are content to juggle ideas and build unrealistic ideals.'

'When a man of action takes an unrealistic ideal to his heart, it becomes a war machine. And Freemasonry could link thinkers and activists in the image of Goethe, who is both a writer and a politician. I want all the information you can get on this Weimar Lodge.'

'From what I know already, Herr Count, it is certainly not going to become a hotbed of revolution. Its members are more concerned with maintaining the established order.'

'Let us hope so, Geytrand, let us hope so.'

*Salzburg, 2 September 1780*

On 29 August, the dazzling symphony in C major,* featuring no fewer than forty violins, mingled light-heartedness and a determination to conquer. So much musical power astonished Leopold. Did it signify a return to optimism and Wolfgang's acceptance of his status as a Salzburg musician?

He soon changed his mind as he saw Wolfgang lapse back into depression. Convinced that his opera *The Seraglio* would never be performed, he stopped composing when he reached the vocal quartet in Act II, at the moment when brave Allazim begged the sultan to spare his daughter Zaïde and his son Gomatz. The young man did not have the heart to write the final scene, magnifying the greatness of the tyrant's soul as he granted his pardon to the three heroes.

Colloredo was hardly likely to behave in the same way.

Disenchanted, Wolfgang put his unhappiness into three short songs on poems by Johann Timotheus Hermes.

* K338.

The first, *To Hope,*[*] moved at a moderate pace, evoking the pain of living and the need to find a friend who would help to bear it. The second, *To Solitude,*[†] celebrated it as the sole refuge of the wounded individual, close to death. The third, *Grace be to the Splendour of the Great,*[‡] was to be sung with indifference and self-satisfaction, advising listeners not to resemble the powerful men of this world, not to allow themselves to be taken in by their lavish excesses and to be wary of their hypocrisy. It was up to experience to teach each individual to be neither audacious nor futile, and not to be reduced to pettiness.

'Do not confuse the power of men who govern with real greatness,' Thamos advised Wolfgang as he walked beside him. 'Expressing solitude, suffering and disappointment liberates you, but I above all am pleased by your decision not to shut yourself away in mediocrity. If you cherish your magic, it will break all bonds.'

'*The Seraglio* – another failure!'

'You are mistaken. Just like *Thamos, King of Egypt* and *Semiramis*, it is the prelude to a great opera.'

'Must I keep waiting for many more years?'

'Two kinds of time rule us: the kind that is imposed on us from outside, and the kind we fashion ourselves. When they join together, you will experience intense joy, as long as you do not yield an inch of ground to

*K390.
†K391.
‡K392.

spinelessness. Otherwise, you will be nothing but a wisp of straw.'

'Colloredo will never commission an opera from me.'

'Correct.'

'And he will prevent anyone else from commissioning one from me!'

'Your solitude will come to an end, and your hope will be crowned with success. Work ceaselessly, for nothing that you have prepared will be wasted.'

Despite the rain, the sun was shining.

# 10

*Strasbourg, 16 September 1780*

Asking himself questions about Cagliostro's qualities regarding initiation and about his true intentions, Thamos went to the capital of Alsace to attend a Gathering led by this strange individual, who boasted of having won over one of France's highest dignitaries, Cardinal de Rohan. The prelate was convinced that Cagliostro could produce gold and would supply him with it if necessary.

Thamos was therefore hoping for an alchemical ritual inspired by ancient Egypt and based upon fundamental knowledge, but he was present at a quite different spectacle.

In the middle of the meeting place, the mage put down a cup of pure water.

Then he sent for a young girl, Colombe, and a young boy, Pupille, and asked them to read the messages from the angels and the prophets in it. Next, they entered into contact with the souls of the dead who were dear to the people present.

At the end of the session, Thamos questioned Cagliostro.

'Is this the fundamental core of your initiation?'

'To you, and to you alone, I can tell the truth: I am collecting funds in order to develop my network of lodges. What is more, Cardinal de Rohan has just granted me more funding. The day when I reveal my true secrets, you will be present and will understand the meaning of my Quest.'

*Salzburg, 17 September 1780*

A man of the theatre to the core, Emanuel Schikaneder was the director of a troupe, an actor, singer, set designer, choreographer and even composed a little when circumstances demanded it. He was twenty-nine years old, with an open countenance and a mop of jet-black hair. His heavy jaw and cleft chin betrayed a determination that could withstand any ordeal.

On this beautiful, late-summer evening, Schikaneder's troupe was performing at the theatre in Salzburg, where the travelling actor was planning to settle for a while. The programme would include Calderon, Goldoni, Lessing and Shakespeare, but also less difficult authors and even some comedies of his own devising, which had only one aim: to please, amuse, surprise and enchant the public!

Giving of himself, Schikaneder oversaw every detail and could play young leads, noble fathers or a simple peasant.

He was determined to conquer the city with a burlesque play, *Joyful Poverty or the Three Apprentice Beggars*, and was playing the leading role, weeping gaily over his lot.

Like the other spectators, Wolfgang smiled. And on 1st October, he was present at the performance of *The Vessel from Ratisbon*, Schikaneder's homeland, which he mocked through the character of a servant singing a song 'in the Turkish style'. The play was packed with special effects, from fireworks to variations in lighting, and the actor brought on monkeys and bears, which proceeded to do all sorts of amusing things.

This excess of marvels enchanted Wolfgang, who made a point of congratulating the director.

The two men immediately struck up a rapport.

'Are you an actor?'

'A musician at court. My name is Wolfgang Mozart.'

'Mozart . . . The child prodigy all Europe was talking about?'

'Nowadays, just an organist in the service of Prince-Archbishop Colloredo.'

'Between you and me, he doesn't look like a lover of good jokes!'

'To say the least.'

'Are there many entertainments in Salzburg?'

'You have brought us a breath of fresh air, Herr Schikaneder! Would you do me the honour of having dinner with us?'

'With pleasure! My wife Eleonore, who is an excellent actress, will tell you a thousand and one anecdotes.'

Despite Nannerl's reservations, Leopold liked the Schikaneders.

The jovial actor proved to be an excellent dart-thrower and, delighted with this new friendship, offered free admission to the Mozart family for the entire season in Salzburg.

*Brunswick, 19 September 1780*

Ferdinand of Brunswick was thunderstruck. He had just finished reading an anonymous pamphlet entitled *The Stumbling Block and the Rock of Scandal Unveiled to All My Fellow German Citizens Within and Without the Seventh Province.*

This abominable text revealed the organization of Strict Observance and its weak points, told its secret history, exposed the content of its grades and criticized its leaders.

Who could be the author of such a betrayal, if not one of the creatures of the Duke of Sudermania, furious at not obtaining absolute power and preferring to scuttle the ship?

After consulting Charles of Hesse, the Grand Master decided to call a meeting of his Brothers at Wilhelmsbad, in order to save the Order, which was gravely threatened. In preparation for the debates at this Assembly, he asked all the lodges several questions:

First, does the Order have real Superiors? Who are they? Where do they reside? Is it linked to an older society, and if so, which one? Is it descended from the Order of the Temple?

Secondly, how should the ceremony and rituals be organized in the most appropriate manner?

Thirdly, can the Order of the Temple be restored economically, in all safety?

Fourthly, should the goal assigned to the Order be public or internal? Can charity, mutual support among Brothers and the education of men for the State constitute external goals which justify the society's existence?

Fifthly, are there certain pieces of knowledge which only the Order possesses?

As his guardian angel had not made any kind of appearance, Charles of Hesse wondered if this startling course of action was well advised.

'Are we not exposing our doubts to all the Brothers?'

'When they become aware of our sincerity, the Unknown Superiors will come to our aid,' replied Ferdinand of Brunswick.

# 11

'Are you joking, Anton?' asked Wolfgang.

'Not at all,' replied Stadler, looking scornfully at the composer.

'You're really getting married?'

'Indeed I am. I'm getting married on the twelfth, to Francisca Bichler.'

'Are you settling down then?'

'Of course, since I'm a decent lad. We have no money, but we shall be very happy and we'll start a really big family.'*

'A magnificent programme, Anton! I'm happy that you're finally taking the right path.'

'So am I,' sighed Stadler. 'Women are so complicated! At least this one knows what she wants. And besides,

---

* Eight children were to be born, between 1781 and 1791.

one piece of good news never arrives on its own. My talents as a clarinettist have been recognized at court, and I'm soon to be granted an official post.'

*Vienna, 15 October 1780*

'The Strict Templar Observance movement is dead!' proclaimed Geytrand, whose sinister face shone with unsavoury delight. 'Look at the Grand Master's incredible response to the pamphlet revealing its turpitude: a questionnaire to the lodges which proves his total confusion!'

Josef Anton read the text slowly.

'This course of action will provoke such a stir that the Wilhelmsbad meeting, if it takes place at all, will not happen soon,' added Geytrand. 'And a new schism has struck the Templar Order: the resignation of the Duke of Sudermania and all the Swedish Brothers who refuse to be mixed up in scandals.'

'So Ferdinand of Brunswick has eliminated his rival,' commented Anton.

'But at what price! He will not recover from this.'

'I am less optimistic than you, for Brunswick and his accomplice Charles of Hesse are steely characters who will fight to the end. They will never again find an army like the Strict Observance movement. Perhaps it is merely going through a bad phase; perhaps it will re-emerge stronger and more united after the meeting. I have reread the Templar rituals and I judge them to be threatening. Does the new Knight not simulate the act of murder, does he not return to the lodge brandishing a "crowned head", does he not wish to avenge Jacques de Molay by decapitating Philip the Fair and all bad kings, does he not advocate equality between men and does he not demand that peoples are granted sovereignty? We must on no account lower our guard, and your informants must remain mobilized.'

*Salzburg, 31 October 1780*

Thanks to his new friend Schikaneder, Wolfgang was able to forget his Salzburg prison a little. He escaped into the fairyland of the theatre and joyful evenings with plenty of drink where various society games were played and saucy banter exchanged.

Although delighted to be taking part, Anton Stadler felt awkward about telling Wolfgang a piece of news which might sadden him.

'How are you feeling today?'

'Not too bad.'

'Do you think we could talk again about . . . the past?'

'How mysterious you are, Anton!'

'It's delicate, extremely delicate, and I wouldn't want to . . .'

'Why don't you get to the point?'

Anton Stadler swallowed hard.

'It's about Aloysia.'

'She's not . . . ill, is she?'

'No, oh no! Unless you consider marriage an illness.'

'Aloysia is married?'

'Yes, to an actor, Josef Lange.'*

'An actor . . . I wish them much happiness and I shall give them a present.'

Wolfgang composed two *Lieder*, notable for their mandolin accompaniment. The first, on words by poet Johann-Martin Miller, was entitled *Happiness*† and sang of serene joy, far from the vanity of the great of the world. The second, *Come, Sweet Cithara (Zither)*‡ was a lover's serenade.

With these small works, Wolfgang once and for all cut the thread that still linked him to Aloysia. His first great love was now no more than a shadow, for ever lost in the mists of oblivion.

*Munich, 31 October 1780*

Karl Theodor, Prince-Elector, was nearing his goal. After a long period of instability threatening to lead to a murderous conflict between Austria and Prussia, he now reigned over Munich and was once again thinking about reviving artistic life, despite the objections from his

* They had six children.
† K349.
‡ K351. It prefigured that of Don Giovanni.

counsellor and confessor, the Jesuit Frank, who wished to see him spend more time in devotion and prayer.

So he summoned several prominent figures in order to collect their suggestions. He came across as a liberal prince, who wished to improve the daily lot of his subjects by providing them with excellent entertainments.

'Count of Thebes! I am pleased to welcome you to Bavaria.'

'Knowing how precious your time is, may I be permitted to submit a project to you?'

'Please do.'

'The next carnival period could host a high-quality opera, which will charm this magnificent city.'

'A . . . serious work?'

'Would that not befit the circumstances? A fine subject with rich and demanding music would serve your fame better than a farce or an *opera buffa*.'

This Count of Thebes is right, thought the prince-elector.

'Little time remains before the carnival. What composer would be capable of carrying through such a project?'

'I know only one: Wolfgang Mozart.'

Karl Theodor frowned.

'A rather rebellious character . . .'

'Nowadays he is a faithful servant of Prince-Archbishop Colloredo and would work with Varesco, a religious from Salzburg Cathedral, in order to provide you with a work which conforms to morality and

68

religion. Moreover, Mozart constantly proclaims his gratitude and his esteem for you, as one of music's greatest protectors.'

Karl Theodor was neither immune to the guarantees nor to the compliment.

'Your proposition interests me, Herr Count, but I must consult further. My decision will be taken swiftly.'

Thamos bowed.

The prince-elector immediately summoned his confessor.

'Do you know this man Varesco?'

'A Salzburg chaplain who is worthy of esteem,' replied the Jesuit.

'And Wolfgang Mozart?'

'Who is he?'

'A musician in Colloredo's court. No files on him, no disastrous rumours?'

Frank the confessor was also one of Geytrand's informants, charged with making a list of Freemasons and gathering as much information as possible concerning them. Gifted with an excellent memory, he could quote their names and their grades.

'No files and no rumours. This Mozart fellow does not belong to any subversive movement.'

# 12

Count Hieronymus Colloredo had not changed. Still icy-cold and terse, he did not bother with polite formalities as he announced his decision to Mozart, his servant-musician.

'The Prince-Elector of Bavaria, Karl Theodor, wishes you to compose an opera, to be performed at the Munich carnival. The libretto is the work of my chaplain Varesco, who will provide you with the text. You will leave today and I am granting you six weeks' absence in order for you to direct the rehearsals and provide the prince-elector with satisfactory music, in the style of Italian opera. Try not to disappoint us.'

With a flick of the hand, Colloredo dismissed his servant.

Jean-Baptiste Varesco was waiting for Wolfgang. Although he had a rather slow intellect, the chaplain had

had the good fortune to receive a text which was already well advanced, reworking a libretto by Antoine Danchet used by Campra,* a French musician.

'What is the theme?' asked the composer anxiously, fearing he would be given something entirely unsuitable.

'The tragic story of the King of Crete, Idomeneo. Returning from the Trojan War, he must ensure the survival of his people by sacrificing his son.'

'Any heroines?'

'Two, both equally in love with the condemned son.'

'What about the gods?'

'Everything rests on the curse and the clemency of Neptune.'

'Give me your work.'

For the first time, Wolfgang was about to set off on a journey alone, for his father did not have permission to accompany him.

*Munich, 6 November 1780*

His head buzzing with music, his hand ready to rush across the paper, Wolfgang raged against Varesco's libretto, which must be profoundly altered by getting rid of slack periods and dramatic errors.

He was welcomed with open arms by his friends from the Mannheim orchestra, who were currently

---

* 1660–1744.

based in Munich. Principal among them was Christian Cannabich, who took him to comfortable lodgings in the Burggasse.

That same evening, his room in Munich was transformed into the island of Crete and he sang the heroine Ilia's first phrase: 'When then shall my cruel misfortune cease?' The daughter of Priam and a prisoner of the Cretans, the beautiful young woman had fallen in love with Idamante, son of King Idomeneo and regent of the country in his father's absence.

Finally, the king was returning safe and sound after fighting in the Trojan War. But he would not survive the storm unless he fulfilled a solemn vow to Neptune: to sacrifice to the god the first person he met when he set foot once more upon the soil of his homeland.

Cruel fate ensured that the expiatory victim was none other than his own son, Idamante. The king, therefore, ordered the unfortunate son, who did not know of his father's promise, to leave Crete for ever along with the sombre, tortured Electra, who was in love with the prince and envious of Ilia.

Supernatural forces proved to be superior to human tricks! A monster rose up out of the deep and threatened to destroy the island of Crete. Faced with his terrified people, King Idomeneo admitted the truth. And everyone demanded that he kill his son in order to appease divine anger.

Ready to die, Idamante attacked the monster . . . and killed it. A happy ending? No, for this victory did not cancel out the vow. Then courageous Ilia wanted to take the place of the man she loved. This time, tragedy seemed inevitable.

'A god can change the face of the world on his own,' declared the libretto, 'and severity shall be swept away in the face of clemency.' Accepting the triumph of love, Neptune freed King Idomeneo from his promise, but on one condition: that he gave up the throne in favour of his son Idamante, who married Ilia, to the great displeasure of Electra, who was mad with pain.

Pure love, self-sacrifice, keeping one's word, the power of the divine . . . All these aspects filled Wolfgang with enthusiasm. And what a strange ending: a worthy father, who loves his son, finds himself condemned to sacrifice him; but divine will alters destiny and causes the son to triumph, obliging the father to abdicate. For one moment, one short moment, Wolfgang thought of Leopold. Then he set to work again, delighted to be able to express a thousand feelings through a 'serious' opera, whose characters he would truly bring to life.

*Munich, 7 November 1780*

Wolfgang was received by Count Seeau, who had been confirmed in his post as steward in charge of theatre and music. This perfect hypocrite, who had formerly dismissed him as a good-for-nothing with no future, now greeted him with smiles and courtesy.

'Delighted to see you again, Mozart. From what I hear, you are giving complete satisfaction to Prince-Archbishop Colloredo, whose excellent tastes in music are known to all. I shall not conceal from you the fact that I am somewhat anxious. You have only the barest minimum of time in which to compose this work *Idomeneo*, which our good city is hoping to hear at carnival time.'

'Are the prince-elector's desires not orders? I like the subject, and I shall work within the time I have.'

'Do you give a firm undertaking to respect the deadlines?'

'Could you doubt it? When a Mozart gives his word, he does not take it back.'

'Perfect, you have reassured me.'

It was clear that Count Seeau was thinking only of his own reputation. In the event of a delay, Prince-Elector Karl Theodor would be certain to reprimand him.

With a laughing eye, Wolfgang watched the courtier walk away, to spend his day listening to gossip and spreading more. Fortunately, technicians and decorators were turning the Munich Opera House into a fine musical venue, where *Idomeneo*'s score would shine with all its brilliance.

Far from Salzburg, Wolfgang could breathe. The previous day, he had met the singers, whose standard seemed satisfactory to him with the exception of the old tenor Raaff, who had been promised the title role. And now he must alter several pages of the libretto, which was still somewhat shaky.

# 13

'Happy to have you here,' said Prince-Elector Karl Theodor to Mozart. 'Is your work progressing satisfactorily?'

'Very satisfactorily, Your Highness.'

'So our *Idomeneo* will be ready in time?'

'Have no fear. I have a clear head and I am thoroughly enjoying the work.'

'A fine subject, is it not?'

'Provided the libretto is improved, for Chaplain Varesco understands nothing of the demands of music.'

'I shall rely upon your sense of diplomacy, Mozart!'

'You may do so, Your Highness.'

'What about the singers? Are there any problems?'

'A few.'

'Easy to resolve, I hope?'

'I shall manage.'

'Perfect, Mozart, perfect! I want this to be a fine success.'

'As do I, Your Highness.'

'You were right to return to Salzburg and serve a prince who is as enlightened as Colloredo. Henceforth, your career is assured.'


*Munich, 20 November 1780*


The tenor Raaff, who had formerly been so friendly, had taken to pestering Wolfgang constantly, asking him to alter his role and adapt it to his declining vocal abilities. As for the castrato Del Prato, who was singing Idamante, the son of King Idomeneo, he was so inexperienced that the composer had to sing with him to teach him every note. Totally devoid of method, he behaved like a child.

Fortunately, the female singers were excellent!

Despite being so busy that he had not a moment's respite, Wolfgang managed to put together an aria for his friend Schikaneder, to insert into an opera by Gozzi, and entitled: *O Love, Why Take This Cruel Pleasure?** and sent it immediately to Salzburg.

Despite the fatigue, the young composer was having the time of his life. Was he not realizing his dream, to write an opera and have it performed? Once again, he tasted hope and a certain kind of freedom.

* K365a, lost.

He owed this happiness to his protector, Thamos. It was he, without a doubt, who had persuaded Karl Theodor to commission *Idomeneo*. True, Wolfgang would have preferred to continue his exploration of the sun-priests' universe, but did the theme of this work not put him in contact with the gods?

*Salzburg, 29 November 1780*

Without a doubt, thought Emanuel Schikaneder, this man Mozart is a good person. The aria he promised has arrived in time. This is a man of his word, and there are very few of those about!

A Freemason, the man of the theatre did not regret having listened to the advice of a Brother, a certain Count of Thebes, who had advised him to head for Salzburg where, that very evening, his new and spectacular play, *An Eye for an Eye*, was sure to unleash the public's enthusiasm.

Created during drinking sessions along with the actors in the troupe, it was seasoned with sparkling comedy so that the spectators would not find it indigestible or unoriginal.

But slapstick and broad jokes did not defrost the audience.

To Schikaneder's great disappointment, Salzburg's nobility and middle classes lacked a sense of humour. An emissary from the prince-archbishop tackled the troupe's manager.

'As you can see, this type of spectacle does not find favour in our principality.'

'But there was much to laugh at in it!'

'Salzburg detests vulgarity.'

'I have other plays in my repertoire.'

'After such a failure, it would be better to try your luck elsewhere.'

Schikaneder choked.

'Am I to understand that . . .'

'Pack your bags with all speed. Our theatre is expecting other troupes.'


*Vienna, 29 November 1780*


The black-clad doctor bowed before Josef II.

'Majesty, God has just welcomed into His bosom the soul of Empress Maria Theresa.'

Now sole master of the Austrian Empire, Josef II showed no emotion. For a long time now the old lady, who listened too much to the Church, had not really governed, although she had retained the ability to block vital reforms.

Long-faced with deeply furrowed cheeks, austere and simply dressed, the emperor called a meeting of his ministers.

'Great things must be done in a single sweep,' he declared. 'All changes arouse controversies sooner or later. The best way to proceed is to inform the public of one's intentions from the outset and, once one's decision is taken, to keep to it resolutely and take no account of adverse opinion.'

His firm tone and clear intentions were surprising. Evidently, Josef II's reign would not be characterized by laxity.

'What is our political line to be, Majesty?' asked the senior figure present.

'It can be summed up in a few words: the State must ensure the greatest good of the greatest number. These are the urgent measures which will be adopted by decree: confirmation of the abolition of slavery and serfdom, improvements in the penal system, equality of taxation, limitation of the powers of the nobility and the Church, abolition of monasteries and convents which do not fulfil any social function, greater tolerance and freedom of thought.'

'Majesty, do you not fear . . .'

'The world is changing. Failure to admit that and a rejection of reform would lead the empire to its ruin. Let us take the initiative and prove to the people that we govern in their favour and not for our own petty glory or personal benefit.'

*Vienna, 30 November 1780*

Josef Anton drank a large glass of red wine. He was in a state of collapse, his stomach in knots. The death of his protector, Maria Theresa, was a catastrophe. She alone had financed his secret service, whose existence the chief of police knew nothing about.

Josef II's first speech left no room for doubt: by declaring himself to be liberal, the emperor had opened the doors to all schools of thought, even Freemasonry!

Anton stared bitterly at the piles of files he had patiently built up. So much pointless work, so much futile effort, so many discoveries, now destined to disappear . . . He could not resign himself to burning the pages covered with tight rows of small, ultra-precise handwriting. They bore no trace of passion or rage, but testified to a scientific meticulousness that excluded all errors or vagueness.

And yet, he must destroy the proofs of his activities.

Then again, no!

Bringing his fist down hard upon the table, he decided to take the initiative. By obeying the late empress, had he not served his country?

Instead of scuttling his work, he would plead his cause, explaining to the emperor why Freemasonry was so dangerous.

# 14

At the end of the first rehearsal of the first act of *Idomeneo*, with a reduced orchestra, there was general satisfaction. The instrumentalists and singers liked Mozart's music.

Mozart himself was feeling unwell.

'My cold and bronchitis are getting worse,' he confessed to the tenor Raaff. 'One becomes more heated when honour and reputation are at stake. But we shall get there if we keep a cool head!'

In fact, the leader of the orchestra demonstrated such fervour that everyone followed suit, to the point of exceeding their technical limits. Only old Raaff was still asking for more alterations, aware that he was having difficulty keeping up the pace.

'Have you heard the big news?' he asked Wolfgang.

'Is there going to be a war?'

'Fortunately not! Empress Maria Theresa of Austria has just died.'

'So there will be an official period of mourning!'

'Do not worry, it will be over before the first performance of *Idomeneo*. You don't seem very upset by the death.'

'Too long a period of mourning does not bring as much benefit to the deceased as it does prejudices to a large number of the living. On the eighth, we shall rehearse the first two acts.'

*Munich, 16 December 1780*

On account of the delay caused by the slowness of a copyist, the second rehearsal had been postponed. If his cold and bronchitis were beginning to improve, another calamity was now threatening Wolfgang: the Grand Mufti! The six weeks granted by Colloredo would soon be over. Now, the premiere of the opera was fixed for 20th January the following year. Consequently, it would be impossible to get back to Salzburg by the planned date.

'The prince-archbishop and his presumptuous nobility are more intolerable to me with each day that passes,' Wolfgang confided to Raaff, who was at last happy with his part.

'Avoid thinking thoughts like that,' advised the tenor. 'If you want a fine career, don't criticize those who lead us. Without them there would be no theatre, no orchestra, no singers and, worst of all, no work!'

Caught up in the joy of being far from Salzburg and seeing

his work performed, Wolfgang forgot the Grand Mufti
and conducted the musicians with an infectious dynamism.

*Munich, 23 December 1780*

At the third rehearsal of *Idomeneo*, there was an important spectator in the front row: Prince-Elector Karl
Theodor himself.

Despite Mozart's promises, he preferred to take stock
himself of how the work was progressing.

Still as dynamic as ever, Wolfgang led the musicians
into a dramatic whirlpool in which, however, not a single
melody line sounded out of place.

'Magnificent,' declared Karl Theodor. 'One would
never imagine something so big hiding away inside such
a little head! On no account relax your efforts, Mozart.'

'Have no fear, Highness.'

*Vienna, 25 December 1780*

'You wished to see me urgently, Count Pergen?' asked
Emperor Josef II in astonishment.

'Indeed, Majesty,' replied Anton, who was tense in the
extreme.

'So what is so important?'

'Empress Maria Theresa appointed me to head a
secret department whose task was to keep watch on

83

the Masonic lodges. With a dedicated colleague and a network of informants which we have patiently built up, I have succeeded in compiling detailed files which are at Your Majesty's disposal.'

'Maria Theresa was extremely religious and detested Freemasonry, which she suspected of wishing to overturn thrones. Since you have undertaken a great deal of work, what are your conclusions?'

'The empress was not mistaken. Several Masonic movements exist, of varying size and influence, and I have studied them all. They present certain features in common: the taste for secrecy, the sharing of conflicting ideals, the determination to form a new elite, the study of mysterious symbols, the practice of strange rituals and political ambitions. Thus, the Strict Templar Observance movement seeks to revive the old knightly Order and give it back its past splendour.'

'Simply a dream, don't you think?'

'I have my doubts, Majesty.'

'Does this Strict Observance movement have a presence in Vienna?'

'Fortunately not, but there are other dangers, and the principal one seems to me to be the appearance of a new Order, uniting Freemasons and intellectuals, the Illuminati of Bavaria.'

The slender report which Anton had received, just before this decisive interview, had chilled his blood. This time, the peril was growing stronger. And he must convince Josef II not to view it lightly.

'Do you know the names of these intellectuals?'

'Not yet, Majesty. This movement remains extremely self-contained. I would require time and skilful diplomacy to discern all its secrets. The only certainty is that the Masonic lodges are forever conspiring.'

'Does Freemasonry not advocate brotherhood, which humanity so sorely needs? Too much authoritarianism and injustice can lead to rebellion and chaos. Let us listen to the people and not close our minds to new ideas.'

Josef Anton turned deathly white.

Clearly, highly placed Freemasons were influencing the emperor, and asking him not to conduct any repressive measures against them.

Josef Anton's enormous toil had been a waste of time. He would have to exile himself to the provinces and rot there while he watched the empire fall into decay, undermined by Masonic ideals.

'That being so,' went on Josef II, 'I intend to govern without weakness and to combat any ideology which might menace the fundamental values upon which we have built our greatness and our prosperity. That is why you are going to pursue your research, Herr Count, and continue to compile your dossiers with the most extreme discretion. I shall not tolerate any incidents. You will report only to me and will maintain absolute secrecy.'

'I shall not make a single mistake, Majesty, and no sovereign in the whole of Europe will be as well informed as you are about the true goals of Freemasonry.'

# 15

*Munich, 3 January 1781*

'*My head and my hands are so caught up in the third act that it would be no miracle if I were myself transformed into a third act,*' wrote Wolfgang to his father. '*It alone is causing me more trouble than an entire opera, for there are practically no scenes that are not interesting in the extreme. I never get dressed before half-past noon, because I must write and cannot therefore go out.*'

This creative fever enchanted the young man. At last, he was giving of his best, in the certainty that his efforts would end in an opera being performed! He now understood better why it had required so many formative journeys and failures. Although sometimes painful, these many experiences had taught him the extremely difficult art of writing sung drama, and the need to bring out the personality of each character. Admittedly the ones in *Idomeneo*, an *opera seria* constructed according to very old criteria, seemed a little fixed, but he gave them as much life as he could.

And Wolfgang received excellent news: because of the death of Empress Maria Theresa, Colloredo was rushing to Vienna to present his condolences to the emperor and, above all, to proclaim his absolute fidelity. The Grand Mufti did not want to be forgotten and risk losing an ounce of his prerogatives.

This had a formidable benefit: Wolfgang did not have to go back to Salzburg! As for his father and his sister, they could leave the principality and come to Munich in order to be present at the first performance of *Idomeneo*.

The door of the trap had swung open.

*Munich, 10 January 1781*

'On account of the circumstances,' announced Count Seeau to Wolfgang, 'the premiere of your opera will be put back by at least a week.'

'On account of what circumstances?'

The aristocrat bristled.

'I am the director of music and spectacles,' he reminded him, 'and I do not have to justify my decisions in any way.'

This delay suited the composer, who still had a few tunes to write for the last ballet. So he would benefit from additional rehearsals.

'I have examined your score closely, Mozart. I am happy with it, apart from the excessive use of the trombones.'

'Excessive?'

'That is indeed the term I used. You will therefore reduce the part they play.'

'Certainly not.'

'What?'

'I repeat: certainly not.'

'Do you know whom you are addressing?'

'An administrator, not a musician. It is not your place to judge the colours one must give to an orchestration, according to the text of the scene and the presence of one or several singers. When I bring in trombones, it is because they are necessary to the intelligence of the work.'

Most annoyed, Count Seeau promised himself that this insolent individual would never occupy the smallest position at the court of Karl Theodor.


*Munich, 25 January 1781*

Wolfgang embraced his father and Nannerl.

'Did you have a good journey?'

'Excellent,' replied Leopold.

'If you knew how happy I am! On the 13th, we rehearsed the third act and on the 18th, the recitatives. The day after tomorrow, the day of my birthday, there's a general rehearsal.'

'No major problems?'

'An infinite number! I have had to fight against the conventions of opera, the mediocrity of certain singers, the inadequacies of the libretto, the defects of the set, the stupidity of Count Seeau and a hundred other obstacles! The most annoying thing is having to entrust the role of Idamante, the son of King Idomeneo and a young virile prince, to a castrato who is devoid of talent and technique. Definitely off-putting as the hero and future sovereign of Crete! Unfortunately there is no other solution. As soon as the opera is performed again, I shall replace him with a valiant tenor.'

'You haven't lost your temper with anyone, I hope?'

'Of course not! As an economy measure, you will be staying in my hotel room. It is so good to see you again!'

Leopold was delighted to be present at his son's success. *Idomeneo* would perhaps mark the starting point of the brilliant career he had imagined. Salzburg, it was true, was nothing but a dead-end, but it was also a reassuring shelter. A good post at the Munich court, whose musical reputation merited respect, would be a true gift from the gods.


*Munich, 29 January 1781*


The attentive audience at the Residenz Theater in Munich watched the first performance of *Idomeneo, King of Crete*, an *opera seria* by Mozart, under the direction of orchestral leader Cannabich.

Not once did the score arouse their enthusiasm.

'Fine music, but a little stilted,' murmured Count Seeau into the ear of his neighbour, a pretentious woman who boasted of her infallible taste.

'Hardly surprising, my dear. Just think, an opera in the old style with a boring libretto! It is impossible to be interested in these puppets whose emotions are so conventional that they seem made of marble.'

'Certain arias are not disagreeable.'

'Really? Which?'

'For example, the ensembles. One has never heard anything like them, in my opinion.'

'Too long, too dramatic! Believe me, this *Idomeneo* will not hold the stage for long and this fellow Mozart will be swiftly forgotten.'

This radical critique spread like lightning. The second-rate musician from Salzburg had all Munich against him, and would never again have the opportunity to have one of his works performed, supposing that he ever composed any more . . .

# 16

*Brunswick, 30 January 1781*

'We have just received the reply from Jean-Baptiste Willermoz,' said Charles of Hesse to Grand Master Ferdinand of Brunswick. 'In exchange for our promise of absolute discretion, he consents to give us documents relating to the secret grade of Professional.'

'So my information was correct! This French mystic writes his own rituals and recruits his own followers outside Strict Observance.'

'Indeed, but he appears to be progressing along the right path, for he is distancing himself from the knightly aspect and advocating an esoteric form of Christianity.'

Ferdinand of Brunswick did not protest. For some time he, like his Brother Charles, had thought that the soul of Freemasonry was Christian and not Templar.

'Willermoz's new Order is made up of Charitable Knights of the Holy City,' Charles of Hesse recalled.

There is nothing threatening about them and the only battle they wish to fight is the total conversion of their souls to Christ. That is why I wanted to introduce you to Count von Haugwitz, whose profession of faith will interest you.'

This twenty-nine-year-old politician was both religious and debauched. Initiated in Leipzig, a member of the Swedish Rite and of the high Templar grades, he was prone to flights of mystical ecstasy.

'My Brother,' declared von Haugwitz, 'I invite you to come back to Christ. He is the way, the truth and the life. If our dear Freemasonry wanders on to the foul-smelling pathways of occultism and magic, it will be damned! On the other hand, if we understand that our Order can become the true Christian Church, we shall give it its authentic grandeur. I beseech you, august Grand Master: bring our Templar Brothers back to the path of righteousness.'

'With von Haugwitz,' said Charles of Hesse, 'we are planning to create a secret lodge* where we shall fashion the new Christian doctrine whose standard-bearer Freemasonry will be.'

Ferdinand of Brunswick did not voice any objection.

And yet, deep within himself, a doubt refused to be silenced: why had the Count of Thebes, one of the Unknown Superiors, not reappeared? Did he disapprove of this direction?

---

* The Lodge of the Brothers of the Cross.

'I have heard the voice of my guardian angel,' declared Charles of Hesse. 'We are not mistaken.'

*Munich, 10 February 1781*

Elisabeth Wendling, who had sung Electra in *Idomeneo*, was not lacking in charm. Her pretty soprano voice had certainly charmed Wolfgang, who gave her a bravura aria filled with virtuoso flourishes, *But What Matters It to You, O Stars!*,* in which passion and rebellion predominated.

'What a marvellous gift, Herr Mozart! Are you reassured, after the second performance of *Idomeneo* on the 3rd of February?'

'More or less. The critics are hardly favourable to me.'

'Do you have doubts about your talent?'

'Personally, I have none. But Count Seeau certainly does. And it is he who decides the programme of operas.'

'Has the prince-elector not intervened?'

Wolfgang shook his head. Moreover he had written a Kyrie in D minor,† with a view to obtaining a post in Munich as a composer of religious music.

'Whatever you do, you must not lose hope!' insisted the soprano.

More than admiration could be read in Elisabeth Wendling's eyes.

---

*K368.

† K341. This may, in fact, be another work, for the musicologist Monika Holl dates this Kyrie to 1791.

'Thank you for your encouraging words. Forgive me for abandoning you, but I have promised to finish a quartet* for a friend, the oboist Ramm.'

Oboe, violin, viola and cello mingled their voices in a way that was sometimes intimate and solemn, sometimes joyful and almost frivolous. After the exhausting work on *Idomeneo*, Wolfgang wished to rediscover working on a more intimate scale and, above all, to drag his father and sister off to enjoy the follies of the Munich carnival, forgetting all his cares about tomorrow.

*Salzburg, 21 February 1781*

Just as he was about to leave for Vienna, Prince-Archbishop Hieronymus Colloredo received a letter from Josef II, to whom he was preparing to pay homage: '*The empire over which I reign must be governed according to my principles: prejudices, fanaticism, arbitrary decisions and the oppression of consciences, all of these must be eliminated, and each of my subjects must be established in the freedoms that are native to them.*'

It was an excellent programme, strengthened by an edict of tolerance ensuring freedom of worship for Protestants and Orthodox Christians, who would no longer have to leave Austria. Moreover, Jews were given permission to leave their ghettos, and could live

* K370.

wherever they saw fit. As for bankers, whether they were Swiss or Jewish, they could now settle in Vienna and engage in new business dealings.

Colloredo was in agreement with the emperor's reforms. The time was coming when the path of progress must be chosen, as long as nothing was yielded in terms of authority. And who would contest his own authority, apart from young Mozart, who still wanted to leave Salzburg and experience adventures with no future? He was constantly overstepping the limits, doing whatever he wanted, and ending up producing only failures which were prejudicial to the principality's reputation.

According to the latest reports, *Idomeneo* would not survive the winter. And Mozart would have wasted his time writing a minor work that would be swiftly forgotten, instead of working for the prince-archbishop's court.

From now on, Colloredo would not tolerate the smallest infringement. He had broken the father, and he would break the son. No musician must forget that he was first and foremost a servant, obliged to obey the demands of his lord. Otherwise, there would be anarchy.

'Are my bags packed yet?'

'Yes, Eminence.'

By securing Josef II's goodwill, Colloredo could consolidate his own position and ensure a long reign which nobody – above all a petty musician with a difficult temperament – was going to disrupt.

# 17

*Vienna, 1 March 1781*

'We are to continue with our mission,' Josef Anton informed Geytrand.

'Is the emperor encouraging us, or merely grudgingly approving of our work?'

'He demands extreme discretion. At the slightest hint of scandal, our department will be dismantled.'

'Then our task is going to become very delicate.'

'Like many other sovereigns, Josef II does not yet perceive all the vices associated with Freemasonry. Here is the document he gave me, a letter from the Queen of France, Marie-Antoinette, to her sister Marie-Christine:

*You worry yourselves far too much about Freemasonry in so far as France is concerned; it is very far from having the importance here that it may have in other parts of Europe, on account of the fact that everyone is in it; so we know everything that goes on there; so where is the danger? One would be right to be alarmed if it was a secret political society; the art of government is on the contrary to allow it to spread and then it is no more than it is in reality, a society concerned with charity and enjoyment; people eat a lot there, and talk and sing, which tells the king that people who sing and who drink don't conspire; it is in no way a society of declared atheists, since, I have been told, God is in all their mouths there; much charitable work is done there, the children of poor or deceased members are brought up, and their daughters married; there is no harm in that.*

'Such is the Freemasons' usual smokescreen,' concluded Anton. 'They present themselves as inoffensive revellers, solely preoccupied with good works, and the naïve fall into the trap! Behind the mass of jolly fellows conspirators are hiding, such as the Illuminati of Bavaria who, according to the latest reports, are continuing to recruit intellectuals. We must follow their every move, Geytrand.'

*Munich, 8 March 1781*

After the third performance of *Idomeneo* on the 3rd, Wolfgang faced up to the obvious: the opera would not remain part of the repertoire.

There was one last chance to obtain a post in Munich: pleasing Prince-Elector Karl Theodor by presenting his mistress of the moment, Countess Baumgarten, with a dramatic soprano aria, *Unhappy One, Where am I? Ah, It is Not I Who Speak,*\* on a text by the poet Metastasio. It evoked the distress of Fulvia, moving from anger to despair because she did not understand either her destiny or the gods' indifference.

Alas, the countess's opinion weighed very lightly compared to the venom distilled at court by Count Seeau and the moral intransigence of Father Frank, Karl Theodor's Jesuit confessor.

With nothing more to hope for in Munich, Wolfgang took his father and sister to Augsburg, where they played the organ in order to forget this new disappointment.

'Orders from Colloredo,' Leopold announced to his son. 'You are to rejoin him in Vienna without going to Salzburg first. Nannerl and I are returning home immediately. Above all, do not delay. The prince-archbishop is becoming more and more authoritarian and will not tolerate the least insubordination.'

Wolfgang would obey, but before leaving Munich, he wanted to get together with his friends from the orchestra and play a work he had been toiling away at for months, and which was particularly dear to his heart, a serenade† for two oboes, two clarinets, two bassoons,

---

\* K369.
† Serenade (No. 10) in B minor, known as *Gran Partita*, K361.

four horns, four basset horns and a single string instrument, the double bass. It was the first time, on the advice of Thamos the Egyptian and Anton Stadler, that Wolfgang had used the basset horn in F. Its sonorous quality opened up a new world to him, a world which he felt was intimately linked to the solemnity and serenity of initiates into the Mysteries.

The score, which was played by thirteen soloists in perfect harmony, stunned Thamos from the very first bars. Lasting almost an hour, it alternated solemnity, smiles, maturity, youthfulness of spirit and controlled dynamism. Colours and melodies created a richness never before attained. Beginning with a slow movement, an adagio worthy of featuring in an initiation ritual, and going beyond the usual forms and conventions with its seven movements – a romance and a theme with six variations – this marvel allowed Wolfgang's creativity to burst forth.

When the emotion became too intense, the gaiety of a popular dance melody brought listeners back to earth.

As an initiator, Thamos did not have the right to reveal his feelings to his disciple who, by attaining this peak, had proved once and for all that he was the Great Magician.

'We are leaving together for Vienna,' he told Wolfgang. 'Important events are about to take place there.'

'Not involving me,' lamented the young man. 'I'm just returning to the ranks of the Grand Mufti's servants.'

'A decisive battle is being joined, Wolfgang. Do not yield an inch.'

'Colloredo . . .'

'Colloredo is no longer on his own territory in Salzburg, but in Vienna, the capital of the empire, a great city of which he is not the master.'

'But he is the one I have to serve, and I have to lodge on his premises.'

'Your work is before you. It will call to you and be your guide.'


*Weimar, 12 March 1781*


Brother Johann Joachim Christoph Bode caused a great stir by publishing a text designed to enlighten Freemasons about how the Jesuits were perverting initiation.

At the start of the century, these kings of trickery and hypocrisy had invented so-called 'symbolic' Freemasonry, in order to fight against Protestantism, which was triumphing in England. These famous symbols were religious disguises, such as the three cups for the Holy Trinity, or the letters J and B engraved on the columns of the Masonic temple, i.e. 'Jesuits' and 'Benedictines'.

Without realizing it, the Freemasons were playing the Church's game and reconstructing the Jesuit Order, whose disappearance was only an illusion. Worse still, the Strict Templar Observance movement, led by fervent believers, wanted to return omnipotence to the Catholic faith!

As for Bode, he saw through the turbulent game of Ferdinand of Brunswick and his principal accomplice, Charles of Hesse. He dreamt of awakening every Brother, gathering together those who were clear-headed and courageous, and no longer giving permission to Jesuits disguised as Freemasons to eat away at the Order from the inside.

The great battle was beginning.

# 18

*Vienna, 12 March 1781*

The son of an African king, and tutor to the princes of Lobkowitz and Liechtenstein, Angelo Soliman had succeeded, despite the colour of his skin, in becoming a respected member of good Viennese society.

That evening, he was taking part in the foundation of a new lodge, To True Union*.

On the advice of Thamos, Count of Thebes, Angelo Soliman was presenting a new follower of exceptional stature, the mineralogist Ignaz von Born.

In accordance with Thamos's recommendations, von Born did not reveal that he had been running a research lodge in Prague for several years. So he was received as an Apprentice, knowing that he would be rapidly raised to the grades of Companion and Master to direct the

---

* *Zur wahren Eintracht*. Sometimes translated as: To True Concord.

destinies of To True Union, which brought together writers, scientists and other notable figures, some Catholic and others Protestant.

Welcomed with 'all the honours of our royal Order', in Soliman's words, Ignaz von Born thanked his Brothers and promised them that he would take a very active part in symbolic research in order to build a lodge whose initiation would be the first and constant preoccupation.

This declaration troubled certain Brothers, who were unaccustomed to such a programme. Perhaps von Born's authority and skills would dispel their reticence.

'Have you read von Bode's work?' Soliman asked the Egyptian during the banquet.

'The violence of his attacks on the Church and the Jesuits will make him many enemies.'

'Doubtless, but he lacks neither courage nor clear-sightedness. Until Freemasonry escapes from external influences, and notably from religious manipulation, it will not truly take flight.'

'Are such thoughts current in the Viennese lodges?'

'Far from it, my Brother! They are filled with religious believers and are still proving very conformist. I hope that Ignaz von Born will free us from that rut.'


*Vienna, 16 March 1781, 9 a.m.*

Wolfgang entered Colloredo's palace, nicknamed the 'German House', at 7, Singerstrasse, a former base of the Teutonic Knights where he would be accommodated along with the other servants, musicians, valets or cooks who formed the prince-archbishop's entourage.

The first imperatives were a concert at the German House on that very day, at 4 p.m., and another the following evening at the house of Prince Galitzin, a very wealthy diplomat upon whom the Grand Mufti was relying to make himself an excellent reputation.

Lunches, at noon sharp, were painful ordeals. Wolfgang had to take his meals along with two cooks and a pastry-chef who spent their time exchanging vulgarities. As a musician, he was subject to the command of a brutal aristocrat, the Count of Arco, 'master of the kitchens'. Were musical productions not akin to digestible dinners?

Wolfgang ate in silence. Being so humiliated was becoming unbearable. '*The Lord Archbishop has the kindness to glorify in his people,*' he wrote to his father. '*He steals their profits.*'

Since his last conversation with Thamos, one project had been obsessing the composer: a plan to organize concerts for his own benefit. And in order to escape from the stifling atmosphere of the Grand Mufti's palace, Wolfgang went to see Mesmer at his house. Now settled in Paris, the magnetic therapist would no longer return to Vienna, but his family received the visitor in a most friendly manner. They advised him to go and see some nobles who enjoyed fine music, beginning with Count Thun and his wife, who were great lovers of anything new.

## The Son of Enlightenment

*Vienna, 16 March 1781*

'Here is the list of the members of the new To True Union Lodge, Herr Count.'

Geytrand handed it to Josef Anton, who consulted it immediately.

One name caught his attention.

'Ignaz von Born ... the mineralogist from the university?'

'The very same.'

'One of the late Empress Maria Theresa's protégés! He hid his game well, that fellow. And see how the Freemasons are infiltrating our country!'

'According to my informant, he will soon be one of the major figures in this lodge, which he is planning to set to work. His speech and attitude shocked several Brothers, who are unaccustomed to studying symbols and rituals.'

'You seem even better informed than usual, Geytrand. Has a Brother betrayed this lodge so soon after its foundation?'

'Indeed.'

'What is his name?'

'Soliman, the tutor to several princes.'

'Why does he behave in this way?'

'He is a mulatto who has suffered many humiliations, and dreams only of avenging himself against the whole of humanity.'

'And yet Freemasonry has admitted him to its bosom!'

105

'Indeed, but without granting him a leading role. From his point of view, the lodges do not do enough. He wants a true revolution. And besides, he is a venal man with a considerable need for ready cash.'

'Keep watch on Ignaz von Born without alerting him,' instructed the count. 'And no mistakes! If he becomes suspicious, give up. The emperor would not forgive us for importuning a brilliant Viennese university scholar. This is precisely the kind of individual I would have preferred to see a long way away, a very long way! Everyone praises his rigorousness and intelligence, and he enjoys an international reputation. If he succeeds, he will lend this lodge a brilliance that will attract other intellectuals.'

'I doubt he will succeed,' objected Geytrand. 'Numerous rivals will get in his way and prevent him consolidating his plans. Fortunately, vanity, jealousy and corruption are not absent from Freemasonry. Otherwise, like the old brotherhoods of initiates, it would produce great works.'

# 19

*Vienna, 23 March 1781*

Armed with a recommendation from the Mesmer family, Wolfgang went to see Count Franz Josef Thun-Hohenstein.

The forty-seven-year-old count was a Freemason in the To True Union Lodge and a Brother of Thamos, who had talked to him at length about Mozart. He was also a follower of spiritualism, magnetism and all the occult sciences. His wife, Maria-Wilhelmine, was extremely cultivated and a former pupil of Joseph Haydn. She kept a famous salon in the Ulfelde palace, a family property near to the Minoritenkirche.

'Herr Mozart!' exclaimed Franz Josef. 'I had a premonition of your visit in a dream. How could a true artist have escaped my dear Wilhelmine? You believe in spirits, naturally?'

'Is music not filled with them?'

'But of course! Come and have a look round. The acoustics are excellent, apparently, and people who play at this salon say extremely good things about it. Then I shall introduce you to my wife and we shall sit down to eat. A belief in the spirits does not harm the appetite.'

Straight away, Countess Wilhelmine discerned that Wolfgang was an exceptional personality. Before even hearing a single note from this young man, she knew that his works would resemble nothing as yet known.

'This house is open to you,' she told him with a kind smile. 'If you wish, come here every day.'

'Prince-Archbishop Colloredo gives me hardly any freedom.'

'You will have to give academies* in order to win over the Viennese,' decreed the countess. 'To begin with, you could take part in the charity concert organized by the Society of Musicians. Colloredo will not forbid you to take part in good works.'

*Vienna, 24 March 1781*

Unable to bear his lunch companions, who were becoming ever-more vulgar, Wolfgang had eaten nothing and was pacing around in the Grand Mufti's antechamber as he awaited his response.

---

*Name given to concerts.

Finally, the Count of Arco emerged from His Eminence's office.

'Has my request been accepted?' asked Wolfgang.

'Refused. You are in the service of the prince-archbishop and nobody else.'

'But this is a charity concert, and I would be just one musician among many others.'

'The prince-archbishop has a perfect knowledge of Viennese artistic life. As a servant belonging to his retinue, you must submit to the rules he decrees. Good day, Mozart.'

The Count of Arco returned to see his august patron.

'I have informed him of your decision, Eminence.'

'And has the young cockerel bowed to it?'

'He has no choice.'

'We shall break him, and he will continue to eat out of my hand. Without the salary I pay him, he would become a beggar. His father will never accept such a fall from grace and will succeed in persuading his son to behave in a docile manner.'

'While I share Your Eminence's views, I feel I must inform you of various rumours that are stirring up the Viennese nobility.'

Colloredo frowned.

'Might these rumours concern me in one way or another?'

'I fear so.'

'Then tell me!'

'Many music-lovers would appreciate a slightly more flexible attitude on your part, and would like to hear some of your musicians at academies, which would enable lovers of music to discover the artistic wealth of the Salzburg court.'

'Mozart, for example?'

'Him and others. Would Your Eminence's prestige not be enhanced by it?'

'There is no question of yielding on tomorrow's concert. Mozart will think I am capitulating. When will the next occasion be?'

'The academy on the 3rd of April.'

'I shall think about it.'


*Vienna, 24 March 1781*


As he read Josef II's decree, Josef Anton could not believe his eyes: the emperor was forbidding all associations, whether religious or civil, to recognise the authority of foreign superiors and to pay them dues.

This concerned the monastic orders, but also the Strict Templar Observance and Swedish Rite lodges which were still based in Vienna.

Anyone who broke the new law would be subject to legal penalties.

Josef II's declared liberalism was accompanied by the exercise of a strong central power, determined to control everything.

# 20

*Vienna, 3 April 1781*

The previous day, Wolfgang had finished a rondo for
violin and orchestra,* with a view to a future concert.
And this evening, at the Carinthian Gate Theatre, he was
making his first public appearance in Vienna, outside the
Grand Mufti's empire! As a child, he had experienced a
certain success, but in the manner of a dream that had
swiftly faded away. This time, he was aware of the difficulties and of the challenge he was issuing to Colloredo.

During this academy, held for the benefit of the
Viennese doctors' widows and orphans fund, in the presence of one hundred and eighty spectators, Wolfgang
conducted a symphony, played some piano variations†
and improvised at length.

*K373.
† K354 (299a).

Charmed, the audience did not want to let go of this young musician, who was both dynamic and thoughtful. Enchanted by this experience, which he planned to repeat, Wolfgang wrote to his father: '*I assure you that it is a magnificent place here and, for my career, the best in the world.*'

*Vienna, 4 April 1781*

'A success, you say?' Colloredo demanded furiously of the Count of Arco.

'Mozart's performance was very well received,' confirmed the Master of the Kitchens. 'But it was merely a charitable event, and the audience would have applauded anyone.'

'Perhaps, perhaps . . . Nevertheless, I will not allow my servant to parade himself in this way!'

The Count of Arco coughed gently.

'You did not issue a formal ban, Eminence.'

In rage, Colloredo snapped his goose-feather pen in two.

'That young rebel is already boasting of his exploit! If he thinks he has won, he will soon have to think again. You will order him to go and play at my father's house, on the 8th of April. If he conducts himself correctly, I shall retain him in my retinue.'

At the same moment, Wolfgang was declaring to Leopold: '*Imagine what I could do, now that the public knows me, if I gave a concert on my own account? Really, the only thing preventing it is our boorish master.'*

*Vienna, 5 April 1781*

Wolfgang rejoiced at the thought of taking part in the important academy on 8th April, which Countess Thun was organizing at her home. Emperor Josef II would be present, and the young man was eager to persuade him of his talent, in the hope of obtaining a post at court.

As he was getting up from the table, without speaking a word, the Count of Arco barred his way.

'The prince-archbishop orders you to give a concert at the home of his father.'

'Gladly.'

'That concert will take place on the 8th.'

'The 8th? That's impossible!'

'How do you mean, impossible?'

'I have already been invited by Countess Thun.'

'That matters not, Mozart. You are in the exclusive service of Prince-Archbishop Colloredo and you owe him absolute obedience. Forget your society obligations and do your work.'

Stunned and furious, Wolfgang hesitated.

If he went to Countess Thun's house, that would constitute an insult to Colloredo. If the emperor took the prince-archbishop's side, the composer from Salzburg would be forced to leave Vienna. Deprived of work, would he not be doomed to poverty?

Once again, he gave in. And on 7th April, between 11 p.m. and midnight, he composed a sonata for violin and piano.* There was no time to write down the piano part, so he would therefore have to play it from memory.

*Vienna, 9 April 1781*

'We missed you greatly,' Countess Thun told Wolfgang. 'As promised, the emperor graced the concert with his presence and gave each musician fifty ducats.'

Fifty ducats, half my salary in Salzburg, thought the composer, deeply upset at having missed such an opportunity.

'A generous gesture on the part of Josef II,' went on the countess, 'for he is conducting a policy of austerity, including the artistic domain. Economizing is his favourite word! According to him, Maria Theresa granted far too many pensions to hordes of people who were completely devoid of talent. Even old horses merited a retirement pension! From now on, each florin will be controlled, and nobody will be a drain upon the public purse.'

'Then it is pointless to dream of a post as a musician at court.'

* K380.

'Indeed, my young friend. The current post-holders will cling on to their prerogatives and will not allow anyone to break into their narrow circle. If you wish to remain in Vienna, you must use your talents to affirm yourself.'

'Prince-Archbishop Colloredo will prevent me from doing so.'

'Will you continue spoiling your talent much longer in the service of that tyrant?'

'I am a servant, Countess, and I must bow the knee.'

She smiled.

'The look in your eyes says the opposite.'


*Brunswick, 10 April 1781*

Duke Charles of Sudermania had confirmed his resignation. He was no longer Grand Master of the seventh province of the Templar Order, which he did not consider legitimate and whose disappearance he now openly wished for. From now on, he would devote himself to the Swedish Rite and to his country's affairs.

'At last we are rid of that careerist!' exclaimed Charles of Hesse.

'A bitter victory,' commented Ferdinand of Brunswick. 'Poland, Prussia, Hanover and the Austrian States have withdrawn from Strict Observance.'

'The responses to your invitation to the Wilhelmsbad Gathering should soon be with us, but those which have already been received are well argued and detailed. All the Freemasons of worth and renown will make their contributions and help us to establish a direction. Strict Observance is not dead, Grand Master, quite the contrary! It has merely withdrawn momentarily, the better to reorganize its forces and set off to conquer new territories.'

Sometimes, the Duke of Brunswick felt tired. True, his balance-sheet was not a negative one but he had hoped for better, so much better! Charles of Hesse, who was much younger than he, gave him back his confidence. His unshakeable determination persuaded him not to give up.

But why did the Unknown Superior from Egypt not show himself?

# 21

*Vienna, 16 April 1781*

Thanks to Countess Thun's hospitality, Wolfgang often escaped from Colloredo's palace where, from time to time, the prelate gave communion to his subjects. Coming from an admirer of the French atheist philosophers, such hypocrisy amused Wolfgang, whose judgement was unswerving: 'an evil-minded prince who swindles me each day'.

And that day, during lunch with friends – the Auernhammers, whose ugly daughter was his pupil – the musician met Gottlieb Stephanie, called the Young, inspector general of Vienna's German theatre, who boasted of having the ear of Josef II.

'Have you by any chance composed a little opera, Mozart?'

'A little.'

'No great successes, it seems. Otherwise I would have heard of them.'

'The Prince-Elector of Bavaria commissioned me to write *Idomeneo, King of Crete*, which was performed in Munich during the last carnival.'

'Ah . . . ! So you know the trade.'

'I am searching for a good text.'

'In Italian or in German?'

'Preferably in German.'

'The emperor would like to have a fine work in our language at last. Up to now, we have had nothing but French comic plays and Italian *opera buffa*. Our talented Salieri has composed *The Chimney Sweep*, which will be created on the 30th of April at the Burgtheater, but that is a coarse farce. His Majesty wishes to have something more serious, without being excessively austere.'

'Do you have a . . . precise idea?'

'That is entirely possible.'

Society talk, thought Wolfgang. Like most of the people I meet, this Stephanie fellow will have forgotten me as soon as he gets up from the table.


*Vienna, 17 April 1781*


Radiating all the magnificence of his forty years, Prince-Archbishop Hieronymus Colloredo was presiding in the vast office of his Viennese palace, where he received many influential members of the court. The prelate was careful to agree with the emperor's policies and his plans for reform.

118

Now, that morning, his visitor was not a member of the elite.

'I am not happy with you, Mozart.'

'Have I not obeyed His Eminence's orders?'

'With obvious bad grace!'

'Nobody has complained about my playing. At the concert given to the glory of your household, did I not improvise for a good hour on a theme which Your Eminence yourself imposed upon me? So my goodwill surely cannot be called into question.'

'Technique is not the only thing, Mozart! In my eyes, the state of mind of my servants is just as important.'

'Does one man have the right to rule another man's mind?'

'That is enough! I do not pay you to talk kitchen philosophy. Prepare to leave Vienna.'

'Leave Vienna, but—'

'Would you dare disobey my orders?'

Wolfgang chose to remain silent.

'The date has not yet been fixed,' stated Colloredo. 'As soon as my decision is made, you will be informed of it.'

Leave Vienna, return to Salzburg, go back to prison to rot there for ever, when a librettist might be about to enable him to compose an opera and his new friends, like Countess Thun, were helping him to consolidate a burgeoning reputation!

Clearly his future was here and nowhere else. But if he disobeyed Colloredo, would that not condemn him to ruin? Alas, Thamos was not around to advise him.

There was only one solution: play for time, get a stronger foothold in Vienna and attempt to make his plans more concrete.

*Berlin, 20 April 1781*

As he gazed at the fine building which Emperor Frederick II had given to the Order of African Architects, its founder, the Prussian officer Friedrich von Köppen, could not hold back a tear.

'Total failure,' he admitted to Thamos the Egyptian. 'The building has returned to administration, and the Order is dissolved. However, I believe that our brochure on the initiations of Egyptian priests into the ancient mysteries could profoundly alter Freemasonry.'

'The ideas have spread, and the adventure is not at an end.'

'For me, it is. None of my initiatives has been crowned with success. The library, the natural history study and the alchemical laboratory have remained desperately empty. And yet, here, we have everything: the protection of the emperor, magnificent premises, the necessary books . . . And look at the result! Our society is incapable of interesting itself in what is vital and placing initiation at the centre of its preoccupations.'

'Would it not be the worst failure of all to give up?'

'If you persist, Count of Thebes, I wish you good luck. But you will not succeed. I intend to withdraw into silence and solitude.'

Thamos sensed that he would not manage to change Friedrich von Köppen's decision. The disappearance of this Order had deprived Freemasonry of a research centre which could have welcomed in the Great Magician.

*Vienna, 25 April 1781*

'Two pieces of good news,' Geytrand announced to Josef Anton. First, the Duke of Sudermania has split once and for all from Strict Templar Observance, which will henceforth be absent from all the Austrian States; second, the extinction of the Order of African Architects, in Berlin.'

'Did the authorities intervene?'

'No, there were too few Brothers, incapable of using the means placed at their disposal.'

'That Order counted only a small number of members, and the Freemasons of other Rites looked down upon it. The return to oblivion of these African Architects will not lead to any kind of schism. Is the Wilhelmsbad Gathering in preparation?'

'With many difficulties! If the Duke of Brunswick cannot organize it, he will have to step down.'

'He will succeed, for Strict Observance is his reason for living. We must never underestimate a man's ideal, Geytrand. Sometimes it makes him capable of moving mountains.'

# 22

*Vienna, 1 May 1781*

Prince-Archbishop Colloredo's messenger did not bother with pleasantries.

'Wolfgang Mozart, is that you?'

'It is.'

'His Eminence orders you to move out immediately. He doesn't want to see you under his roof any longer.'

'Where am I to go?'

'I couldn't give a damn. The important thing is that you push off immediately.'

'Is he giving me a little time?'

'You pack your bags and you go.'

As Colloredo's emissary had not mentioned Salzburg, Wolfgang decided to remain in Vienna to await developments.

Several solutions presented themselves. The musician chose the simplest, in other words the Eye of God, the middle-class dwelling near to St Peter's Church, kept by Frau Weber. She lived there with Aloysia's three sisters, and Aloysia was emerging just as the expelled musician arrived.

'Wolfgang! How are you?'

'Almost well. And you?'

'Marvellously well! Allow me to introduce my husband, the actor Joseph Lange.'

The two men greeted each other.

'What are you doing here?' asked Aloysia, intrigued.

'Colloredo has driven me out of his Viennese palace, so I am looking for somewhere to stay.'

'You are knocking at the right door; my mother has a pleasant room available. Forgive me, we are in a hurry. No doubt we shall see each other again.'

'No doubt.'

It was the timid and reserved Constance Weber who greeted the musician. Aged nineteen, she had a slender face, a pointed nose and a small mouth. She welcomed the visitor in a sweet, distinguished voice.

'May I see your mother?'

'I shall go and fetch her.'

A seasoned businesswoman, the matriarch approved of this new lodger, whose honesty she knew.


*Vienna, 9 May 1781*


'This situation has lasted long enough, Mozart,' opined the prince-archbishop. 'Here is a packet which you are to take immediately to Salzburg, where you will remain. Your stay in Vienna is at an end.'

'Eminence, I am not your messenger.'

'Enough insolence, Mozart! Be silent and obey.'

'I am a musician, not a carrier of parcels. I shall not demean myself to perform this kind of task and I refuse to be swindled in this way!'

'That is enough, you filthy, depraved, devilish, villainous, moronic scoundrel!'

'Since you treat me in an unworthy manner, I shall no longer work for you.'

'Then be gone!'

'Tomorrow, you shall receive my resignation.'

Trembling, Wolfgang ran to his new lodgings and wrote an account of the drama for his father.

'*Impossible to get a word in,*' he explained. '*He was going off like a firework. I am still full to the brim with anger, my patience has been so long tried! Today was for me a day of joy. It is now that my happiness begins, and I hope that it is also yours.*'

That same evening, Wolfgang was seized by a violent fever. The emotion had been so intense that he shivered like a man on the point of death.


*Vienna, 10 May 1781*


Miraculously recovered, an elegant Mozart headed for Colloredo's palace and approached his direct hierarchical superior, the Count of Arco, master of the kitchens.

'I have come to submit my resignation,' he declared with gravity. 'From this moment, I am no longer one of Colloredo's servants but a free man.'

'Come, come, Mozart, don't get carried away like this! You are wrong to behave aggressively towards His Eminence, whose great Christian goodness will cleanse you of this lamentable sin. In future, maintain your calm.'

'You do not understand, Herr Count. My decision has been made after mature reflection. Please accept my resignation.'

'Impossible.'

'Why?'

'Because I require the written consent of your father. You are nothing but a big, irresponsible child, ready to spoil your life for a stupid headstrong outburst. Come and see me with that document or, better yet, when you have changed your mind.'

Wolfgang ate lunch with Countess Thun, who encouraged him to submit no longer to Colloredo's demands. With burning determination, the musician exaggerated somewhat in writing to his father: '*All Vienna knows of my adventures. The entire nobility is declaring that I must no longer allow myself to be duped.*'

Incapable of composing, waiting impatiently for the paternal agreement that would at last deliver him from the prince-archbishop, Wolfgang roamed the streets of the city.

Leopold would be bound to understand his attitude and would grant him the vital permission. At last, his son would take flight!

'Tonight,' said Thamos the Egyptian's peaceful voice, 'try to sleep a little.'

'I could have benefited from your help, these past few days!'

'You managed very well on your own.'

'You can't imagine the violence of the argument I had with the Grand Mufti! That filthy fellow is a monster of vanity. Now, I shall hesitate no longer! Since the gates of the prison are opening, I shall take my freedom and never again turn back.'

'Have you considered all the consequences of this decision?'

'I shall have to struggle and struggle again, but it will no longer be for Colloredo's benefit. You of all people will not reproach me for breaking my chains!'

'On the contrary, Wolfgang. But do not let yourself be carried away by this intoxication.'

'My adolescence is ending, and my life as a man begins. Vienna has forgotten the child prodigy, and so have I. Either I am capable of asserting myself as an independent musician, or I do not deserve the chance which destiny is offering me.'

# 23

*Vienna, 19 May 1781*

Wolfgang was devastated.

Instead of giving him his agreement and approving of his desire for freedom, Leopold was urging him to submit to Colloredo, in order to keep his post in Salzburg!

Cruelly disappointed, he allowed his heart to speak: *I do not recognize my father in any of the lines of your letter! And should I allow myself to be regarded as a cretin and the archbishop as a noble lord? If it is satisfying to be rid of a prince who does not pay you and swindles you to death, then yes, it is true, I am satisfied. I have been forced to take this decisive step and can no longer withdraw an inch. My honour must be above all else.*

Would Leopold finally understand his true aspirations? Whatever happened, Wolfgang would bow the knee no more.

*Munich, 20 May 1781*

Professor Adam Weishaupt congratulated himself on having recruited Baron Adolph von Knigge, who was devoting himself with constant ardour to the development of the secret Order of the Illuminati of Bavaria.

'At this moment,' declared the baron, 'we have a membership of more than three hundred and, besides Bavaria, we have members in Swabia, Lower Saxony, the Upper and Lower Rhine, and even in Vienna. This is only a beginning, for many Freemasons are at last beginning to detach themselves from the Church and fight the rampant influence of the Jesuits. Justly, they reproach the Catholics for predicting a better fate for a murderer, a debauchee or an impostor who believes in transubstantiation than for an honest, virtuous man who has the misfortune not to understand how a morsel of flour paste can be at the same time a piece of flesh. The time for these superstitions is past, and we – Illuminati and Freemasons – must prepare for the birth of an era in which the light of knowledge will replace the darkness of belief.'

Adam Weishaupt was jubilant, but wanted to go much further.

'Do you not think, my Brother, that emperors and kings protect and encourage this obscurantism?'

'We must condemn bad rulers, whether they are kings or commoners,' said von Knigge, 'and above all we must provoke an evolution in morality. This immense task may take us millions of years. I tell you again, any violent revolution would end in disaster. Overturning the regimes in place will achieve nothing until we have changed the hearts of men.'

Millions of years, an evolution in morality ... Weishaupt, for his part, was hoping for decisive political action, but he preferred to keep quiet about his real designs as long as he needed Adolph von Knigge and Freemasonry.

'I have constructed the architecture of our Order,' the baron went on. 'It will consist of three classes: the Nursery, Freemasonry and the Mysteries.'*

Von Knigge did not know that Adam Weishaupt controlled the Order of Illuminati of Bavaria with an iron fist, by using compartmentalization, denunciation and espionage.

With the establishment of the Nursery, absolute control would become more difficult. Nevertheless, it must recruit and persuade large numbers of brilliant and influential minds to join a spiritual, intellectual and social movement whose goal was the happiness of humanity.

In reality, Weishaupt hoped to implement his revolutionary plan, whose scope the naïve, easily manipulated Freemasons were unaware of. Despite them, they would

---

* First class: the Nursery (three grades: Novitiate, Minerval, Illuminatus Minor). Second class: Freemasonry (five grades: Apprentice, Companion, Master, Illuminatus Major, Leading Illuminatus or Scottish Knight). Third class: the Mysteries, comprising the Small Mysteries (Priests and Regents) and the Great Mysteries (Mages and Kings).

become the vectors of a conflagration capable of setting the whole of Europe aflame. Doubtless they themselves would become victims of it, but that mattered little. Bringing down the Church and royalty, bringing forward a new political power, that was the important thing.

'Has the Grand Master of Strict Templar Observance responded to your comments on his circular?' he asked the baron.

'His entourage did not much care for them. Our Templar Brothers deceive themselves by imagining they are capable of resuscitating a far-off past instead of interesting themselves in the present. During the meeting at Wilhelmsbad, we shall take vigorous action and point Freemasonry in the right direction.'

*Vienna, 25 May 1781*

'Spartacus, Brutus, Philon, Lucian, Abaris . . . Is this some new Masonic madness?' Josef Anton asked Geytrand, who had just handed him a most curious list of Brothers.

'Those are the code names of several Illuminati, behind which highly placed individuals are hiding. They meet at Athens, Eleusis, Heliopolis or in Egypt, other code names for cities in Germany or Austria, which I have not yet managed to decipher. All of this remains very mysterious, and I have obtained only crumbs of information. These Illuminati form an almost hermetically sealed society. But as it develops, it will inevitably supply us with loudmouths and traitors.'

'Are these Illuminati allied to the Freemasons and the Templars?'

'The majority seem to be Freemasons themselves, and several lodges are beginning to talk about their movement as one which could rouse the Brothers from their torpor.'

'Exactly what must be avoided! Do they have a precise doctrine?'

'I am experiencing difficulties in pinning it down, for the Illuminati do everything covertly. They criticize the Church, while at the same time recognizing the existence of an esoteric Christianity.'

'Do they approve of the emperor's reforms?'

'Apparently.'

'That does not suit me at all! If Josef II likes them, he will forbid me to attack them. No openly subversive declarations that we can keep in reserve?'

'Not yet, Herr Count.'

'We must follow this file very closely, Geytrand. These Illuminati seem to me to be more dangerous than the followers of Strict Templar Observance. Certain of them may not be content with hazy intellectual theories and bizarre beliefs.'

# 24

*Vienna, 28 May 1781*

Still in a state of shock after his violent altercation with Colloredo, Wolfgang took refuge at Countess Thun's house. She continued to lavish comfort and encouragement upon him.

'My father has abandoned me,' lamented the young man.

'Do not worry yourself so,' advised Count Franz Josef. 'I have consulted the spirits on your behalf, and they proved very favourable. Your father will not oppose your wishes, since it is just and right. Most importantly, you must not change your mind, for that would be fatal to you! Dear Wolfgang, it is in Vienna that your career will blossom. I am going to introduce you to two good friends who will support you.'

Caught up in a whirlpool, the musician met Joseph von Sonnenfels and Baron Gottfried van Swieten, who were extremely different from each other.

Josef von Sonnenfels, professor of political sciences at the University of Vienna, the first Austrian lawyer to defend the theses of the philosophy of Lights, and director of the periodical *Man without Prejudices*, had obtained the abolition of torture in 1776. On the emperor's orders, he had worked to promote the Burgtheater, the German national theatre. A Freemason, the eminent university teacher also belonged to the Order of Illuminati of Bavaria, under the code name of Fabius.

'My friend Franz Josef Thun has told me a great deal about you, Herr Mozart. It appears you can no longer bear Prince-Archbishop Colloredo's tight rein?'

'I would prefer to call it tyranny.'

'Great prelates are often pretentious, and when they get mixed up in politics, they become completely odious. I share your sentiments and agree with your course of action. The author of *Idomeneo* should not remain locked away in Salzburg.'

'You . . . you know my opera?'

'It is full of promise. It is vital that you go forward. Count Thun will keep me informed.'

Josef von Sonnenfels left Mozart with Baron Gottfried van Swieten. A well-built fellow, the director of the Imperial Library was a curious mixture of good humour and severity.

'I am happy to see you again. So, you are setting off to conquer Vienna.'

'I do not have that much ambition, Baron. I would simply like to make a living here from my music.'

133

'That will not be easy.'

'I am aware of that, but this destiny does not frighten me, whereas the prison of Salzburg condemns me to a slow death.'

'Destiny . . . It sometimes takes surprising turns. I very much like music and prize composers who are little known to the Viennese public. If you settle in the capital, perhaps you will come and play at my house.'

'Gladly, Herr Baron.'

Gottfried van Swieten remained sceptical, for the Great Magician did not look like one. Was this nervous little man, with the continually alert expression, really the exceptional man who was capable of breathing new life into Masonic initiation? Perhaps Thamos the Egyptian was gravely mistaken.

A surprising promotion had delighted van Swieten; because of his good and loyal services, the emperor had just entrusted him with a new job which had already aroused many other people's envy: the office of President of the Committee of Studies for Education and Culture, in other words head of the committee which censored all publications.

He would get rid of anti-Masonic pamphlets and allow texts to be published which spread the ideas of the lodges, as long as they respected the State and its laws.

Would this post finally enable him to unearth the man responsible for hunting down the Freemasons, a man placed at the head of a department so secret that no information filtered out of it? And did that department really exist?

The late Maria Theresa had dreamt of closing the lodges and had certainly ordered police officers to compile dossiers, now in the hands of Josef II whose liberal tendencies were opposed to such manoeuvres. But the emperor was still the emperor, and he probably did not disdain the use of such precious information.

Step by step, with the greatest caution, Brother van Swieten continued his investigation.

*Vienna, 2 June 1781*

'*The archbishop is fulminating against me before the whole world*,' wrote Wolfgang to his father,

> '*and he does not have sufficient judgement to notice that this does him no honour. For here I am prized more than he, an arrogant and presumptuous priest who despises all that is Viennese, whereas I am held to be an agreeable man. It is true, I am proud if I notice that I am being treated with scorn or as a joke, and that is how the archbishop treats me. By talking to me correctly, he would have obtained what he wanted from me. Be sure that it is not idleness that I love, but work. Nevertheless, for such a mediocre salary, I cannot and I will not serve any longer.*'

135

After such strong words, he hoped for explicit agreement from Leopold, which would permit him finally to break his chains. So he headed confidently for Colloredo's palace, where he encountered the Count of Arco.

'Have you gone back on your decision, Mozart?'

'Of course not.'

'I have received a letter from your father.'

'At last! So, you accept my resignation.'

'That is not the meaning of his message. On the contrary, he asks me to make you change your mind. Consequently, I refuse your request.'

'I shall remain in Vienna and I shall succeed.'

'I know the Viennese well, Mozart. They are changeable and like only new things and the taste of the day. Their favours do not last. Perhaps you will experience a small success which will intoxicate you. Then they will forget you and you will sink into poverty. At Salzburg, like your father, you will lead a decent, quiet existence. Present your apologies to His Eminence, and all will be as it should be again.'

'Out of the question! My father will eventually agree with me and you will be forced to accept my resignation.'


*Vienna, 8 June 1781*


Wolfgang set out again to win over the Count of Arco.

This time, the exchange was as brief as it was violent. Exasperated, the master of the kitchens dismissed him once and for all '*with a kick up the backside, by order of our dear prince-archbishop,*' as Wolfgang wrote immediately to his father, in the hope of being able to kick the backside of that petty noble should he encounter him in the street.

Never again would Wolfgang work for Colloredo, even if he did not send him a formal letter of dismissal.

'*I who must now compose constantly,*' he concluded, '*require a serene head and a tranquil mind.*'

# 25

*Vienna, 20 June 1781*

'Are you certain you have several pupils?' asked the suspicious Frau Weber.

'Thanks to Countess Thun and other wealthy friends,' replied Wolfgang, 'I shall be giving lessons in return for the correct remuneration.'

The matron appeared satisfied. An independent musician, without fixed employment, risked becoming an undesirable tenant. But she had heard good things of this serious little man.

As he was returning to his new, rather pleasant room, pretty Constance greeted him.

'I am very happy that you are remaining with us.'

'So am I, Fräulein.'

'You are very brave, Herr Mozart. To oppose a noble like that . . .'

'Only the heart ennobles a man. If I am not a count,

I perhaps have more honour in me than many counts. Whether he is a valet or a nobleman, a man who insults me is scum.'

Happy to savour his freedom at last, Wolfgang would for ever ignore Colloredo and the Count of Arco. In a *galant* style, he wrote charming variations on French airs, *La Bergère Célimène** and *Au bord d'une fontaine*,† and a march from Grétry's *Mariages samnites*.‡

True, Thamos would criticize this return to light-heartedness, but must he not first and foremost please the Viennese, in order to ensure his financial independence?

'Get your breath back in your own way,' advised the Egyptian, as his protégé was emerging from a lunch at Countess Thun's house.

'Do I really have a chance of success, in your opinion?'

'The great adventure is beginning, Wolfgang. It is up to you to create your own path towards the temple, to fashion your own destiny as a man and as a musician.'

*Cobenzl, 13 July 1781*

As he finished a sonata for piano and violin§ with a tumultuous start but a calming development, Wolfgang was

---

* Twelve variations for piano and violin, K359.
† Six variations for piano and violin, K360.
‡ Eight variations for piano, K352.
§ K377.

enjoying a happy, tranquil period at the house of Count Cobenzl, cousin of one of his pupils, who had invited him to sample the charms of the countryside at the foot of Mount Reisen, an hour's journey from Vienna.

During his numerous journeys, Wolfgang had not often had the opportunity to appreciate nature. This time, he took the time to gaze upon it, to ramble through the vast gardens, to sit beside the lake and meditate in the artificial grotto, where he thought of the delicious face of Constance Weber, enlivened by her sparkling dark eyes. She had neither the beauty nor the bearing of her elder sister, Aloysia, but her delicacy enchanted him.

Several times, during July, Wolfgang returned to this place, '*sumptuous and very pleasant*' as he described it to his father. For a few sun-filled days, he relaxed and no longer worried about the future.


*Vienna, 25 July 1781*


Wolfgang composed two sonatas for piano and violin[*] which were rather feverish and agitated, dominated by the feeling of a struggle against oneself and the outside world.

His father must allow him the time to settle in Vienna and plough his own furrow. Success would not come in a day.

[*] K379 and K380.

And above all, why suspect him of having settled in the Webers' house so that he could seduce one of the three daughters who lived there with their mother! The eldest, Josefa, he did not like; the youngest, Sophie, was barely more than a child; and Constance, the middle daughter, had no thoughts of marriage.

Moreover, Wolfgang did not feel in love with her. Or at least, not entirely. Whatever the case, he had no intention of marrying her. All that mattered was this German opera, whose libretto he was awaiting.

*Vienna, 30 July 1781*

'Here is the promised text,' declared Gottlieb Stephanie the Young, full of his status as inspector of the German theatre in Vienna. 'I have talked to His Majesty the emperor about it, and he has approved the subject: *Belmonte and Constance, or the Abduction from the Seraglio*. In a few words, a noble young woman, Constance, is a prisoner of the sultan, as is her English servant, Blonde, and Pedrillo, the servant of the man she loves, Belmonte. Belmonte tries to free them, but the tyrant and the guardian of the seraglio are watching! I shall leave you to discover the dramatic moments.'

Wolfgang remained silent.

Constance . . . Like Constance Weber and like the high virtue of the *Dream of Scipio* – Constancy, which was superior to Fortune!

'You seem astonished! Do you not like the story?'

'Oh no, on the contrary! This is a fine hymn to liberty.'

'Try to write music halfway between serious and buffoonery. The emperor does not want a vulgar farce, but he would not wish to be bored listening to a sombre drama either.'

'What date is the first performance planned for?'

Stephanie coughed.

'We in Vienna are going to have the joy of receiving Grand-Duke Paul of Russia, son of Catherine II and the future tsar. On that occasion, the emperor wishes to present some new operas to him, including *The Abduction from the Seraglio*.'

'What is the date of this visit?' persisted Wolfgang.

'Mid-September.'

'A month and a half . . .'

'It is not long, I agree, but it is said that you write very quickly.'

'What about the singers?'

'Prima donna Caterina Cavalieri will sing the role of the heroine, Constance. Despite her slight weight problem, she is, at twenty-six, at the peak of her powers and can interpret the most difficult arias with gusto. Although he is forty-one, Valentin Adamberger will be a superb Belmonte, as romantic and valiant as one could wish. The famous Ludwig Fischer will make the appalling Osmin both odious and comical. The pretty, sparkling Theresa Teyber will take the part of Blonde and Johann-Ernst Dauer will make an amusing Pedrillo. You will not find a better cast.'

Stephanie was not exaggerating.

'The 15th of September . . . I shall be ready.'

Taking the libretto under his arm, the composer ran off in search of a piano. There was not a second to lose.

'I shall place a salon and an instrument at your disposal,' said Thamos the Egyptian's calm voice.

# 26

*Vienna, 30 July 1781*

On the piano, Wolfgang played the overture, the chorus from the first act and a few arias from *The Abduction from the Seraglio*, not forgetting a little 'Turkish-style' music, a convention often practised in Vienna which wanted to forget that in 1683, the Turks had almost taken the city.

'A miracle!' exclaimed the composer. 'This *Abduction* is so much like *Zaïde* that I already have many pieces ready.'

'Miracle is not the correct term,' Thamos corrected him. 'To launch your career in Vienna, you needed an opera. That is why I contacted Stephanie the Young, guiding him towards the libretto of a certain Christoph Friedrich Bretzner, a trader in Leipzig. He got hold of it without too much trouble, and has now imposed an impossible task upon you. If you fail, he envisages that there will be a replacement, using one of his own libretti. Of course, Stephanie does not know that you have already made a start.'

'The couple, Constance and Belmonte, enchant me,' confessed Wolfgang. 'Together, they confront terrible ordeals, including death. Even the worst threats do not frighten them, for their mutual fidelity proves unshakeable.'

'Pedrillo, Belmonte's servant, will introduce him as "a skilful architect",' explained Thamos, with a Masonic wink of the eye. 'And the pasha Selim, who is at first depicted as a tyrant, will be an entirely spoken role. Purely an orator, he will conduct himself with exemplary goodness, like a monarch who is capable of forgiving his enemies and governing wisely.'

'The audience will think of Joscf II,' ventured Wolfgang.

'Why not? Against him will be the harem guard, Osmin, who is choleric, narrow-minded, violent, and a slave of his own fanaticism to the point where he becomes pitiful as a result.'

'This is the beginning of Belmonte's first aria: "*O heaven, answer my desires: give me back rest! I have borne sufferings only too heavily, O Love. Bring me joy and lead me to the goal.*"'

'May heaven answer that prayer, your own and your hero's,' commented Thamos.

'Belmonte's task is not an easy one. True, he manages to track down his betrothed Constance, her servant

Blonde and her valet Pedrillo, who have been kidnapped
by pirates, but they are locked away in a seraglio and
reduced to the status of slaves. Worse still, Pasha Selim
wishes to make Constance his mistress!'

'She wears her name well,' said Thamos, 'for she
dares to resist him, at the risk of losing her life.'

'Constance . . . Yes, it is a beautiful name and a fine
virtue.'

'Blonde, who was born in England, the land of freedom, is promised to the abominable Osmin, but she
rejects him with the same vigour as Constance, who is
given an order by Pasha Selim: either she yields, or the
next day she will die.'

'After being presented to the pasha, the great architect
Belmonte manages, with Pedrillo's help, to get into the
palace. But Osmin dreams of ridding himself of this visitor, whom he detests. And that is our first act!'

*Berlin, 8 August 1781*

For Frederick-William II, who had been called upon to
become King of Prussia, this was the greatest of evenings.
Having enabled the Golden Rose-Cross to conquer the
principal German lodges to the detriment of Strict Templar
Observance, he was about to obtain the reward he had so
hoped for: at last to enter into contact with the spirits.

The two patrons of the Rose-Cross, Wöllner
and Bischoffswerder, arrived at the entrance to

Charlottenburg Castle along with a small, dumpy man just as a storm was unleashed and flashes of lightning cleaved the ink-black sky.

'An excellent omen, Majesty,' said Wöllner, who was proud of heading twenty-six circles comprising more than two hundred members. 'This is how the higher powers are indicating their approval; tonight, you will be able to question them.'

Following the initiation of Frederick-William II into the Masonic and Christian rites of the Rose-Cross, Wöllner and his acolyte presented him with a priceless gift: the participation of an authentic medium.

Heralded by a thunderclap even more violent than its predecessors, the mage launched into a series of incantations whose results went far beyond the future sovereign's hopes.

Spirits actually manifested themselves and spoke to him!

'As soon as I come to power,' said Frederick-William II to Wöllner, 'I shall appoint you Minister for Religions. And Bischoffswerder shall be my Minister of War.'*

*Vienna, 15 August 1781*

'Impossible!' declared Josef Anton. 'This time, Geytrand, you are making it up!'

---

* The promise would be kept.

'Unfortunately not, Herr Count. According to the servant who is acting as my informant, the scene occurred exactly as I have described it to you.'

'A medium ... Surely Frederick-William II is not quite as credulous as that!'

'The two manipulators are astute and convincing members of the Rose-Cross, and they knew exactly what to do.'

Anton was stunned. How could one of the future leaders of a great power sink so low?

'So he listens to the voices of Leibnitz, an annoying and unimportant thinker, and of Marcus Aurelius, a Roman emperor who believed in wisdom but had few illusions about the human race. It could have been worse! If the future spirits with whom Frederick-William II communicates are Nero, Caligula or Attila, he will become an arsonist, a madman or a bloodthirsty bandit!'

'As long as the Rose-Cross and the Freemasons lose themselves in such reveries, they will not bother with politics.'

*Vienna, 22 August 1781*

As early as 7th August, Wolfgang had played Countess Thun the first arias from *The Abduction from the Seraglio*. That day, she had the privilege of savouring the entire first act.

'Superb, Mozart! It is spirited, gay and dramatic at the same time. You will win the hearts of the Viennese public.'

'The 15th of September is rapidly approaching, and I still have two acts to compose, not to mention my dissatisfaction with the libretto. But I do not have sufficient time to alter it.'

'You will succeed, as long as you have focus and concentration on your task.'

'That is indeed my intention, Countess!'

'Even while you are being besieged by a would-be suitor, it seems?'

Wolfgang blushed.

'I . . . I don't understand.'

'You can tell me everything.'

'Who dares spread such gossip?'

'A certain young lady called Auernhammer.'

The composer struck himself on the forehead.

'Oh no, not her!'

'Is she not a charming person?' asked Countess Thun worriedly.

'She is merely my pupil, and I dare not describe her to you for fear of being extremely unkind.'

Too fat, squeezed into her luxurious clothes, sweating profusely whenever she played quickly, and slow-witted to boot, Fräulein Auernhammer was not really Mozart's ideal woman.

'Please believe me, Countess, when I tell you that I have never had the slightest feeling for her. Her inventions displease me to the highest degree, for I care a good deal about my reputation.'

'You are right, Mozart. But it would not be a sin to fall in love.'

# 27

*Vienna, 29 August 1781*

Constance Weber seemed sincerely moved.

'Are you leaving us already, Herr Mozart?'

'I needed larger, furnished accommodation in order to work there comfortably. I must swiftly finish an opera which will establish me as a composer.'

'Will you live far from here?'

'No, very close by, next to St Peter's Square.'*

She was touching, with her small dark eyes and her slender face.

'Perhaps we shall see each other again . . .' Constance hoped in a soft voice.

'Certainly! Walking relaxes me. Would you care to explore the gardens of Vienna?'

---

*At the present day 1175, Am Graben.

'If my mother does not forbid it, gladly.'

'Then I shall see you soon, Constance.'

The accommodation which Thamos had found suited Wolfgang very well. Several intellectual Freemasons lodged in the building, notably a Jew called Isaac Arnstein, a specialist in the Kabbalah, in part the heir to the esoteric teachings of ancient Egypt.

He made immediate contact with Wolfgang. Several times, the young composer had an opportunity to ponder the words of this expert in sacred numbers.

'In the beginning', revealed the Kabbalist, 'when the king's will was made manifest, he wrote signs upon the celestial sphere. Those signs became creative powers. For you, as a musician, it is notes and melodies which enable you to travel to the centre of the flame and rediscover. Wisdom, the primordial starting-point.'*

'The wisdom of the sun-priests and priestesses?'

'It is incumbent upon the seeker after initiation always to be simultaneously male and female. In this way, the divine Presence never abandons him. Woman makes that Presence endure in the home.'

Marriage was a serious, decisive act, and woman played an essential role at all stages of life. Why did religion grant her so small a place, why did it forbid her all sacred office?

---

*We quote extracts from the *Zohar* according to G. Scholem, Paris, 1980.

'The stars of the firmament are the guardians of the world,' continued the Kabbalist. 'Each object has a star which is assigned to it and protects it. It performs the function of an elixir of life and guides us towards the wisdom of the East. Just as wine must be poured into a jug to preserve it, truth must be wrapped in an external garment, composed of fables and tales.'

Meditating on the scholar's words, Wolfgang went for dinner at Countess Thun's house.

'Bad news,' she told him without preamble. 'The visit of Grand-Duke Paul of Russia has been postponed until November.'

'So much the better – I shall have time to alter the libretto and give the dramatic situations more depth.'

'People are already whispering against you,' lamented the Countess. 'A grand opera, in Vienna, composed by such a young artist . . .'

'Hypocrites and those who are petty-minded or jealous have stood in my way ever since I wrote my first note. This time, they will not prevent me from succeeding.'

'My husband, my friends and I myself will help you with all our strength.'

With such support, Wolfgang felt stronger than ever.


*Vienna, 5 September 1781*


Although he did not enjoy a cast-iron constitution, Wolfgang did possess a fine degree of energy which had enabled him to overcome smallpox, the beginnings of pneumonia, bouts of influenza and bronchitis, as well as helping him to battle rheumatic problems. Unlike so many artists with loose morals, whom he openly condemned, he did not suffer from any venereal diseases, led a healthy existence and therefore could not bear the insinuations made by his father, who was so prompt to believe the gossip concerning his son the seducer!

So he called him back to reality: '*People can write until their eyes pop out of their heads, and you can listen to them as much as you want. I shall not change my attitude one jot and shall remain, as usual, the most decent of lads.*'

Because he had won his independence, he was accused of sleeping with all the singers, the better to ruin his reputation. A free musician could be nothing other than a debauchee! He who dreamt of a marriage of absolute fidelity, he who had known only one great, unhappy love, he who placed women on a pedestal and respected them more than anyone, saw himself reviled as a miserable womanizer.

How difficult it was to bear injustice and falsehood! Fortunately, there were the walks with sweet Constance.

Constance, the heroine in *The Abduction from the Seraglio*. Constance – like Constancy, the most beautiful of virtues. Constance, who vowed eternal love to Belmonte.

'My father does not understand me,' lamented Wolfgang. 'At heart, he disapproves of my fight and wishes to see me return with all speed to Salzburg, where I will beg the prince-archbishop's pardon.'

'Is that your intention?'

'I shall never go back, Constance, for I have sworn to succeed in Vienna and not to betray myself.'

'You are very brave.'

'I want to live by my art and to regret nothing, even if I upset my father.'

'Mine was a good man and I miss him greatly. Like me, he was deeply upset by Aloysia's behaviour towards you.'

'What does the past matter, Constance?'

'Do you not hate her?'

'I hope she is happy. Your sister has a great deal of talent.'

'When I tried to sing, next to her, I felt ridiculous.'

'Be yourself! Each voice is unique, and it is the composer's task to show it at its best.'

'Do you really think so?'

'I don't know how to lie.'

'A grave defect, today! Whatever you do, don't change.'


*Saverne (Alsace), 22 September 1781*

As promised, Cagliostro had invited Thamos, Count of Thebes, to experience the birth of the new Egyptian Rite which was going to conquer Freemasonry.

This time, there was no Colombe or Pupille to decipher the spirits' message in the clear water, but there was a copy of the rituals of the Charitable Knights of the Holy City and of the invocations of the Lyons mystic Jean-Baptiste Willermoz, with whom Cagliostro corresponded.

Originally the perfect work of God, Man had abused his power over the angels and all living beings. So the Lord punished him by rendering him mortal. How could he escape this terrible fate, if not through initiation, which brought back his lost dignity?

Cagliostro's Rite claimed to regenerate initiates by getting them to drink an elixir and droplets of white liquid to which he added a balm. Then they learnt the science of Numbers, inherited from Pythagoras.

'Are you satisfied?' the mage asked Thamos.

'I have learned nothing.'

'My revelations must be progressive, for the majority of beings are slaves of materialism.'

'Then I shall await the next stage.'

'You will be astonished.'

# 28

*Vienna, 13 October 1781*

Before resuming work on the libretto of *The Abduction from the Seraglio* and attempting to convince Stephanie to undertake several alterations, Wolfgang put his father firmly in the picture. If the '*opera was dragging*', he was in no way responsible. This delay was due to political and social circumstances, and was enabling him to carry out refinements on the text, for example by portraying properly the enraged outbursts of the violent Osmin, guardian of the seraglio,

*for the man who finds himself in such a violent rage
goes beyond all rules, all measures, all boundaries.
He no longer knows himself. And it is necessary
that the music also no longer knows itself. However,
the passions, whether they are violent or not, must
never be expressed to the point where they arouse*

*disgust. And the music, even in the most terrible situations, must never offend the ear but charm it and remain always music.*

Moreover, the composer must clearly assert his predominance and not submit to the yoke of pretentious authors. '*In an opera,*' declared Wolfgang,

'*it is absolutely essential that the poetry is an obedient daughter to the music. Why, with all the miserable content of their libretti, are Italian* opera buffas *popular everywhere? Because in them the music rules unchallenged! Yes, an opera will please people all the more if the plan of the play has been better established, if the words have been written for the music and one does not encounter unfortunate rhymes here and there or entire strophes which spoil the composer's idea. Rhymes for rhymes' sake, there is nothing more harmful! The pedants who write like that will sink without trace, they and their music. The best thing is when a good composer, who understands the theatre and who is himself capable of suggesting ideas, meets a judicious poet, a real phoenix. Then, one does not have to worry about the opinions of ignorant people! With their pot-boiler farces, poets have something of the same effect on me as trumpets. If we composers were always to follow their rules, we would produce as mediocre music as they produce mediocre libretti.*'

# The Son of Enlightenment

*Vienna, 31 October 1781*

After his last, popular and vigorous serenade* was played three times in the open air without offending Viennese taste, Wolfgang listened to *Iphigenia* by Gluck, the musician currently in vogue. On that day, St Wolfgang's Day, he went to see Baroness Martha Elisabeth von Waldstätten, a thirty-seven-year-old eccentric who was separated from a State adviser. She was a wealthy woman who lived in a vast apartment at 360, Leopoldstadt, and wished to help young Mozart to conquer Vienna.

Sometimes using extremely coarse language which reminded Wolfgang of the way his little cousin from Augsburg spoke, the baroness proved extremely talkative, eccentric and nonconformist.

'Happy saint's day, Mozart! When is your *Abduction* going to be performed?'

'Mid-November, I hope.'

'In the meantime, I have a surprise for you.'

'What is it?'

'This evening, you shall see.'

At the end of a long day's toil, Wolfgang was worn out. As he was undressing, he heard the first bars of his serenade in B flat major!

Leaning out of the window, he spotted a group of poor fellows, street musicians who were playing his work

*K375.

very pleasantly and thereby wishing him an excellent saint's day.

This gift from Baroness Waldstätten, and first homage from Vienna, lulled him into a delicious slumber.

*Vienna, 18 November 1781*

'The Duke of Brunswick's affairs are not working out well for him,' Geytrand announced to Josef Anton. 'Now he is being challenged in Brunswick itself, on his own territory!'

'Is it a serious rebellion?'

'So serious that he is transferring the government of his Templar province to Weimar, where he can count on solid support. The Grand Master is vacillating and, with him, so is the entire Order.'

'The Gathering could restore its strength and vigour.'

Geytrand looked astonished.

'Saving your respect, Herr Count, you have just used a Masonic expression.'

'After reading so many of their rituals . . . Is there any precise news about this Gathering?'

'The responses from the lodges are taking some time to reach the Grand Master, and nothing seems to have been decided yet.'

'Has your network of informants in Weimar been put on alert?'

'Of course, but I am not satisfied. The information

reaches me in dribs and drabs and seems suspect to me. I must strengthen that network and make it more reliable.'

'Brunswick is a great wounded wild beast, and he is therefore very dangerous. I want to know everything about his real plans. Let us not forget his colleague, Charles of Hesse. For the moment, he remains in the shadows, awaiting his moment. If his very dear Brother Ferdinand happened to stumble and fall, he would pick up the torch.'

'According to reliable indications,' stated Geytrand, 'Charles of Hesse is a true mystic who would like to turn Strict Observance into the new Church, faithful to the message of Christ.'

'In that case, he is not at the end of his difficulties, and we run the risk of having to face a fearsome fanatic! The only good Church is the one made up of ordinary believers who ask themselves no questions, respect the accepted customs and preoccupy themselves with nothing but their own salvation.'

# 29

*Vienna, 22 November 1781*

At last, Grand-Duke Paul of Russia was arriving in Vienna with his wife!

Wolfgang eventually succeeded in tracking down Stephanie the Young.

'My poor Mozart, I don't have a moment to myself any more. Can you imagine, a visit of such importance?'

'*The Abduction from the Seraglio* can be performed in its current state, but I would like several alterations because . . .'

'You will have time to think them over. The emperor wishes his illustrious guest to hear operas that are a little more . . . serious. So we thought of Grétry and, above all, of our great Gluck, whose numerous successes have conquered all minds. His works will certainly delight the grand-duke.'

'And . . . what about *The Abduction*?'

'It will be performed at the Burgtheater, do not worry, but not immediately.'

'Do you give me complete freedom to improve the libretto?'

'As you wish, Mozart, as you wish! Forgive me, I am swamped with work.'

Far from being discouraged, Wolfgang decided to put this delay to good use in order to transform the text into a faithful servant of the music.

The following day, the 23rd, he gave a concert with the aid of the perspiring Josefa Auernhammer, who still enveloped her teacher with languorous looks, but held her tongue. Together, they played a concerto for two pianos* and a sonata in D major†. These dazzling scores pleased the audience, which included Countess Thun and Baron van Swieten.


'Are you not downcast, Herr Mozart?' asked Constance worriedly.

'On the contrary! I dared not hope for this period of respite, which enables me to reflect and to make progress. *The Abduction from the Seraglio* will no longer be Stephanie's work, but mine.'

'Does he really want to stage your opera?'

'The emperor does.'

'Are the great of this world not changeable?'

---

\* K365.
† K448.

'Not Josef II. I understand that he should favour a musician as famous and established as Gluck. Then my turn will come, and I shall not disappoint him.'

'I am certain of it!'

'Your friendship is precious to me, Constance.'

'And yours is even more so, Wolfgang . . . Oh forgive me! I did not intend to be so familiar!'

'Since we know each other better now, why should we not be so?'

'Gladly! May I . . . may I kiss you on the cheek?'

She did not wait for his consent.

It was a furtive and decent kiss, but a great deal more ardent than a simple mark of friendship.

For the first time, Wolfgang looked at Constance with different eyes. Although timid and reserved, she was also a charming young woman.

'Constance . . .'

'Yes, Wolfgang?'

'I am twenty-five years old, and you are nineteen, and . . .'

'Is our youth a sin?'

'Indeed not, nevertheless . . .'

'If Wolfgang Mozart wished to marry me, I would give him my consent,' she whispered, lowering her eyes. 'And if he was as much in love as I am, he would not hesitate to tell me.'

'Constance, I . . .'

Her delicious look demanded an answer.

'I shall speak to your tutor,' he promised.

Smiling and radiant, she escaped.

Numb, not understanding what was happening to him, the musician walked along aimlessly and almost knocked over Thamos.

'You seem lost in your thoughts, Wolfgang.'

'No, well . . . yes . . .'

'Your *Abduction* has been put back, I know, but I have no fear of another failure. According to my contacts at court, the play will be staged, although a precise date has not yet been fixed.'

'Would you be willing to go over the libretto again with me?'

'Before that, I am going to introduce you to some friends who will play an important role throughout your career.'

'Performers?'

'No, publishers. You must think about publishing your works so that they can be passed on to posterity. The profession includes many incompetents and thieves. But the Artaria brothers will deal with you correctly.'

Originally from the region of Lake Como, the Artaria family had arrived in Vienna in 1769 and had opened a flourishing business on Michaelerplatz, near to the Burgtheater. Both Freemasons, Francesco and Carlo greeted Mozart warmly and agreed to publish several of his sonatas for piano and violin, thus conferring on him the status of a professional, worthy of the Viennese public's interest.

It wasn't yet glory, but it was an important step forward. Moreover, the author would receive a little money, that commodity which was so essential to his independence, so far from Salzburg and Colloredo!

*Vienna, 15 December 1781*

Would Nannerl detect Wolfgang's intentions, half-revealed in his letter? He wrote: ' *"The Secret in the Light of Day" is not acceptable except when considered as an Italian play, for the princess's condescension towards the servant is completely unconvincing and contrary to all that is natural. The best thing, in this play, is certainly the secret in the light of day, that is to say the way in which the two lovers, mysteriously and yet publicly, make themselves understood to each other.*'

So that was what love was. Not an all-consuming fire like what he had felt for Aloysia, but a peaceful flame, nourished by tenderness and complicity. Constance brought him balance and calm, she left his mind free to compose. Between them there was neither competition, nor confrontation, nor storms; only a profound communion, which grew richer day by day.

Now he knew. Destiny was granting him a true and reasoned love, beyond frivolity and destructive passions.

That was why Wolfgang was walking with a firm step towards the Webers' house, where he was greeted by Constance, who was visibly tense, her mother and her tutor, a cold, disagreeable fellow whom the musician detested.

He went straight to the point.

'Constance and I love each other. I would like to marry her, Frau Weber, and officially request her hand.'

'Marriage is a serious matter,' cut in the tutor. 'A young girl runs great risks and must therefore be protected. Do you admit that, Mozart?'

'Of course.'

'I demand your signature at the bottom of a contract which will signify your irreversible engagement. If you back out, you will have to pay damages and compensation.'

# 30

Constance's tutor presented Wolfgang with the document he had drafted along with the young woman's mother: 'I promise to marry Fräulein Constance Weber within the space of three years; if it becomes impossible for me to do so or if I change my mind, she will have a right to demand from me three hundred florins per year.'

The musician read the document out loud.

Constance was trembling, on the verge of tears.

'Do you agree to it?' asked Frau Weber hoarsely.

'I agree and I shall sign.'

'Here is a pen.'

Constance snatched it from her mother's hand, then tore the paper into a thousand pieces.

'Dear Wolfgang,' she exclaimed, 'I do not need this written assurance! I believe you at your word.'

'Be quiet, little idiot!' raged her mother. 'Spoken promises are worth nothing. This musician may be content to seduce you and, when he has obtained what he wanted, he will abandon you. With a proper contract, you will be protected.'

Wolfgang would never slap a woman, even if the abominable Frau Weber hardly merited the description.

'I shall not allow you to doubt my word!' he declared, outraged.

'I don't give a damn about your word! Only your signature interests me.'

'Mother,' shouted Constance, 'you are odious and grotesque. I shall not remain another minute in this house.'

The young woman fled. Wolfgang followed and caught up with her.

'Where will I take refuge?' she asked him in anguish.

'Baroness Waldstätten will take you in.'

'Me, a poor girl?'

'The baroness is a charitable person and she will come to our aid.'

'I am sure she will not!'

Constance was wrong. Martha Elisabeth von Waldstätten embraced the weeping young woman and offered her a room where she could regain her spirits.

'You can remain here as long as necessary, and Wolfgang will come to comfort you.'

'I cannot pay you, Baroness!'

'It is not a question of money, little one. On the other hand, you are going to explain all your misfortunes to me.'

Knowing that his beloved was safe, Wolfgang rushed to write to his father, weighing each word carefully so as not to anger him. He must present his marriage plans without painting his fiancée in too glowing a light, or he was likely to be criticized as nothing but a dreamer.

*I have revealed my desire to you; permit me also to reveal my reasons, which are very well founded. Nature speaks rather loudly within me and perhaps more loudly than in tall, vigorous oafs. It is impossible for me to live like the majority of young people today. First, I have too much religion, then I have too much love for my neighbour and feelings that are too decent to be able to seduce an innocent young girl; lastly, too much horror and disgust, repulsion and the fear of illnesses and too much love for my health to go and associate myself with whores. Moreover, I can swear that I have never frequented women of that sort! For my nature, which is more attracted by the quiet life and the home than by fuss and noise, for myself, someone who has never since my childhood been accustomed to looking after my affairs, my laundry, clothing and all that entails, I can imagine nothing more necessary than a wife. I can assure you how often I make futile expenses because I do not keep a check on anything. I am completely convinced that with a wife – and the same income as for myself alone – I would fare better. And how many futile expenses would fall at the same blow! It is true that it occasions others, but we know those, we can cut our cloth according to them and, in a word, lead a regular life. A bachelor, in my eyes, lives only half a life.*

*The object of my love? Constance Weber. The eldest of the Weber sisters, Josefa, is lazy, coarse, deceitful and sly. Aloysia is deceitful, spiteful and coquettish. Sophie, the youngest, is too young to be anything. She is merely a good creature, but too dazed! May God guard her against seduction. The middle one, on the other hand, my good, my dear Constance, is the martyr and, for that reason perhaps, the most generous, the most sensible, in a word the best of them. She is not ugly, she is nothing less than beautiful. All her beauty is contained in her two small dark eyes and in a fine bearing. She has no wit, but sufficient good sense to fulfil her duties as a wife and mother. She knows how to keep house and has the best heart in the world. I love her and she loves me heartily.*

*Vienna, 24 December 1781*

Wolfgang's father's reply cruelly disappointed him. It contained nothing but reproaches and suspicions, notably regarding a written promise of marriage. Who had told Leopold about that horror?

He hastened to explain the truth to him by describing Constance's magnificent conduct, and also talked of his work as a composer and teacher, so as to reassure him. This letter seemed so important to him that he did not send it immediately, in order to allow it to mature.

Then he prepared himself for a strange duel, imposed by the emperor to amuse Grand-Duke Paul of Russia: confronting the virtuoso Muzio Clementi on the piano. At twenty, the latter displayed an incredible speed.

On the evening of the battle, Wolfgang chose to play on other registers: invention, expression and sensitivity. As his adversary launched into a frenzied race which stunned the audience, Mozart improvised a dazzling series of variations, alternating slow and fast movements.

No victor was proclaimed, and the emperor handed each pianist fifty ducats. At least having confronted that soulless machine of a man had brought him in a fine sum while he waited for *The Abduction from the Seraglio* to be staged!

*Vienna, 25 December 1781*

In truth, it was a strange Christmas!

Happy to find himself far from Salzburg, although unhappy to be on cold terms with his father, Wolfgang comforted Constance who refused to return home, for fear of being locked up and never again seeing the man she loved.

'My mother terrifies me,' confessed the young woman. 'She listens too much to my tutor and thinks of nothing but money. If they search for me, you will have problems!'

'I do not fear Frau Weber,' declared Baroness von Waldstätten.

'We shall marry as soon as possible,' promised Wolfgang, 'but I must have my father's consent. Then I shall persuade Constance's mother to allow her to make a free choice.'

'After such a drama,' objected the young woman, 'she will take revenge by refusing.'

'Do not be so pessimistic,' advised the baroness. 'If your love is deep and sincere, it will overturn all obstacles.'

'That is also my opinion,' added Wolfgang.

Constance grew calmer.

All things considered, it was not such a very bad Christmas.

# 31

*Vienna, 25 December 1781*

In the apartments of the Grand-Duchess, wife of Paul of Russia, Josef Haydn* was playing his latest string quartets. Among the audience were the admiring Thamos and Mozart. As he approached his fiftieth year, Haydn was at the very peak of his craft.

That evening, Wolfgang dared not approach him. He allowed the music to rest within him, so that it would later become integrated into his own creation.

The Egyptian showed him a strange document.

'It is time to know yourself properly, by means of an ancient science, astrology. This is your heavenly chart.'

Around a bottle of Tokay, Thamos revealed to the

* Josef Haydn (1732–1809) worked at Esterháza, the residence of the Esterhazys, a rich Hungarian family. He had an orchestra and a five-hundred-seat theatre at his disposal.

174

musician the strengths and weaknesses which the gods had determined.

'There are three points which it is vital to emphasize: a dominant sign of the zodiac, your ascendant and the master of your birth chart.'

'Where does your knowledge come from?'

'From Abbot Hermes, who had it from the Egyptian sages. It enables every man to discover himself, not within the narrow limits of his individuality, but in accordance with his relationships with the celestial powers. The Great Architect of the Universe is made up of the twelve signs of the zodiac and thus symbolizes perfect harmony. We humans are only a partial – and more or less discordant – expression of it.'

'Is my own expression negative?' asked Wolfgang anxiously.

'Negative or positive, that means nothing. The heavens offer you a raw material whose nature you must perceive in order to use it to the best. The Sun, Mercury, Venus and Saturn inhabit Aquarius, that is, four planets! A whole host of them, which makes you a superb representative of that sign.'

'What does that signify?'

'A sense of rhythm, resonance and of the creative flux flowing from the two vases of the god Hapy, the spirit of the Nile flood. It brings abundance and prosperity. Never will you lack for the source of life, never will you lack for inspiration, as long as you fulfil the whole unity of your being, without concessions, and remain upon the path where you build yourself around an axis.'

'Music!' exclaimed Wolfgang. 'That is my unity and my axis.'

'From that starting point your existence is organized, from the unity of your creation the multiplicity of your works is made manifest, from the most amusing to the most profound. You think the world and your own life through the architecture of your music. In it and by it, you discern a subtle energy which you alone can make audible. In it resides your supreme duty. It is up to you to develop a kind of intelligence sensitive enough to open you up to the universe's vibrations. This course of action will take you far from ordinary reality. Then, your work will not belong to any era. But will you be able to go beyond the letter of such an ideal, and not confound purity and rigidity? Integrating yourself into present-day society presents you with numerous difficulties, for you prefer authenticity to duplicity and lies. However, you feel a visceral need for others and you dream of belonging to a community, each one of whose members would be faithful to his undertakings.'

'That of the sun-priests?'

Thamos smiled.

'You have still to attain the end of your Quest and adapt to constraints without losing your spontaneity.'

'That is tantamount to walking on a sword's edge!'

'Insolence, anger and passions would condemn you to the abyss, if your energy was poorly controlled. But the sign of your ascendant, Virgo, your rising sign at the time of your birth, provides you with remarkable help, at the price of hard labour. You will not know a moment's rest until your last breath and you will not wander off on to side paths. Precision and the feeling of a job well done make you the opposite of a dreamer. Nothing vague; scores with drawn ledger lines, where every note is in its rightful place. You cannot bear imperfection, to the point that you wound yourself. Be careful not to become too thin-skinned, even if criticism, which is so often stupid and blind, injures your sensibilities. The jealous and the sterile will not cease to attack you. Forget them and pursue your own path.'

'It is not as simple as that,' objected Wolfgang. 'My career depends upon them!'

'Only in part, for your dominant planet will enable you to escape from them, a planet which the astronomer Herschel has just discovered and which he has named Uranus. As certain Ancient peoples had already detected it, its field of action is not unknown to us.'

'What does it encompass?'

'A formidable energy, which passes through phases of extreme intensity. That is why your destiny will be neither linear nor tranquil. Tension, exaltation and intense emotions will be your daily lot. Your lucidity, at once a strength and a handicap, will make you see the world and men the way they are, and you will sometimes lose hope. You possess neither lukewarmness nor indifference, but a sense of the absolute which will cause you many difficulties since you have no sense of diplomacy.

You will imitate no one, you will resemble no one, and you will fight fiercely to preserve your independence. No one will succeed in subjugating you. And you will bring to our humanity so many new things that it will take several centuries to assimilate them. True, you will suffer profound heartbreaks, for the power of this planet contradicts the sense of measurement embodied in the sign of Virgo.'

'The sword's edge again!'

'Your lunar house promises you important creations, whose beneficial results will last well beyond your own lifetime. Despite success, you will maintain a real distance from yourself and will not be duped by your own gifts. Nevertheless, alone, you will not attain your goals. Others will be vital to you in order to make your aspirations become reality.'

'I am in love with Constance Weber,' confessed Wolfgang.

'Because of the presence of Venus in Aquarius and its harmonic link with Mars, this love will be lasting.'

'But it will not be sufficient, I can sense it. Others . . . they are also initiates into the Mysteries!'

'The most difficult thing, for a Uranian, is to learn patience.'

# 32

*Vienna, 1 January 1782*

'You must be reconciled with your mother, child,' Baroness Waldstätten advised Constance Weber. 'A situation like this must not be allowed to go on for ever.'

'She will beat me!'

'If she dares, inform me immediately.'

'She will lock me up!'

'Mozart will go and see you regularly. If your mother shuts her door to him, I will intervene. Does that reassure you?'

'A little . . .'

'He is going to take you back home and calm things down. What mother would not be happy to see her daughter again?'

'But I want to get married!'

'Your fiancé sets great store by his father's consent, and I think he is right. If you are to build a life together,

179

it is better that your respective families approve of your actions and get along with each other. And also, a small delay will give your feelings a chance to deepen.'

Wolfgang and Constance's course of action was crowned with success. Despite her sullen appearance and her speech, slurred by too much alcohol, the widow Weber seemed content to welcome back her daughter and consented to embrace her.

'We wish to become husband and wife,' declared the musician. 'As soon as my father sends me his written consent, we shall prepare for the ceremony.'

'In the meantime, work and earn money! I shall not give my daughter to a good-for-nothing.'

'Wolfgang is already honourably known,' protested Constance.

'Possibly, but a reputation still has to bring in money!'

'I shall see you very soon,' said the young man to his beloved.

*Vienna, 15 January 1782*

Caught up in the whirlwind, Wolfgang had omitted to send his father the traditional New Year's wishes. His letter of 9th January was explicit: '*Without my very dear Constance, I cannot be happy and content. And without your own satisfaction, I could be only half-happy. So please make me entirely happy.*'

Leopold's long-awaited reply was stinging and deeply wounded his son. Mother Weber and her sinister 'lawyer man' ought to be sentenced to sweep the streets with signs round their necks, inscribed 'seducers of youth'. It was out of the question to marry a Weber girl, ruin the Mozarts' reputation and ruin himself into the bargain.

In the face of such resolute, hateful opposition, what was he to do? Wolfgang loved Constance, Constance loved him, and he would not give up this marriage. But he did not want to break with Leopold, who had always wanted the best for him, even in a clumsy way.

How could he reconcile the irreconcilable? The task promised to be an arduous one, particularly since the conquest of Vienna was far from won! Thamos the Egyptian had been right when he promised him no rest.

*Vienna, 16 January 1782*

The founder* of the Brother Initiates of Asia was proud to receive two followers into the supreme grade:† Ferdinand of Brunswick and Charles of Hesse, the leaders of Strict Templar Observance.

The Order welcomed in Jews who rejected the formalism of the Talmud and wished to explore an esoteric interpretation of the Bible, through the study of the Kabbalah.

* Hans Heinrich von Ecker-und-Eckoffen.
† The Order comprised five: Seeker, Suffering One, Knight, Master of Sages and Royal Priest or Melchisedech.

True, the success of this new ritual system was limited and the number of Brothers remained small. But the arrival of two great lords might do much to favour its expansion.

The Grand Master of Strict Observance was stunned to discover his own initiator there: Thamos the Egyptian!

'You, at last! Why such a long absence?'

'The Great Magician remains my priority.'

'Our Order is in danger. Attacks are coming from all sides, and I must search for supporters, such as the Asian Initiated Brothers.'

'The Gathering at Wilhelmsbad will mark a decisive step.'

The Duke of Brunswick at last glimpsed a way out, thanks to the path traced for him by the Unknown Superior.


The Grand Master and his second in command drank the elixir of regeneration, were judged worthy to receive the major texts of the Kabbalah and to toil for the reconciliation of the Christian and Jewish religions.

Thamos had no illusions about the future of this unusual Order. Too few Jews belonged to it, preferring to follow their tradition without mixing with Christians; and the great majority of the Christians continued to regard the Jews with a suspicious eye. This Masonic experiment would at least have served to open a few minds, including those of the two leaders of Strict Observance. Would they succeed in freeing the Templar Order from the mire into which it was sinking? Thamos would wait for the answer to this question before deciding upon how precisely to direct the Great Magician who, for the moment, must resolve his emotional problems and take his first steps as an independent musician.

*Vienna, 23 January 1782*

For eighteen ducats a month, Wolfgang gave lessons to three pupils, a task which he regarded as particularly disagreeable but which brought him in enough to live on. It was a means to an end, however much he loathed teaching!

Frau Weber had not closed her door to him, so he often saw Constance and thus appreciated that their sentiments were gaining a firm footing. Why was Leopold proving so intransigent? Wolfgang did not want to marry the Weber family, only Constance, who was so different from her mother and her sisters!

Convinced that he would eventually obtain the consent of his father, he put this wait to good advantage by following various trails, one of which was bound to lead to success: organizing public concerts, responding to commissions, playing in the salons where people wished to hear him, and, in particular, attempting to enter the service of a liberal patron who would grant a musician his rightful status.

As a priority, Wolfgang was aiming at the court of Emperor Josef II. He thought also of those of the Prince of Liechtenstein and of Archduke Maximilian Franz, the future prince-elector of Cologne.

Endowed with a good supply of energy, he feared only one hindrance: ill health.

# 33

Invited with Thamos to dinner at the home of his Jewish friend, Wolfgang sensed immediately that this evening would be an enriching one. The Kabbalist placed a candle at the centre of a low table and questioned the musician in a tranquil voice.

'Were you the ally or the enemy of the day you have just experienced?'

'I . . . I attempted to live it the best way I could, without wasting my time!'

'If a man adopts right-mindedness, the day finds its rightful place. If not, it joins the external chaos and causes him trouble. If a man proves righteous, the day is his good companion. If not, it becomes his adversary and will not feature among the total number of days when he appears before the All-Powerful One. Woe to the man who has not

185

preserved sufficient days to be crowned in the other world!'*

Impressed, Wolfgang gazed at the strange flame that changed colour constantly and took on fascinatingly beautiful shapes.

'As you gaze upon this aspect of the secret fire,' said the Kabbalist, 'you feel the ineffable moment when the Cause of causes engenders life. Its source, the Crown, is a fountain of light which is never spent. Were we not created in order to serve it?'

That night, Wolfgang received the greater part of the teachings of the Asian Initiated Brothers, little suspecting that he understood their meaning more than many of the movement's followers.

'On your birthday,' said Thamos, 'we have an appointment at van Swieten's house. He has a very special present for you.'

*Vienna, 27 January 1782*

Baron Gottfried van Swieten spoke in hushed tones to his Brother Thamos.

'The emperor has complete trust in me and does not seem bent on taking radical measures against Freemasonry, as long as it approves of his reforms and does not disturb public order in any way. Nevertheless,

---

* Words from the *Zohar*, according to G. Scholem.

he is suspicious of certain trends, such as the Illuminati of Bavaria or Strict Templar Observance.'

'Has he confirmed the existence of a secret department, whose task is to keep watch on Freemasons?'

'No, but however much of a liberal and a reformist he may be, the emperor is a true Head of State and nothing escapes his control. He would not allow Freemasonry to develop without knowing its objectives.'

'No theories about the identity of the man in charge of this shadowy army?'

'None. Not the smallest indiscretion, or a single word let slip.'

'Surprising and worrying,' commented the Egyptian.

'I shall continue to search,' van Swieten assured him. At that moment, his butler announced the arrival of Mozart.

The musician entered the baron's official apartment, within the Imperial and Royal Library. An entire room was reserved for musical instruments and scores.

'This place is open to my musician friends every Sunday at noon,' said Gottfried van Swieten, 'and from now on you will be welcome too, my dear Mozart. We shall listen to your new works and play those of the great geniuses whom I venerate: Handel and Bach.'

'Johann Christian Bach, my protector in London?'

'No, his father, Johann Sebastian.'

'I have never heard a note written by that particular Bach!'

'He has been completely forgotten over the last thirty years. I had the good fortune to discover a certain number of his works, including *The Well-Tempered Clavier*, *The Art of the Fugue*, some sonatas in trio form and several other marvels. Would you like to study one of his scores?'

'I'd be delighted!'

Intrigued, Wolfgang played one of the preludes and fugues from *The Well-Tempered Clavier*.

Right from the opening bars, a new universe opened up. It was like a new birth, a blood transfusion,* like passing into another dimension, whose existence the young man had never imagined.

This was not just an encounter with a kind of art that was both unusually rigorous and capable of touching the deepest parts of the soul, but above all a communion with a genius who had attained the very essence of music.

Overwhelmed and on the verge of tears, Wolfgang asked himself if it was still possible for him to compose. No, he must not react like this! On the contrary, it was up to him to assimilate these fantastic riches, to share Johann Sebastian Bach's being and make it live again without imitating it.

'My best birthday ever,' he murmured.

---

* The expression was used by Georges de Saint-Foix (see Bibliography at end of book).

# The Son of Enlightenment

Jean-Baptiste Willermoz was jubilant. According to the latest messages received from Ferdinand of Brunswick and Charles of Hesse, the two leaders of Strict Templar Observance were in desperate straits. Particularly flattered to receive the confidences of such great lords, whose titles and renown impressed him, the wealthy trader nevertheless congratulated himself on holding them in the palm of his hand. He, the commoner from Lyons, was about to decide the destiny of two German princes!

The strategy used by the Grand Master and his lieutenant seemed chaotic to him. They held the best cards, yet they were playing to lose. Why destabilize the Brother Knights by denying all affiliation to the Order of the Temple, the very basis of the brotherhood, and send them a questionnaire proving that the Grand Master himself was succumbing to the disarray?

There was only one solution: to impose a new Masonic system capable of carrying the maximum number of Brothers with it. And Jean-Baptiste Willermoz held the key to success.

If Ferdinand of Brunswick and Charles of Hesse wanted to remain at the head of a powerful and respected Masonic Order, they must rally to the theses of the mystical School of Lyons, and recognize the Charitable Knights of the Holy City and the Grand Professionals as the only holders of the high grades.

So Willermoz sent the leaders of Strict Observance a note clearly indicating the path to follow, the return towards esoteric Christianity, from which the Templars had been wrong to distance themselves.

His conclusion summed up his long years of research: *'The only man who has known and practised the true Masonic science is Jesus Christ.'*

# 34

'Look at this document,' said Anton Stadler to Mozart. 'Take a good look at it!'

'It is a decree from Emperor Josef II . . .'

'Exactly! And what is it about?'

'You and your brother have been engaged as clarinettists in the court orchestra.'

'Isn't it wonderful? Happy in love, and now a professional musician in His Majesty's service! What more could I hope for?'

'Become the top expert in that wonderful, misunderstood instrument.'

'So, will you write for me?'

'Why not?'

'How could you resist the spell of the clarinet? There is no warmer, more magical sound. In the meantime, we shall celebrate and drink enough for four! Then I shall beat you at darts, since this is my lucky day.'

*Vienna, 13 February 1782*

Wolfgang wrote to his sister Nannerl, setting out his daily timetable. This was so that she would intervene with his father and explain to him that his son was working himself to the bone to make a place for himself in Vienna.'

He rose at 6 a.m. At seven, completely dressed, Wolfgang wrote until nine, then taught until one. Either he lunched at home, or honoured one of the many invitations he received. According to the circumstances, he sat down to eat around 2 or 3 p.m. If he was not giving a concert, he composed between five and nine, then went to the Webers' house, where he conversed with Constance before returning to toil, between 11 p.m. and 1 a.m.

This infernal pace had given him a feeling of perfect balance. Sensing that he was living rightly, he hoped that these days would be accounted as good ones by the All High One.

That evening, Frau Weber was slow in opening her door. He had to knock loudly before a red-faced ball of flesh appeared, visibly inebriated.

'What do you want?'

'To see Constance.'

'Constance, always Constance!'

'She is my fiancée, Frau Weber.'

'Fiancée, you say! How much have you earned this month?'

'Sufficient.'

'With all the expenses there are, people never earn sufficient. And I have three daughters to raise!'

'May I see Constance?'

'She is ill.'

'What is wrong with her?'

'An illness.'

'Who is taking care of her?'

'We're getting by.'

'I really would like to see her, Frau Weber.'

'Do you want to fall ill too?'

'Are you closing your door to me?'

The drunken woman hesitated.

'Come in, but don't stay long. That would tire her.'

Constance was dabbing away at her tears, but Wolfgang succeeded in consoling her.

'Life is becoming impossible,' she confessed. 'My mother drinks too much. When she is drunk, she gets angry and talks rubbish. Then she becomes nice again, almost gentle. I love her and hate her at the same time. Since my father's death, she has been getting worse.'

'Be brave, my love. I shall get you out of this.'

'Have you obtained your father's consent?'

'Not yet, alas!'

'My mother doesn't like you very much, Wolfgang. She wants to marry me to somebody else.'

193

'Her plans will fail, I swear it!'

'How much longer must I submit to her?'

'Be patient, I beg of you. I shall manage to make my father bend. If the situation gets worse, take refuge with Baroness Waldstätten.'

*Vienna, 3 March 1782*

After composing a soprano aria, *Love's Celestial Feeling*\* Wolfgang went to see Baroness Waldstätten who, faithful to her reputation as a good friend, had taken in the young Auernhammer girl, whose father had just died. Utterly helpless, Mozart's pupil – who was still just as much in love with her teacher – was desperate for affection.

'How is she?' asked Wolfgang anxiously.

'I have given her a sedative and she is sleeping. The poor little one will not recover easily. And what of your Constance?'

'She is holding fast, but the atmosphere in the Weber house is becoming unbreathable.'

'If need be, my home is open to her.'

'I do not know how to thank you, Baroness.'

'By making a success of your concert this evening and charming the whole of Vienna! What will you play?'

\*K119.

'A piano concerto in D major written in 1773,* whose first two movements I have retained. The third seemed too complex to me, so I have replaced it with a very alert rondo,† in which I have attempted to mingle humour and virtuosity.'

Wolfgang was quite right.

The audience at the Burgtheater applauded the programme warmly. It was made up of extracts from *Idomeneo, King of Crete*, an improvisation and the concerto, whose final rondo enchanted even the most world-weary listeners. The Viennese had discovered a surprising pianist, with a disarming simplicity. He did not seek to produce any effects and moved little, remained perfectly calm and did not abandon himself either to extravagant movements or to the contortions favoured by his colleagues. The player did not externalize his feelings and allowed the music to speak for itself.

*Vienna, 10 March 1782*

'Things are moving,' Geytrand informed Josef Anton. 'At Weimar, Goethe was raised to a higher grade and now features among the leaders of the Amalia Lodge which has just initiated Duke Charles-Augustus.'

* K175.
† K382

'Another dignitary at the forefront!' lamented Anton. 'Freemasonry is gaining ground every day.'

'Yes and no,' Geytrand reassured him, 'for this lodge is suffering upheavals which could lead to a sort of explosion. Bode's violence offends many Brothers, who are weary of his vulgarity and his incessant attacks on the Jesuits. Even if he is destined to lead the oldest lodge* in Germany, that fellow Bode seems very gifted in sowing discord.'

'Let us wish him good luck! What else?'

'According to Brother Angelo Soliman, who is as greedy as ever, the mineralogist Ignaz von Born is to be the Venerable of the To True Union Lodge. As planned, his rise has been very swift, and he will carry out his programme: to put the Brothers to work, teach them the meaning of symbols and build an authentic initiation.'

'Unfortunately, Ignaz von Born enjoys an excellent reputation, and the emperor likes him. That mineralogist will give Viennese Freemasonry a good image and favour its expansion. What could we blame him for?'

'There is no gossip circulating about him,' lamented Geytrand. 'Impeccable morals, a tireless worker, a scientist esteemed by his peers . . . He is respected, admired and feared.'

'Von Born will not be content just to head a Viennese lodge,' prophesied Josef Anton. 'He may well become our principal enemy.'

* The Absalom Lodge.

# 35

*Vienna, 10 March 1782*

Emperor Josef II's reforming zeal was endless. Having just promulgated a decree relating to the freedom of work, he was now studying documents relating to the problems of the peasantry as he headed for the fields closest to the city. Everyone in Vienna knew his green-lacquered carriage, drawn by two pairs of horses.

Simply dressed, the emperor liked to walk around, meet his subjects and listen to them. Since false rumours were announcing bad harvests and a rise in taxes, Josef II must dispel people's fears.

So his carriage halted in the middle of a field, around which numerous curious passers-by were gathered.

Josef II jumped down and walked towards an abandoned plough in the middle of the field.

When he lifted it up, everyone applauded.

And the words ran over everyone's lips: 'The emperor is the god of peasants!'

*Berlin, 11 March 1782*

The Templar Order was going through a worryingly turbulent period. 'We are leaderless,' complained several Knights. Each month there were numerous defections, and even the Most Serene Brother Ferdinand of Brunswick himself was suffering criticism!

Before answering Jean-Baptiste Willermoz, whose demands were constantly growing, Charles of Hesse wanted to consult Dom Pernety, former chaplain of Bougainville, author of *Egyptian Fables Revealed* and the *Mytho-hermetic Dictionary*. Curator of the Berlin Library, he directed his Hermetic Rite* and dispensed teachings based on the revelations of the Swedish mystic Swedenborg, whom the German prince venerated.

On the doorstep of Dom Pernety's home, there were many trunks. His face drawn, the sixty-six-year-old mage was thrusting piles of books into leather bags.

'Forgive my disturbing you, my Brother. I am Charles of Hesse and I would like to speak with you regarding serious matters.'

---

*It comprised two high grades: Novice and Illuminatus.

'I am leaving Berlin once and for all, to return to Avignon with my faithful Illuminati,' revealed Dom Pernety. 'The Holy Word has ordered me to do so, and I have always obeyed it.'

'Praise be to it,' nodded Charles of Hesse.

'A terrible revolution is coming,' prophesied the mage, 'because of the baseness of the Churches, who are guilty of betraying the message of Christ. Terror and desolation will fall upon our corrupt world.'

'Will the New Jerusalem follow the Last Judgement?'

'Those who believe in the immortality of the soul, who pay homage to the Virgin and obey the Holy Word will have nothing to fear.'

'Can we trust Jean-Baptiste Willermoz and so save Strict Templar Observance?'

Dom Pernety hesitated.

'He is extremely active and no doubt is concealing a great deal of ambition.'

'Should we not return to the way of Christ and found the new Church, which will at last respect His teaching?'

'Indeed, as long as alchemy is not forgotten. How can mortal individuals be transformed into celestial beings without philosophical gold? The great Swedenborg was emphatic on that point. Organize the Assembly, hold fast to what is vital, and you will succeed. But do it quickly, for the revolution is coming.'

*Brunswick, 13 March 1782*

Von Haugwitz emerged from the bed of a beautiful woman, and called in at a confessional before honouring the two leaders of the Strict Observance movement with his presence. Having obtained forgiveness for his sins, he could devote himself once more to the pleasures of the flesh, at the same time praising the Lord.

'We have just replied to Willermoz,' declared Charles of Hesse, 'and specified our course of action: to commit the Templar Order once and for all to the way of Christ.'

'Perfect,' nodded von Haugwitz.

'However, we do not wish to give up alchemical experiments, for Christ himself symbolizes the supreme gold.'

'My disciples* are hostile to these occult practices,' replied von Haugwitz indignantly. 'Only devotion can obtain the favours of the All-Powerful One.'

'So that we may be united within the bosom of the same Order,' continued Charles of Hesse, 'I have suggested to Willermoz a secret agreement between him and us three here present. Thus we can point the next Masonic assembly in the right direction.'

Baron von Haugwitz's face turned purple.

'How dare you? I shall submit to no one, do you hear, no one! Christ is my only master, I receive orders from Him alone. From this moment on, I am leaving this

---

* The Brothers of the Cross.

subversive, dangerous Freemasonry. From now on, I shall fight it without respite.'

Von Haugwitz slammed the door of the great salon.

'This defection does not call our strategy into question,' said Ferdinand of Brunswick. 'A secret alliance with Willermoz is the only way to save Strict Observance.'


*Vienna, 20 March 1782*


'Great news, Herr Count!' proclaimed Geytrand. 'The Masonic Assembly arranged by Strict Observance is to begin in mid-July. All the dignitaries have given their agreement to the Grand Master and announced that they are coming. The debates will last several days, if not weeks.'

'And what will be their outcome? That is the main question.'

'Given the quarrels between the different Masonic tendencies, we may hope for a fine state of chaos.'

'Ferdinand of Brunswick and Charles of Hesse are not imbeciles. In order to hold on to power, they must be preparing some underhand trick.'

'A brochure has just been published in Berlin, entitled *The Rose-Cross laid Bare*. It accuses the Rosicrucians and the Templars of being puppets, manipulated by the Jesuits.'

'If Bode did not write it, he must be reading it with delight.'

'The said Cagliostro is planning to found a mother lodge in Paris, adopting high Egyptian Freemasonry,' added Geytrand.

'Seriously?'

'It is a simple adaptation of rites already known, with added magic. Cardinal Rohan and a few members of court would be interested. If that fellow Cagliostro plays with fire, he is liable to burn his fingers.'

'So much the better! Collect as much information as you can about the participants in the Wilhelmsbad Assembly and increase the payments to our informants. I want to know every word exchanged, and every decision adopted.'

# 36

*Vienna, 22 March 1782*

The capital city of the Hapsburgs was in turmoil. For a month, Pope Pius VI was to dwell within its walls and confront Emperor Josef II.

The head of the Catholic Church, a slow-talking sixty-five-year-old, had decided that this journey was vital in order to defend personally his point of view in the face of the master of the Austrian Empire. By putting the weight of his authority into the balance, he planned to win the day.

At their first private meeting, the Pope set out his fears.

'Majesty, you have undertaken a considerable number of reforms, and I salute your courage. May I nevertheless ask if you are perhaps going too fast and too far?'

'I seek for peace, justice and social cohesion. Without these vital advances, grave upheavals will occur.'

'Is it necessary to attack the Church?'

'I spoke of justice, Most Holy Father, and no one is above it, not even the Church or the State.'

'All the same, closing monasteries and placing the clergy under the yoke of temporal power!'

'Whatever religious institutions may be, they must fulfil a social function and not encroach upon the government of a country. That is why I am carrying out these measures, which the people appreciate.'

'The people . . . Their judgement cannot be clear-headed!'

'The happiness of my subjects is my foremost preoccupation.'

'Empress Maria Theresa venerated the Church and—'

'May her soul be at peace, Most Holy Father. Shall we go and have lunch?'

Pope Pius VI had not been expecting such a formidable adversary. Negotiations had not begun very well at all.

*Vienna, 23 March 1782*

How was he to re-establish a dialogue with his father and sister? Wolfgang did not regret having won his independence at such a high price, but he lamented his family's hostility and very much wanted to obtain his father's consent to marry Constance.

'Give them presents,' advised the young woman. 'What are your father's tastes?'

'Let us send him a snuff-box and a pair of watch-cords.'

'And what about your sister?'

'Nannerl is sure to like two bonnets in the Viennese style.'

'I shall make them myself. Let us add a little cross, as proof that we will marry in the Lord's faith, and a little heart pierced by an arrow, evoking our love.'

Wolfgang embraced his fiancée.

'Your soul is good and generous, my darling! Thanks to you, our two families will share our happiness.'

Constance added a few very humble words to Wolfgang's letter.

This initiative was crowned with success, for the stiff and starched Nannerl, who had become Leopold's confidante and adviser, consented to reply, couching a few banalities in writing.

No actual approval yet, but the dialogue had recommenced.


*Vienna, 10 April 1782*


To his father's latest letter, which advised him to get himself hired by the Viennese court on any terms possible, Wolfgang replied: '*Josef II must pay me, for the happiness of belonging to him is not sufficient on its own. If the emperor gives me a thousand florins and a count two thousand, understandably I make my compliments and go to the count with my sureties.*'

The emperor granted more consideration to Gluck and Salieri than to young Mozart, a remarkable pianist and pleasant composer, but without any real fame.

Someone knocked at his door.

'Aloysia!'

'I am leaving for a long tour abroad. Could you provide me with a dazzling aria which would make the most of my voice?'

'Of course!'

The singer was delighted with *Accept my thanks, kind benefactors.** She kissed Wolfgang on both cheeks and fled with the score.

After her came the postman, bearing sad news.

On 1 January, Johann Christian Bach had died in London. 'A misfortune for the world of music,' murmured Wolfgang. He would never forget the friendship and encouragements of the son of Johann Sebastian, whose genius was currently lighting up his research.

*Vienna, 20 April 1782*

Wolfgang no longer confined himself to playing Bach during the Sunday concerts at van Swieten's house. Now, he was attempting a particularly difficult experiment: to assimilate his science and his style, incorporating them into his own language.

*K383.

The works he developed, an adaptation of five fugues for string quartet* and four preludes for string trio,† were not destined for the public. With humility and patience, knowing that he would need a long period to mature, Mozart placed himself in the service of Bach and asked him to train him. Beginnings of unfinished fugues and sketches of themes followed each other like laboratory formulae.

From the outside, these looked like failures and giving up, but Wolfgang regarded them as a thorough apprenticeship, which would one day bear fruit. With his extraordinary sense of polyphony and his perpetually demanding attitude, Bach cleansed and purified him, removing all traces of vain seduction. He forced him to dig deep into his creative will, far from fashion and the prevailing ambience.

While notating a fugue in C major, he composed the complementary prelude‡ as if his mind was functioning independently of his hand.

At his fiancée's insistence, he agreed to give the score to his sister Nannerl: '*When Constance heard the fugues,*' he told her, '*she was totally taken with them. She now only wants to hear those by Handel and Bach. As she asked me if I had written any yet, and I told her*

---

*K405.

† K404a, to accompany fugues by Johann Sebastian and his most talented son, Wilhelm Friedman.

‡ Prelude and fugue K394.

*no, she very heartily scolded me for not wanting to write what is the most artistic and the most beautiful thing in music; she has been on at me incessantly to compose a fugue, and this is it.'*

*Vienna, 22 April 1782*

As he left Vienna, Pope Pius VI brooded on his total failure. Despite several meetings and many warnings, Emperor Josef II had not yielded an inch of ground. And it had even been whispered in His Holiness's ear that, quite unlike the late lamented Empress Maria Theresa, the new master of the Austrian Empire allowed Masonic lodges to prosper, in which people uttered barely veiled criticisms of Rome and Peter's successor. Did Brothers not speak of the necessity to revive the Church of John, faithful to the initiation teachings of Christ, far from official Catholic doctrine?

Doubtless Josef II would soon encounter difficulties which would make him less liberal and persuade him to take a backward step.

In the meantime, Pius VI was in an extremely bad mood, and the heavy-handed homage he received from Prince-Archbishop Colloredo, whom he met in Bavaria on 25th April, did not brighten it. A follower of Rousseau and Voltaire, and a supporter of the reforms of Josef II, that prelate was infatuated with himself and benefiting from supporting all sides.

# 37

*Vienna, 29 April 1782*

When the incident occurred, it was as unforeseeable as it was shocking.

As Constance and Wolfgang were taking part in an evening of dance and forgetting their cares, the young woman, who had become separated from her knight, allowed a stranger to wind a ribbon around her calf!

The scandal unleashed Wolfgang's anger. If that boor had persisted, he would have intervened.

Constance, his sweet Constance . . . How could she have dared to behave like that?

'My dear, I consider your conduct unseemly.'

'Unseemly . . . Whatever are you imagining?'

'I am not imagining anything, I saw everything!'

'Yet there was nothing to see.'

'Please never do anything like that again.'

'Your reproaches wound me gravely, Mozart. I shall never speak to you again!'

Constance fled while Wolfgang just stood there, rooted to the spot.

What a dreadfully stupid thing he had just done! Was he about to lose his future wife because of his foolish suspicions?

In desperation, he wrote to her immediately: '*From this, see how much I love you! I do not rage as you do, I think, I reflect and listen to my feelings. What I want to be able to say about you is: this is the beloved of decent, good-hearted Mozart, virtuous, jealous of her honour, level-headed and faithful.*'

Anxiously, he paced up and down before the Eye of God, the Weber house.

Twice the door opened. Tenants emerged and greeted him.

The third time Constance appeared.

'Will you forgive me?'

She smiled.

'I will, but do not be so possessive, and trust me properly.'

Wolfgang took Constance tenderly in his arms.

Back at his lodgings, he composed a fantasy for piano in D minor,* which was tragic at the start but ended joyfully.

---

* K397.

# The Son of Enlightenment

*Vienna, 7 May 1782*

After working hard on the libretto with Thamos, Wolfgang played the second act of *The Abduction from the Seraglio* for a very attentive Countess Thun.

Blonde, the English servant of Constance, the heroine imprisoned in Pasha Selim's harem, repulsed the advances of the odious Osmin, guardian of the harem. Boldly, she reminded him that one did not seduce a woman by force. And Wolfgang made this pretty English girl proclaim her rule of life: '*A heart born for freedom never allows itself to be treated as a slave and, even when it has lost its freedom, it retains its pride in it and laughs at the universe.*'

Not content with this revolt against misfortune and servitude, Blonde laughed in Osmin's face and even promised that she would intervene herself so that the pasha would punish him. And if necessary, she would put out the torturer's eyes!

Impressed, Countess Thun shared the distress of Constance, whose future seemed very sombre. '*Torments of all kinds may well await me,*' declared the heroine, '*I laugh at the tortures and sufferings, nothing can shake me. Death, in the end, will deliver me.*'

This *Singspiel*, a half-sung, half-spoken German opera, was taking a strange turn! Happily, the pasha admired Constance's firm character and did not know about the escape plans devised by Belmonte, who was determined to save his beloved, her servant Blonde and his servant Pedrillo, who succeeded in getting Osmin drunk. The Muslim discovered the wonderful taste of the wine, without noticing that it contained a narcotic.

At last, the two couples met again! But Belmonte and Pedrillo were in anguish: had Constance and Blonde yielded to their jailers?

The two women were indignant: '*It is unbearable that men should nourish doubts about our honour and regard us with suspicion!*' Shamefaced, the two suitors repented and asked for forgiveness, which their beloveds were kind enough to grant.

'Very moving, Mozart,' said Countess Thun. 'Just like experiencing the situation oneself!'

Wolfgang made no comment.

'Will your heroes succeed in escaping?'

'You shall find out when I play you the third act, Countess.'


*Vienna, 25 May 1782*

Since the heavens authorized it, Wolfgang and the other guests ate lunch in Countess Thun's garden. That evening, the rehearsal took place for the grand concert the next day which, thanks to intervention by Thamos and the Freemason Adamberger, the future singer of Belmonte, was to be organized by Martin, a good professional.

Placed under the aegis of the Concert of Dilettantes, an association of musicians the majority of whom were Freemasons, this open-air academy enabled Wolfgang to be heard by a vast audience, both cultivated and popular.

'The spirits are very favourable to you,' revealed Count Franz Joseph. 'The weather will be fine, there will be a large audience and you will be on excellent form.'

'I have been preparing for weeks! A failure would destroy me.'

'Believe in the spirits, Mozart. They have never disappointed me. You will see, all will be well.'

'Everything is absolutely ready,' confirmed Adamberger. 'The musicians are of high quality, and the instruments have been checked.'

Wolfgang thought of the happy times he had spent in Mannheim with the members of an exceptional orchestra. In Vienna, the level was equally remarkable; but this time, heavy responsibilities weighed upon the composer's shoulders.

'This will be a decisive step,' said Adamberger. 'After this, we shall think about the first production of *The Abduction from the Seraglia*.'

'Will it really happen?' asked Wolfgang worriedly.

'Without a doubt, since the emperor continues to be favourable to it. Whatever you do, do not relax your efforts!'

Mozart had heard that piece of advice before.

*Vienna, 26 May 1782*

On the door leading into the Augarten Park, opened to the public in 1775, Josef II had had an inscription placed: 'To all men, from their protectors.' Within the park stood a pavilion where concerts were held.

'At last,' Wolfgang confided to Thamos, 'I am getting out of the salons and going out to meet ordinary people!'

The programme featured the elegant and easy *Parisian Symphony*,[*] and a concerto for two pianos,[†] joyful and dazzling, which he was to play with Josepha Auernhammer, his lovesick pupil.

The presence of Constance dispelled the unfortunate girl's hopes, and she respected her teacher's instructions to the letter.

Everything had been organized down to the smallest detail, the musicians were excellent, and the audience delighted: this open-air academy was a thoroughgoing success, and the name of Mozart began to be heard upon people's lips.

[*] K297.
[†] K365.

# 38

'At last, the third act of *The Abduction from the Seraglio*!' exclaimed Countess Thun, who was delighted to be welcoming Wolfgang and Constance, who were still as much in love as ever. 'I can't wait to find out how this story ends. Will the two couples, Constance and Belmonte and Blonde and Pedrillo, escape death?'

'They think they have succeeded, but Osmin, the harem guard, catches them and brings them back to Pasha Selim.'

'What punishment does he have in store for them?'

'Hanging. Then Belmonte reveals that his father, a Spanish grandee named Lostados, will pay an enormous ransom to free them.'

'Does the pasha accept?'

'Alas, Lostados is Selim's worst enemy. He pursued him with unjust hatred, kidnapped his wife and forced him to become a fugitive and a renegade.'

'What a superb opportunity to wreak his revenge by killing his son and the woman he loves!' commented the countess.

'Constance does not fear the fatal outcome,' declared Wolfgang, 'since Belmonte is by her side. *"What is death?"* she asks herself: *"The path to rest. At your side, my beloved, it is the foretaste of happiness."* '

'Your Constance is a wonderful woman, Mozart. She will touch many hearts. Save her, I beg of you!'

'She will owe her salvation to the love which the pasha feels for her, and which he renounces when he admits that Constance and Belmonte are united for ever. So he declares: *"It is a much greater pleasure to respond to an injustice one has suffered with an act of goodness rather than by answering vice with vice."* And the four escapees conclude: *"Nothing is viler than vengeance. On the other hand, to be human and good, to forgive without self-interest or resentment, that is how one recognizes great souls! He who does not agree with this deserves only scorn."* '

'You have a pure heart, Mozart,' said Countess Thun. 'May destiny preserve you from wounds that are too deep to bear.'

'*The Abduction from the Seraglio* is finished,' said Constance, 'and I know all the main arias by heart! When will we see it on the stage at last?'

'In the wings, unpleasant rumours are being spread about your fiancé,' revealed the countess. 'But the emperor is so happy to have a German play at last, one that is both spoken and sung, that the rehearsals will begin very soon. And I can even give you a precise date: the 3rd of June, at the Burgtheater.'

*Weimar, 21 June 1782*

Raised to the dignity of Master Freemason on 2nd March, Goethe was present at an incredible Assembly. He who had joined this Order to discover the secrets of initiation found himself plunged into a free-for-all worthy of the worst political situations.

Unable to believe his eyes or his ears, Goethe witnessed the violent altercation between Bode and a dignitary regarding the real goal of Freemasonry.

'Enough hollow discourse and meaningless words!' thundered Johann Joachim Christoph Bode. 'When will you understand at last that the Jesuits are poisoning Freemasonry? Fortunately, Zinnendorf died on the 6th of June while opening the works of his lodge* and his Christian Rite disappears with him!'

'Scandalous words, unworthy of a Brother!' protested the dignitary.

'The unworthiness,' snapped back Bode, 'consists of our bowing before Catholic dogmas and refusing to think for ourselves! Freemasons, free men! What a joke!'

The Master of the Lodge brought down his gavel.

---

* The Three Keys.

'Our work is suspended. The Brothers are to withdraw in peace.'


*Vienna, 25 June 1782*


'The Amalia Lodge in Weimar has just been closed,' Geytrand informed Josef Anton. 'No date has been fixed for reopening it.'

'What is the cause of this schism?'

'Bode's incendiary declarations.'

'That man is a real Attila the Hun! Let us hope that he will visit as many lodges as possible. After he has passed through, there will be nothing left but ruins.'

'All the Freemasons are impatiently waiting for the Wilhelmsbad Assembly,' said Geytrand. 'The participants will have to define the nature and the goals of their Order.'

'Ferdinand of Brunswick wishes to restore the temple, which has cracks all over it. To my mind, this will not merely be one more gathering, but a real turning point.'


*Vienna, 1 July 1782*


'My dear Constance, you shall sing the soprano part; Jacquin, my friend, you shall sing the bass; and I shall sing tenor.'

The trio sang through Wolfgang's burlesque work, *The Little Ribbon,*\* telling of a lost scrap of fabric which two spouses were looking for, explaining their painful problem to a trader friend, who could obtain as many for them as they desired. Fortunately, the lovers found their precious possession.

At the end of their performance, the three singers burst out laughing.

Thamos the Egyptian had instructed his Brother Jacquin to entertain Wolfgang, whose nerves were tense. Although he was convinced that he had written an opera which was both pleasurable and serious, how would music-lovers and critics react?

The composer was obsessed by another concern: his marriage. Leopold was still refusing to send him his consent and Constance, with an admirably firm disposition, was continuing to put up with her mother's dreadful personality.

When Jacquin had left, Wolfgang took his fiancée into his arms.

'If your father rejects me,' she whispered, 'will you give up all thoughts of our marriage?'

'Of course not! Before the end of this year, we shall be united before God.'

Constance's beautiful smile overwhelmed Wolfgang.

'You will do without his agreement?'

\* K441.

'If he persists, yes. And I am making a solemn vow, here and now: if Leopold receives us in Salzburg as husband and wife, I shall have a Mass played there in your honour.'

# 39

While the rehearsals for *The Abduction from the Seraglio* were continuing, Wolfgang was invited to dinner by one of his admirers, Johann Valentin Günther, along with the tenor Adamberger and the librettist Stephanie.

Günther was the secretary of the emperor's secret cabinet for war affairs and one of his intimate friends. His support would help Wolfgang to establish himself.

'Are you pleased with your singers?' he asked.

'In the presence of the future hero Belmonte, I could not wish for better! We work together in an excellent atmosphere; nobody tries to take all the credit.'

'It's a kind of miracle,' commented Adamberger. 'Ordinarily, divas tear each other's hair out! Mozart's music calms tensions and makes us want to celebrate it by overcoming our usual pettiness.'

Someone knocked violently at the door of the apartment.

Scarcely had a servant opened it when several policemen poured in and their leader approached Günther.

'Kindly consider yourself a prisoner, Herr Secretary.'

'What am I being accused of?'

'Spying on behalf of Prussia.'

'That is insane!'

'Your mistress, Eleonora Eskeles, daughter of the chief rabbi of Bohemia and Moravia, extorted extremely confidential information from you. As your complicity has been established, the emperor is placing you under house arrest.'

'I wish to speak to His Majesty!'

'Out of the question.'

'I am innocent, and I protest vigorously against this injustice!'

The police officers forced Mozart, Adamberger and Stephanie to leave the apartment.

'Our friend Günther has been imprudent,' commented Stephanie. 'The seductress has led him to disaster!'


*Vienna, 5 July 1782*


'One of those close to the emperor was arrested last night,' Geytrand informed Josef Anton.

'Why has such an incident attracted your attention?'

222

'Because the Freemason Günther was dining with two Brothers, the singer Adamberger and the librettist Stephanie the Young.'

'Any other guests?'

'Mozart, a young composer.'

'Also a Freemason?'

'No.'

'Mozart . . . That name has appeared in my files before.'

'He is working on an opera with Stephanie.'

Just in case, Josef Anton opened a new file in the name of Mozart.


*Wilhelmsbad, 11 July 1782*


Jean-Baptiste Willermoz arrived in Wilhelmsbad, a small spa town in Hesse, four days before the opening of the Assembly, in order to meet in secret with the Grand Master of Strict Observance, Ferdinand of Brunswick, and his second in command, Charles of Hesse.

What an honour for a merchant, to be so regarded by two illustrious lords! The true saviour of Freemasonry was himself, Willermoz, and he knew how to make the two aristocrats bow to him: by promising them his secret rituals without ever giving them to them.

To his great satisfaction, they greeted him with deference.

'The discussions promise to be stormy,' declared the Grand Master, 'and together we must adopt a line of conduct which will enable us to save Strict Observance.'

'We have decided to rally to your vision of spirituality,' added Charles of Hesse; 'to reject Templar references, rationalism, scientism and the esoteric tradition.'

'Are you well aware, venerable Brothers, that only the Charitable Knights of the Holy City can regenerate Freemasonry?'

'We are,' replied Ferdinand of Brunswick.

'You will encounter strong opposition.'

'Since we are concluding an alliance, I shall be able to impose my authority and reduce opponents to silence.'

'Must we abandon all alchemical practices?' asked Charles of Hesse anxiously.

'Christ is philosophical gold. I shall offer you that revelation when I initiate you, after the Assembly, into my Rite's supreme grade.'

The duke and the prince drank in Willermoz's words. Even if the Brothers believed that Brunswick was still Grand Master, the Lyons mystic held real power and would point the assembly in the right direction.

Within a few days, or at worst weeks, his triumph would be total.

# 40

As soon as the Assembly opened, two Illuminati from Bavaria unleashed hostilities. Facing delegates who had come from all over Europe and represented numerous tendencies, Adolph von Knigge stated: 'This world was not made to philosophize, but to act', and von Dittfurth attacked with rare violence the mystic Christians, who were capable of polluting Strict Observance. 'Was it not vital at last to oppose the powers and privileges of aristocrats, to bring forth a fixed society, promote humanitarian equality and dispense with religious superstitions?'

These speeches were extremely badly received, except by Bode. Once again, he accused the Jesuits of having got their hands on Freemasonry.

At the end of this first engagement, which caused a dreadful atmosphere, Bode approached the Illuminati

225

and decided to join that movement, which corresponded fully to his ideals. The revolution was in motion.

'You see,' Bode said to Thamos, 'we are making progress!'

'It seems the Grand Master did not care much for his opponents' declarations.'

'He is very much mistaken! Strict Observance is done for, and only the Illuminati can give real impetus to Freemasonry and give it the place it deserves. Come and join us.'

Thamos listened attentively to Adolph von Knigge, the author of the Illuminati rituals, and arranged a meeting in order to find out about them.

'Strict Observance is destroying itself,' von Knigge declared. 'Fierce competition between the systems of high grades, the defection of the Duke of Sudermania, attacks by the Swedish Rite, false secrets, the Brothers' profound dissatisfaction . . . What a lamentable state of affairs! Let us turn our backs to the past and commit ourselves resolutely to the future.'

'How do you envisage doing so?' asked the Marquis de Chefdebien, colonel of the hunters, a Knight of Malta and an experienced Freemason, delegated by the French Philalethes Lodge in order to gather information.

'No understanding is possible with Willermoz, the Rose-Cross and other more or less disguised Christians! It is because of them that we are bogged down.'

'Will you go as far as breaking away?'

'If necessary, yes.'

'Do we not cruelly lack their secret rites?' asked the marquis anxiously.

'Empty vessels! The only future of Freemasonry,' hammered home von Knigge, 'lies in the Illuminati of Bavaria.'

Under the authority of Ferdinand of Brunswick, who had not yet been personally attacked, the debates recommenced.

Who will win the initiation? wondered the Egyptian.


*Vienna, 16 July 1782*

To combat the spasms, Wolfgang took tincture of rhubarb with ethereal alcohol. This remedy did not prevent him dropping the score of the first act of *The Abduction from the Seraglio* in a muddy puddle as he was heading for the Burgtheater to conduct the first performance of his opera.*

The composer was not thinking of the precious hundred ducats which the work would bring him but of the multiple conspiracies aimed at breaking him. Even the emperor himself had had to calm down certain opponents.

When the small, pale, scrawny composer with the shining eyes and the long, strong nose summoned up the first bars of *The Abduction from the Seraglio*, he became immersed in the music.

---

* K384.

That evening, he was gambling his career, and – beyond success – with his creative freedom.

He missed Thamos the Egyptian. In these decisive moments, his presence would have comforted him. But had destiny not decreed that he must confront the main ordeals of his life alone?

Towards the middle of the first act, there were whistles. At first discreet, they grew louder. But bravos answered them and eventually carried the day.

'Just what is needed, Majesty.'

The emperor gave a small smile. Decidedly, this music had character!

Everyone waited impatiently for the critics' opinions, which Count Karl Zinzendorf, an observer of Viennese cultural life, summed up in one sentence: 'This music is a hotchpotch of stolen things.' Mozart? He was a looter, whose opera was a paltry imitation of respected compositions, such as those of Gluck.

*Vienna, 19 July 1782*

The second performance of *The Abduction from the Seraglio* came close to disaster. In the absence of the emperor, the anti-Mozart clique was strengthened and the whistles sounded with all the more malice since Fischer, the actor playing Osmin the harem guard, sang lamentably badly. With the agreement of the tenor and Freemason Adamberger, who was as furious as himself, Wolfgang

demanded a new rehearsal before planning a third performance, which was to be announced as the last.

'Surely not!' prophesied Adamberger. 'Only the
critics' reviews are bad. The public likes it, and word-of-
mouth communication works well. If we sing our parts
properly, the whistlers will lose heart.'

At Wolfgang's instigation, the team set to work again.
The cause was not yet lost.

Despite his fatigue and his worries, he composed a
strange serenade* for a wind octet, which presented
the peculiarity – unique in this genre of work – that it
answered to the solemn key of C minor. The rigour of
Bach declared itself, before the final joy burst forth.

And then the young man could not reject the pressing
request from his father, who was demanding a symphony
for the celebrations of Burgmeister Sigmund Haffner's
elevation to the nobility.

This return to Salzburg, however strictly musical it
might be, bored Wolfgang, but he still hoped to obtain
Leopold's consent to marry Constance, so he bowed to
his demands.

Overcoming his lassitude, he slept for a short time and
began writing the *Haffner Symphony*.†

Would his father finally understand that his son loved
and respected him, so much so that he would not marry
without his consent?

* K388.
† K385.

# 41

*Vienna, 20 July 1782*

'The Wilhelmsbad Assembly promises to be a real disaster,' declared an almost joyful Geytrand.

'Do you have any reliable information?' asked Josef Anton, ever the sceptic.

'I have bought two delegates and they are providing me with accounts. Right from the very first day, the confrontations have been violent.'

'Is the Grand Master succeeding in silencing his opponents?'

'For the moment, yes. The Illuminati of Bavaria made the mistake of revealing their radical positions all at once, and this has met with objections from the majority of Brothers.'

'What do these hotheads want?'

'A revolution, Herr Count. To destroy the Church and royalty is becoming Freemasonry's first goal.'

'How is the Grand Master reacting?'

'He formally disapproves of this line of conduct, and the majority of the Brothers follow him.'

'In other words, the Illuminati are heading for failure.'

'The debates have only just begun.'

'Have you identified their leaders?'

'This assembly is giving us a chance to make progress. I can already cite the names of Adolph von Knigge and von Dittfurth.'

'Even if this tendency fails,' said Joseph Anton, 'it will not go away completely.'

'Bode is prepared to leave Strict Observance to help the Illuminati to develop,' said Geytrand.

'The danger is becoming specific, but we must add to the file before presenting it to the emperor. He will demand proofs and irrefutable documentary evidence before attacking these intellectuals who dream of changing the world.'

*Vienna, 26 July 1782*

Wolfgang had just settled himself in at the Red Sabre* and *The Abduction from the Seraglio* was to be performed again that evening; then Constance arrived in tears.

'I cannot stay at my mother's house any longer! She is drunk again and threatening to beat me.'

---

*Today, 19, Wipplingerstrasse.

He took her in his arms.

'You are not going home ever again. I am taking you to Baroness Waldstätten's apartment.'

'My mother will have me fetched back by the police and will accuse you of corrupting a minor.'

'Do not worry, our friends will defend us.'

'She will be mad with rage!'

'We shall resist her.'

Baroness Waldstätten greeted the couple with her usual kindness, and Constance's tale sickened her.

'Calm yourself, my child. Neither your mother nor the police shall cross the threshold of my home. I shall make it known that I have granted you hospitality, and nobody will importune you.'

'I so wish I was married!'

'You will not have to wait much longer,' promised Wolfgang. 'First thing tomorrow, I shall write again to my father, begging him to give me his consent at last.'

*Vienna, 31 July 1782*

The performances on 26th and 30th July had not been disturbed by the clique opposed to Mozart. *The Abduction from the Seraglio* was becoming a success and its creator was gaining the status of a respected composer.

However, his father's latest letter wounded him deeply. On the one hand, he still refused his consent; on the other, he barely acknowledged his Viennese suite.

Taking up his pen again, he reproached Leopold for his indifference and coldness. Then, one last time, he begged him to allow him to be united with Constance Weber, stating that in any event the marriage would take place.

Wolfgang could not make his fiancée wait any longer, for her situation was becoming untenable. Why was his father preventing his happiness and not rejoicing at the growing audience for *The Abduction from the Seraglio*?

The musician dared not think of professional jealousy. Driving away this dreadful thought, he went to Baroness Waldstätten's house to announce to Constance that they were soon going to live together in the full light of day, as husband and wife.

*Vienna, 4 August 1782*

On 2nd August, *The Abduction* was performed again, to lively applause. Wolfgang and his fiancée received communion at the Théatins,* after making their confessions. On 3rd August, he sent his father the end of the *Haffner* symphony and signed his marriage contract. And on 4th August, the couple entered St Stephen's Cathedral to celebrate their union before God.

---

* Congregation of regular clerics founded in Rome in the sixteenth century.

'Have you received your father's consent?' asked Constance worriedly.

'Unfortunately not.'

'Are you not risking a break with him?'

'Think only of our joy, my darling. We were made for one another, and God, who orders everything and consequently this too, will not abandon us.'

Constance, Wolfgang and their witnesses could not hold back their tears. The young couple were well aware that they were promising to build a family.

'I shall provide your marriage feast,' declared Baroness Waldstätten.

The celebrations were accompanied by an unexpected gift: Mozart's sublime serenade in B minor* for twelve wind instruments and double bass, the work which had so moved Thamos.

Where was he, at this important time? Wolfgang would gladly have chosen him as a witness, but the Egyptian clearly had a more important task to carry out. Was he conversing with the sun-priests, contributing to the creation of a kind of wisdom without which the world would be uninhabitable?

Constance was happy. Her pretty dark eyes expressed a degree of trust and tenderness that Wolfgang would never betray. With her at his side, he would be able to lead a tranquil and harmonious life, far from the excesses of passion which were so harmful to true creativity. Excess

*K361.

and torments led nowhere, and hard work was going to be essential.

Would he find a way to unite his inner song with the rigour of Johann Sebastian Bach, the impulse to reach for the light with masterly control of every note? Constance understood and shared his ideal. Thoughtful and level-headed, she had now given him a priceless gift: the peace of soul and heart, vital for the balance he would need in order to build his work.

# 42

*Vienna, 6 August 1782*

'I place my hope in you, my beloved wife,' Wolfgang sang to Constance as he composed a soprano aria* in the luminous key of C major.

He was experiencing the happiest morning of his life, and this happiness was no illusion for, the previous day, he had finally received the consent of his father, who was most impressed by the help and protection given to the young couple by 'the high-born and kind lady Waldstätten', of whom Leopold had heard great things. Since a Viennese baroness approved of this marriage, he surrendered.

The confirmed success of *The Abduction from the Seraglio*, Constance's love, the reconciliation with his father, a promising career . . . The heavens were fulfilling

---

*K440.

all Wolfgang's wishes; however, he was impatient to see Thamos again.

*The Abduction* was not an end in itself, but a starting point. Knowing he was capable of mastering the complex art of opera, he wished to return to the path that led to the sun-priests' and priestesses' temple. But without the help of the Egyptian, how could he succeed?

'You seem concerned,' observed Constance.

'No, I am savouring the good fortune we have to be living together. And I am going to thank God by keeping my promise: to give you a Mass. It will be played in Salzburg when my father and sister receive us.'

'Do you think they will eventually accept me?'

'You will charm them, I am sure of it!'

*Salzburg, 7 August 1782*

The *Haffner* symphony surprised Leopold, who had been expecting a work that was as light and entertaining as anyone could wish for. But his son had changed greatly. Time and time again, his work broke the mould of convention.

Here and there, there were signs of rebellion against this hated city of Salzburg and its good folk, who were so attached to their routine! The andante seemed almost peaceful, but the presto echoed the victory song of the harem guard, Osmin, a perfect incarnation of the Grand

Mufti Colloredo. An illusory victory, since in the end he was ridiculed and overcome.

'Your brother is no longer the same man,' Leopold said to Nannerl. 'I hope he will manage to control himself and integrate into good society.'

'That woman Constance exercises a bad influence over him. You should never have given your consent. Wolfgang would have given up all thought of this disastrous marriage.'

'No, he was firmly decided, and the vigilance of Baroness Waldstätten reassures me.'

'Well it does not reassure me,' snapped Nannerl. 'My brother is a fantasist who has no sense of reality. This union will not last long; he will fail in Vienna and return here, with his tail between his legs.'


*Vienna, 8 August 1782*


There were foreign language dictionaries all over Wolfgang's desk.

'What are you doing?' asked Constance.

'I am revising my knowledge of French, which I have almost mastered, and learning English.'

'Are you planning to travel?'

'Why not? Following the success of *The Abduction from the Seraglio* and my first Viennese concerts, I am writing to Le Gros, a second-rate but influential figure in Paris, and offering him my services during the next

Lenten period. Then we shall plan to visit London, the musician's paradise!'

'For the moment, you should concentrate on getting ready for lunch. Let us hope this invitation is not a trap!'

Indeed, as he headed for Gluck's house, Wolfgang's spirits were not high. Why would Vienna's most fashionable and Europe's most famous musician grant him such an honour?

Mozart's fears were unfounded. Gluck wished simply to get to know him, to congratulate him and to say that he was supporting attempts to repeat *The Abduction from the Seraglio* at the Burgtheater.

*Vienna, 9 August 1782*

Wolfgang got up without making the slightest noise and wrote a little note, which he left next to the bed: '*Hello, dear little wife! I hope you slept well, that nothing disturbed you, that you don't have any difficulty in getting up, that you aren't getting cold, and that you don't have reason to get annoyed with the servants. Save the problems for when I get back.*'

What a joy it was to ride on horseback to the outskirts of Vienna at five in the morning! Wolfgang took advantage of this enchanting summer and the immense space of creation which opened up before him. Gluck's recognition had enthroned him as a real composer, and his detractors scarcely raised their voices any more, with the exception of the 'official' critics. He must learn to bear the jealousy, wickedness and stupidity of sterile individuals whose sole occupation consisted of denigrating other people's work.

Only one thing mattered: putting into music the celestial harmonies evoked by the Kabbalah, and known to those who were initiated into the Great Mysteries.

*Vienna, 17 August 1782*

Baron Gottfried van Swieten was stamping around angrily. True, in revealing to Mozart the major works of Johann Sebastian Bach, he was contributing to the training of the Great Magician. And his position as chief censor gave him access to large numbers of files and documents. In the event of danger, he could alert his Brothers.

But the baron still could not identify a single clue leading to the secret department charged with spying on Freemasons. Neither the chief of police nor the Minister of the Interior seemed to know of its existence. Of course, they could be lying, with the fine assurance of politicians who no longer knew how to recognize the truth when they saw it.

Nobody seemed to be menacing the existence of the Viennese lodges, which were preserved from the upheavals which the Wilhelmsbad Assembly was attempting to calm down. Van Swieten was hoping for positive decisions.

Perhaps this secret, invisible department existed only in nightmares?

Countess Maria-Wilhelmine Thun approached the baron.

'A fine society soirée, is it not? All we lack is Mozart's music.'

'The success of *The Abduction from the Seraglio* gives me the greatest delight. Now he has been recognized as one of our most brilliant musicians.'

'Yes and no,' replied the countess. 'Despite my actions and yours, Emperor Josef II has not granted him an official post at court, which would free him from all material concerns and enable him to compose in complete serenity.'

'Josef II practises a policy of economy and refuses to increase the State budget,' van Swieten reminded her.

'When one has the good fortune to encounter an exceptional individual, ought one not to take care of him as a priority? The emperor lacks lucidity, surrounds himself with second-rate people and allows talented people to get away. In the end, this blindness will lead to a catastrophe. A man who neglects a Mozart can have no idea how to properly govern an empire!'

# 43

*Wilhelmsbad, 20 August 1782*

At the fourth session of the Assembly, a fundamental question was asked and submitted to the delegates for consideration: who are we, and how long have we existed?

Convinced of Strict Observance's future potential, several Knights put forward solutions. The first advocated the material resurrection of the Order of the Temple and his own desire to make a fortune. The second advocated raising twenty thousand warriors in order to drive the Turks from the islands of Lampedusa and Linosa. The third urged the Brothers to leave Europe and settle in Australia, an immense, empty continent where Templar Freemasonry could develop openly. The fourth spoke of the true leaders of the Order, the Unknown Superiors, without whom initiates would never discover the Philosopher's Stone.

Everyone was waiting for the contribution by Ferdinand of Brunswick, elected Grand Master General on 15th August and put in charge of the new Masonic system which was to be set up.

'My Brothers, the founder of Strict Observance, Charles de Hund, lied to us. He did not possess any documents proving our Templar provenance. Consequently, we must give up this illusion and all thoughts of restoring a knightly Order which is dead and buried, without any links to the Freemasonry to which we belong. The Temple will remain as a simple reference point of a moral and mystical nature.'

The Assembly was stunned.

'I agree with the most serene Grand Master!' roared Bode.

'As do I,' added Willermoz, delighted with the turn of events.

'What concrete proposals do you make?' asked Bode.

'The name Strict Templar Observance no longer means anything,' said Ferdinand of Brunswick. 'Consequently, we must follow another path, traced for us by Brother Jean-Baptiste Willermoz and his institution of Charitable Knights of the Holy City.'

'A return to an archaic Christianity!' exclaimed Bode in fury.

'We have heard the words of the Illuminati of Bavaria,' the Grand Master reminded him. 'Their goals are not ours; their ideas have not been accepted.'

*Vienna, 20 August 1782*

'Aren't you shocked?' Constance asked Wolfgang.

On the 18th, in Augarten park, a transcription for wind instruments of *The Abduction from the Seraglio* had been played, and it had not been written by Mozart. Ought he to be enraged, or pleased by this popular craze?

'This evening, my opera is being performed again at the Burgtheater. The day before yesterday, people walking in the Augarten stopped to listen to it. Gifts from heaven! Before, I was the prisoner of a tyrant and condemned to shrivel away in Salzburg. Today, everyone in Vienna from the common man to the aristocrat is listening to my music! Why should I complain?'

'You have a feeling for happiness, Wolfgang.'

'Certainly, since you love me.'

*Wilhelmsbad, 21 August 1782*

When the new session of the Assembly opened, everyone knew that the main decision had been taken: from now on, the reforms devised by the mystics from Lyons would be imposed on everyone.

The Unknown Superior, Thamos the Egyptian, had raised no objection, so Ferdinand went ahead. He instructed four Brothers to draw up a plan for a 'General Code of the Order' and granted them a year in which to do so. And Willermoz was to write the texts of the new ceremonies to be celebrated in Strict Observance lodges.

'I have nothing in common with this credulous rabble whose minds have been pushed out of shape by the Jesuits' gossip,' Bode confided to Thamos. 'These are not Masonic rituals that they are going to concoct, but parodies of the Mass! Believe me, my Brother, only the Illuminati can pull us out of the mire.'

Jean-Baptiste Willermoz was triumphant. Wisely, however, he waited until the end of the Assembly to be certain of his total victory.

*Vienna, 24 August 1782*

Baroness Waldstätten did not tell Mozart about the letter which Leopold had just sent her, describing his son as '*too passive, too somnolent, too nonchalant, sometimes perhaps too proud, too impatient, not knowing what to expect. Too much or too little, no middle point. And alas it is the most intelligent people, the most extraordinary geniuses who are presented with the most obstacles along their way.*'

Did this father really know Wolfgang? Did he love him with all the desired tenderness? Could he help him to succeed in such a demanding city and such a difficult profession?

'Constance and I wish to go to Salzburg,' Wolfgang told the baroness. 'I would so like to introduce my wife to my father and my sister! We only make up a small family, and it would be good to reunite it.'

'Have you been invited?'

'Not yet, but it won't be long.'

'Do not leave before the future tsar's new visit to Vienna. His coming will occasion a great deal of musical activity. This time, Grand-Duke Paul will listen to *The Abduction from the Seraglio*.'

'In other words, it is impossible to leave Vienna in the immediate future . . . Moreover, I have a feeling of apprehension that holds me back from going to Salzburg.'

'What do you fear?'

'Being arrested by Colloredo's police. Does the prince-archbishop not detest me sufficiently to throw me into prison?'

The baroness did not reject the theory.

'Take precautions and be prepared,' she advised him.

# 44

After *The Abduction from the Seraglio* had been performed again on the 27th, with continued success, Wolfgang sketched out three sonatas for piano and violin[*] – the first dedicated to his 'very dear wife' – and an adagio for the same instruments.[†]

He did not finish any of these works, which were laboratory experiments designed to master the counterpoint technique which Johann Sebastian Bach had brought to perfection.

Constance admired these attempts in an archaic, even rough style.

'A difficult task,' confessed her husband. 'Bach does not allow himself to be simply swallowed like common food! But I shall manage it.'

[*] K403, 402, 404.
[†] K396.

His friend the horn player Leutgeb, a dull-witted bon viveur, interrupted this research. He had an urgent need for music scores.

'Understood,' said Wolfgang. 'As long as we can get our friends together and enjoy an excellent dinner!'

Leutgeb understood that kind of language very well. Copiously supplied with wine, the night was riotously happy. From it resulted a quintet for horn and strings* and a concerto† which the instrumentalist would have no difficulty in playing.

Constance loved to see Wolfgang enjoying himself and spreading open gaiety while thinking of a rigorous work inspired by Johann Sebastian Bach. He was both here and there, earthly and celestial.

*Wilhelmsbad, 1 September 1782*

On this last day of the Assembly, all the participants had a terrible feeling of failure.

'This constitutes a conjuration against the social order,' said the Marquis de Chefdebien – representative of the Philalethes – to Thamos. 'And France will be its first victim.'

'Have the ideas of the Illuminati of Bavaria not been rejected?'

* K407.
† K412.

'Only in appearance. What is more, all they are doing is relaying a current of ideas whose strength is growing every day. Strict Observance has been unable to take Freemasonry beyond its weaknesses and its contradictions.'

The Grand Master wore the expression of a defeated man. For twenty years, Ferdinand of Brunswick had attempted to build an international system which would dominate all European lodges. Today, the mountain had given birth to a mouse, a new Christian Rite* now under formation, whose guarantor would be a French mystic, Willermoz.

To general surprise, the great victor of the Assembly looked uncomfortable. All of a sudden, the weight of responsibilities seemed much too heavy to him. Could he and his disciples succeed in constructing the ritual edifice expected of them and impose it on all the countries formerly allied to Strict Observance?

And Jean-Baptiste Willermoz, proud of not communicating the real content of his secret ceremonies to the German Brothers, had received no information about the other Rites, with which he would have liked to be familiar. A dialogue of the deaf and a market for tricksters, the Wilhelmsbad Assembly marked the end of an era.

Thamos had gathered nothing constructive for the initiation of the Great Magician. He would however

---

* It has survived under the name of Rectified Scottish Rite, fundamentally different from the Ancient and Accepted Scottish Rite.

continue to follow the development of the Illuminati of Bavaria, who were planning to open themselves up to the outside world.

Just before their respective departures, the eyes of Ferdinand of Brunswick and Thamos the Egyptian met.

'Will we meet again?'

'I do not know, Most Serene Grand Master.'

'Why did you not intervene more and advocate another way?'

'Because the decisions were already taken before the start of the Assembly.'

'I thought I was acting in the interests of the Order. And Willermoz may perhaps succeed!'

'Initiation rests on the quality of the rites and the spiritual power they transmit,' declared the Egyptian. 'Without a tool of real worth, which is constantly improved, we fall into credulousness, accepted behaviour and vanity.'

'That will not be the case with us,' declared Charles of Hesse, flying to the assistance of the Grand Master, 'for Christ will guide us.'

*Vienna, 12 September 1782*

'A veritable explosion!' Geytrand congratulated himself as he handed Josef Anton the reports from his informants on the Wilhelmsbad Assembly. 'Strict Templar

Observance is dying. Even if its death-agonies last for years, even if Ferdinand of Brunswick and Charles of Hesse hang on to their prerogatives, the Order is no more than an empty shell in which puppets dance. They themselves have scuttled their boat by cutting all links with the Templar tradition and by entrusting the Frenchman Willermoz with the task of preparing a new Rite, strongly tinged with Christianity.'

'This man Willermoz – is he dangerous?'

'He is a rich merchant, a mystic who parades his charitable deeds but does not disdain women, a man imbued with the superiority conferred upon him by his privileged contacts with God, proud of rubbing shoulders with the nobility and very embarrassed by his apparent victory!'

'Will Ferdinand of Brunswick resign?'

'I think not, since he is so attached to his title of Most Serene Grand Master. But he seems to me to be broken and will yield government of the tattered Order to Charles of Hesse, who is younger and more dynamic. Hesse is convinced that Freemasonry is a privileged path towards Christ.'

'That may be good news,' nodded Anton. 'What of the bad?'

'The Illuminati of Bavaria will follow neither Willermoz nor the Grand Master, whom they consider supporters of the Church. They want a revolution and use the lodges like instruments of conquest.'

'Then the hardest still remains to be done,' said Josef Anton. 'Eradicating Freemasonry does not promise to be easy, for the most formidable adversaries advance masked, like that man Johann Valentin Günther, whom the emperor has sent into exile, while his mistress, the Jewess Eskeles, has been extradited to Berlin.'

'Do they not both vigorously state their innocence?'

'Josef II is very fond of the secretary of his secret cabinet. So he is carrying out an in-depth investigation. But I am intrigued, Geytrand. Just before his arrest, the Freemason Günther had invited his Brothers Adamberger, the singer, and Stephanie, the librettist. The fourth guest was Mozart, the composer, who as we know does not belong to the brotherhood. All the same, his presence at that curious dinner seems suspicious to me.'

'I have checked again, Herr Count. There is nothing of the conspirator about that young man. His only desire is to use influential aristocrats to establish himself in Vienna.'

'Let us hope so.'

# 45

'I would like to have everything that is good, pure and beautiful!' exclaimed Wolfgang before kissing Constance passionately.

On 6th and 20th September, there had been two new performances of *The Abduction from the Seraglio* at the Burgtheater. On the 24th, Emperor Josef II had listened to the opera in private, so signifying his admiration. And on the 25th, the Prague court had offered Mozart one hundred ducats for a copy of the work.

'Your *Abduction* will be performed all over Europe!' predicted his wife. 'We shall earn lots of money and be able to move into a bigger apartment.'

'Today, we are playing host to many of our friends and celebrating our happiness. Will there be any smoked Alpine trout on the menu?'

'I know your favourite food, my darling.'

The meal was Rabelaisian, and the wine flowed in abundance. As there could be no rejoicing without music, Wolfgang composed several canons, beginning with '*Eating and Drinking Keeps You Going*'* and ending with one of the texts currently in vogue in Vienna, '*Lick My Arse Clean, Nothing Delights Me More*'†, which the revellers sang together at the tops of their voices.

*Vienna, 1 October 1782*

After lunch at Baroness Waldstätten's house, Wolfgang and Constance questioned each other.

'We can't hide the truth from her,' he said.

'But I daren't tell her.'

'What is shameful about it, dear little wife?'

'Nothing, nothing at all, on the contrary! This new happiness crowns all the others.'

'Come on, I shall write to her, but in her style. Our good baroness, who likes saucy jokes so much, would not enjoy a conventional letter. This is how I shall tell her about your pregnancy: '*Very dear, very kind, very beautiful, in gold, in silver, in sugar ... My wife has cravings – and only for beer prepared in the English style! If Your Grace could have a pitcher brought to me, I would be much obliged.*'

* K234.
† K231, 233.

The pitcher soon arrived, and the mother-to-be was able to satisfy her craving.

*Vienna, 5 October 1782*

On examining its accounts, the Mozart household noted – not without bitterness – that the creator of a musical success was paid very little. In fourteen days, the theatre had earned four times more than the composer of an opera applauded by a large audience!

'It is no use being bitter,' said Wolfgang, 'but neither should I behave like an idiot who lets others derive the profit from his work, which cost him enough trouble and fatigue, and who nevertheless gives up all his future rights.'

'How can the situation be improved?'

'I must negotiate better contracts, obtain more fitting remuneration from publishers and ensure that the work survives for posterity! The battle will be harsh and difficult, but I shall win it.'

Wolfgang was very disappointed by Josef II's latest decision: to appoint the mediocre Summer as piano teacher to Princess Elisabeth, a post which he had hoped to secure. In the eyes of the emperor, this unknown offered an enormous advantage: his tiny salary!

*Vienna, 19 October 1782*

On 8th October, Wolfgang had – from the keyboard – conducted *The Abduction from the Seraglio* in honour of Grand Duke Paul of Russia and his wife. Was Leopold not finally proud of his son? Besides, Wolfgang had just composed some piano concertos* occupying the middle ground between too difficult and too easy, in order to charm the Viennese public with the aid of a small orchestra or even a simple string quarter backing the soloist.

In his letter, Wolfgang also rejoiced at the outcome of the Battle of Gibraltar. '*I learnt and it really was to my great joy – for you well know that I am an arch-Englishman! – about the victory of the English over the Spanish.*'

Unfortunately, Wolfgang had to put back his trip to Salzburg again, for the musical season was beginning in Vienna. In the midst of his rise to fame, he could not allow himself the luxury of an absence. Even if this justification was to a large part true, the composer still feared he might be arrested by henchmen of Colloredo, who was capable of ruining his career.

However, he wanted to see his father and sister again, introduce his wonderful Constance to them and add this family happiness to all the others he had been enjoying over the last few months. How right he had been to leave Salzburg and try his luck in Vienna!

---

* Concertos nos. 11, K413 and 12, K414. Dating from the same time, the rondo for piano and orchestra, K386.

But he must renew these links and once again confront the city of his birth as soon as he felt capable of doing so.

What advice would he have been given by Thamos, who had been absent for so long? For a moment, Wolfgang thought he disapproved of his conduct, which was too worldly in his eyes, then he set to work again, composing pretty music for Viennese ears. Whatever else he did, he must not slacken, and he must continue to win them over!


*Vienna, 4 November 1782*


Venerable Master Ignaz von Born took a revolutionary decision: to call a Gathering each month of the Master Masons who truly wished to perceive the secrets of initiation by setting to work.

The candidates were few, for by no means everyone wanted to conduct intensive research into the symbols which surrounded them without their understanding the significance. The majority of Freemasons did not come to the lodge to make a sustained effort. Nevertheless, von Born's patience was rewarded, since an elite began to take on these duties.

That evening, each Brother read out his work, which the others listened to attentively. Thamos established a synthesis, adding essential elements which nobody had thought of. An editor was instructed to conserve the ideas which would serve as a basis for the next Gathering.

This unusual method won over certain progressive spirits, and put off conformists who were satisfied with the ordinary life of the lodges, where people developed contacts by taking part in banquets.

'A group of individuals capable of initiation does exist,' Ignaz von Born confided to Thamos. 'It does not matter that they are few in number. The important thing is their commitment, their rigour and their solidity. What happened at the Wilhelmsbad Gathering?'

'It was a disaster. Our only chance now of initiating the Great Magician consists of building one or several Viennese lodges worthy of that name.'

'I am hopeful of success. The months to come will be decisive. If the emperor does not change his attitude and continues to advocate tolerance, we shall attain the beginnings of unity. According to Gottfried van Swieten, the secret department we fear so much may be no more than a mirage.'

'While I hope I am mistaken, I do not share his optimism. Let us remain on our guard.'

'Mozart is enjoying great success. Last night, he gave a concert at the Gate of Carinthia Theatre and he continues to attract the favours of the Viennese public.'

'This is his new trial,' said the Egyptian. 'If this glory intoxicates him, it will take him further from the temple, and he will rejoin the ranks of puppets fed by their own vanity.'

# 46

*Vienna, 10 November 1782*

'Ignaz von Born is taking some worrying initiatives,' Geytrand revealed to Josef Anton. 'According to my informant, Brother Angelo Soliman, he has assembled a small group of Masters and is urging them to decipher the language of symbols.'

'Does this smokescreen conceal political ambitions?'

'Certainly not, Herr Count! Von Born is an idealist who really believes in the spiritual dimension of Freemasonry, beyond ideologies and doctrines.'

'If this small group devotes itself to esoteric research, in what way does it threaten the established power? Ignaz von Born reassures me, and I wish him full and entire success. Above all, I hope he confines the Freemasons in their lodges and ties them to their symbols!'

'This course of action does not seem anodyne to me. It could shape strong minds, in revolt against all authority.'

Josef Anton did not ignore this remark by Geytrand, who could not confess to him just how much he regretted not taking part in such an adventure. And his bitterness dictated his behaviour: he must destroy the lodges which wished to experience the Great Mysteries.

'Follow Ignaz von Born closely,' ordered Anton. 'If he puts a foot wrong, I shall inform the emperor.'

*Vienna, 4 December 1782*

The whirlwind continued: the previous day, Wolfgang and Constance had moved into a new apartment on the third floor of a house belonging to Baron Wetzlar, and this evening he was playing at the house of one of the most visible members of the Viennese aristocracy, Prince Galitzin. His palace on the Krugerstrasse often played host to musicians, whom he introduced to eminent individuals from the world of culture.

'I am happy to have you in my home!' he told Wolfgang with a broad smile. 'Your *Abduction from the Seraglio* is a marvel, and you will provide us with many magnificent works, I am sure of it! Now, we shall hold our tongues and listen to you.'

So many melodies were permanently singing inside the composer's head that he had little difficulty in developing variations of such richness that the audience fell under his spell. The unconditional support of Prince Galitzin was helping to establish Mozart as one of Vienna's favourite composers.

In the corner of one of the palace's eleven large rooms, Wolfgang spotted two men in deep discussion: one was the influential steward of events and the other was . . . Thamos!

At first hesitant, he approached.

'Come, my dear Mozart,' advised the Egyptian. 'Count Franz Xaver Rosenberg-Orsini would like to talk to you about a project.'

'Wouldn't you like to write an Italian opera?' asked the steward. 'After the success of your German opera, such a work would win you an even broader audience.'

'The idea charms me,' confessed Wolfgang, 'but I need an excellent libretto.'

'The court does not lack for talented poets.'

After exchanging a few polite niceties about society life, Count Rosenberg-Orsini moved on to talk to some of the notables.

Mozart remained alone with the Egyptian.

'Do you disapprove of my marriage and my attempt to conquer Vienna?'

'As long as you do not forget what is vital, why should I condemn you?'

'Your absences trouble me. Do not doubt that I am seeking the path leading to the sun-priests' temple.'

'Here, in Vienna, your destiny is being played out. For the moment, you are not doing so badly. Founding a family and becoming a popular musician are difficult tasks which demand a great deal of energy.'

'Only the music guides me, you well know that, and I shall not allow myself to be caught in the trap of fleeting glory!'

'A fatal trap, be certain of that.'

'Even if my latest compositions yield to dazzling effects, I have not given up either my true Quest or the teachings of Johann Sebastian Bach. But integrating them into my own thoughts will take more time.'

'Be both patient and impatient, and you will not stray.'

'The sword's edge again!'

'One day, I hope, you will fully comprehend that symbol.'

*Weimar, 10 December 1782*

Following the closure of the famous Amalia Lodge, what would be the reaction of its illustrious members, such as Goethe, who was so proud of being ennobled on 10th April and of hobnobbing with the aristocracy, or indeed Bode, one of the key figures of Strict Templar Observance, which was now moribund in the wake of the Wilhelmsbad Assembly?

Thamos hoped that a few Brothers would take advantage of this episode to rebuild the temple and shed the dross of the past.

He was disappointed.

Far from choosing symbolic research, the Freemasons of Weimar gained access to what remained of the

'Internal Order' of Strict Observance and enjoyed themselves celebrating ceremonies which were as pompous
as they were empty. All that counted were the trappings,
the decorum, the sumptuous raiment and sonorous titles.

Ferdinand of Brunswick and Charles of Hesse had
neither the courage nor the desire to reverse this tendency.
Conservatives, bogged down in their outdated prerogatives, the Freemasons of Templar Obedience contented
themselves with their shattered dream.

### Vienna, 31 December 1782

'*In order to obtain success*,' Wolfgang declared to his
father, '*one must write things that are so comprehensible
that a hansom cab-driver could sing them afterwards,
or indeed so incomprehensible that they please people
precisely because no reasonable creature can understand them*', and he held to the line of conduct he had
already expressly chosen: to heed neither the praises
nor the blame of anyone, and to trust only in his own
feelings. He would have liked to write a small book of
musical criticism with examples, although not under his
own name. And then no, he had a better idea!

As he finished off a new piano concerto,* Wolfgang
thought back to his last conversation with Thamos.
Enough dazzling effects, enough charm. As he had done

---

*No. 13 in C major, K415.

nine years before, he entrusted his demands to the string quartet,* choosing the key of G major and making it very sombre. In Salzburg, he had rejected this musical genre. Listening to Haydn's recent works had prompted him to come back to it, now that his own musical language had reached maturity.

Right from the start, Wolfgang knew that this would demand a long and laborious effort. Unusually, he made many crossings-out, corrected himself, went back and allowed his own questions to nourish his music.

What use were success and wealth to him if Thamos did not open the door of the temple to him? Would he succeed in truly unifying his work, his life and his spiritual quest?

Despite the difficulties he envisaged, the composer decided to create a series of six quartets which he would dedicate to Josef Haydn. As this was not a commission and he wanted to explore several different paths, Wolfgang would take as much time as was necessary. Throughout the months to come, the art of the quartet would serve as his guide towards a new horizon, devoid of concessions.

* K387.

# 47

*Vienna, 8 January 1783*

Constance's pregnancy was progressing marvellously. Happy that she was soon going to create new life, the young woman rejoiced in the successes of her husband, who now had four wealthy pupils.

The previous evening, there had been a new performance of *The Abduction from the Seraglio*, which had now become part of the repertoire. And Wolfgang was setting up a subscription fund, in support of his three latest piano concertos, in the hope of bringing in a fine sum.

He was achieving all his objectives: growing fame, financial independence, creative choice. And yet he seemed tormented.

'What is bothering you?'

'Salzburg, always Salzburg! I do not yet feel ready to return there. This is what I have written to my father to reassure him about my determination and my commitment to create a work for you which will be played during our stay there: '*I have truly made this promise in my heart and truly hope to keep it. When I made it, my wife was still ill, but as I was firmly resolved to marry her as soon as she was recovered, I could easily promise it. As a proof of the reality of my vow, I have the score of half a mass.*'

Then Wolfgang set to work again and composed a dramatic aria,* '*My adored hope . . . Ah, you know not what pain!*'

'Who is it for?' asked Constance.

'Your sister Aloysia, who is back in Vienna. She is going to sing it on the 11th at the Mehlgrube, the casino at the flourmill.'

'Aren't the words a little . . . ambiguous?'

'Oh no!' exclaimed Wolfgang. 'It is you I love, and no one else. Aloysia made me suffer a great deal, and I no longer have any feelings for her, neither affection nor hatred, only esteem for an excellent singer who is capable of interpreting difficult arias correctly.'

'Fortunately,' said Constance, 'you are incapable of lying.'


*Munich, 11 January 1783*

In Athens, the code name for Munich, in the presence of Adam Weishaupt, Adolph von Knigge, the philosopher Franz Xaver von Baader, Grand Master of the local

---

* K416.

lodge, and Thamos, Count of Thebes, Bode was initiated into the higher grades of the Order of the Illuminati of Bavaria, the only Masonic organization which contained no Jesuits.

However, the texts* praised the example of Jesus, who was courageous to the point of sacrificing his life for his ideal. And the ceremony ended with an imitation of the Last Supper, in which the Brothers took communion by eating bread and drinking wine.

Already worried, Bode was even more so when he discovered a grade reserved for the true Illuminati: the Priest!†

The teaching dispensed during these Little Mysteries reassured him, for it stigmatized the Christian religion and dogmatism, rejected the tyranny of the Churches whatever they were, denounced the trickery imposed by beliefs and advocated the free exercise of reason. Man could raise himself up from his fall and build on Earth a celestial kingdom from which despots would be excluded. They must disappear without violence.

Any political revolution was futile and destructive, declared von Knigge. Only the secret schools of Wisdom could make men come of age and enable them really to take control of their destiny. Then the world would be home to rational beings and would at last know happiness.

---

* Grade of Scottish Knight or leading Illuminatus.
† First grade of the third class.

Then Bode was chained up and taken into the lodge as an escaped slave, asking to be delivered from the State, religion and society. His only demand was freedom. By means of initiation, he was at last becoming a man and no longer established any distinction between kings, nobles and simple people. The true 'Prince'* abolished all castes.

Bode was delighted.

He subscribed fully to these ideas and planned to spread them with his usual loquaciousness, attracting as many Brothers as possible to the Illuminati, the only Masonic branch capable of altering reality.

During the banquet which brought the initiates together, Adam Weishaupt revealed his plans.

'I wish to set up a system of confederated lodges, for it is in our interests to establish an eclectic architecture within Freemasonry. Then we shall have everything we want.'

'We must be wary of aristocrats,' cut in Bode, 'and keep them in the lower grades.'

Weishaupt appeared to agree with this hard line, but he knew that it was better to adapt to circumstances and win the trust of certain great lords.

'May we be *Aufklärer* [heralds], propagators of light,' declared the Christian philosopher von Baader, 'and not violent revolutionaries. Our priority shall be to establish a balance between a reasoned religion and the demands of

---

* Grade of Prince or Regent, second of the Little Mysteries.

logic. The Church of St Peter and temporal Catholicism have corrupted our society, which must learn to think for itself and rid itself of all forms of oppression.'

This was a thousand leagues from the Wilhelmsbad Assembly and its deliquescent atmosphere. Prompted by Weishaupt and von Knigge, the Illuminati of Bavaria formed a united front, in marching order, with precise objectives.

Thamos consulted the writer of the rituals, Baron Adolph von Knigge.

'Once the ideal has been declared,' observed the Egyptian, 'it is fitting to give it the ritual tool capable of making it concrete. I assume we are talking about the Great Mysteries, in which the esotericism of the Order will be revealed?'

'There I shall reveal the true nature of magic and of royalty, terms unfortunately used wrongly and out of context.'

'Have you finished writing them?'

'I am a long way from finishing! The most urgent thing at the moment is to recruit as many Brothers as possible, either among outsiders whom we shall train in the Nurseries, or among Freemasons, who will be directly admitted to the higher grades.'

'Are the grades of Mage and King not just as urgent? According to the initiatory tradition, it is fitting to begin the work with the highest and most essential part.'

Baron von Knigge looked uncomfortable.

'For the moment, in full agreement with Weishaupt, we are concentrating on strengthening the Order, giving it solid foundations and conquering Freemasonry. The more Illuminati there are, the more influential our ideas will be.'

# 48

*Vienna, 15 January 1783*

'Are you certain the guests will come?' asked Constance anxiously.

'Certain!' declared Wolfgang. 'The Viennese love original ideas.'

'A ball at our home, from six o'clock this evening until seven o'clock tomorrow morning, perhaps, but making them pay an entrance fee of two florins!'

'The sum will cover our expenses in organizing it. You will see, they will eat and drink a great deal.'

Baroness Waldstätten was first to arrive and kissed Constance.

'The mother-to-be is looking splendid. How jolly it is to spend a mad night at your home!'

She was followed by Aloysia and Josef Lange, Baron Wetzlar, owner of the building and an admirer of the musician, the tenor and Freemason Adamberger, the

271

librettist Stephanie the Young and many other people who knew the Mozarts and did not want to miss this little celebration.

As the atmosphere grew increasingly relaxed, Thamos made a discreet appearance. Despite a little too much punch, Wolfgang still retained some clarity of thought.

'A fine night is in prospect,' commented the Egyptian.

'I assume you do not have much time for this kind of entertainment.'

'A long, long time ago I was young too, and I do not reproach you for making the most of life.'

'I have not forgotten the path to the temple!'

'Your guests are asking after you.'

*Vienna, 27 January 1783*

On his twenty-seventh birthday, Wolfgang reworked the first of the six quartets he had decided to compose for himself, without knowing if they would one day be played in public. It mattered little to him, for he wanted to explore a new landscape without worrying about an audience's reaction.

Beyond happiness and unhappiness, joy and sorrow, the andante cantabile of the quartet in G major* conjured up a universe which Wolfgang did not yet know but which he was approaching with great strides. This music

*K387.

272

was bringing him towards the temple, making him overcome obstacles and pass through doors. Perhaps even the entire quartet was like a vast gateway, whose contours he had finally succeeded in drawing.

In making it visible through notes, he perceived its solemnity and importance. Even in the gaiety of the finale,* he sensed a presence. Although far away, its voice was becoming almost audible.

*Vienna, 5 February 1783*

The previous evening had seen a repeat performance of *The Abduction from the Seraglio* at the Burgtheater, confirming the opera's success. On the other hand, there was no reply from Paris, which clearly had little interest in Mozart, even now that he was recognized as a brilliant composer. Never again would he set foot in that land of boors, so imbued with their own importance that they disdained the rest of the world and thought only of teaching him a lesson!

England continued to attract him, but he was not planning to travel there in the immediate future, for he must consolidate his success in Vienna. Nobody had given him a good libretto in Italian and his own research had not turned up anything, so Wolfgang began writing a

---

* The end of this movement prefigures the theme from the trio '*How? How? How?*' from *The Magic Flute*.

new German opera,* after a comedy by Goldoni, whose first act had already been translated. A new success would confirm him as a specialist in the *Singspiel*, the half-spoken, half-sung German drama which Emperor Josef II had so long hoped and prayed for.

A project for the general public, his series of quartets, other concertos already written in his mind, commissions, small works for special occasions ... Wolfgang had no thoughts of rest. Fortunately, a few hours' sleep gave him back sufficient energy to accomplish his many tasks.

*Vienna, 11 February 1783*

Baron Otto von Gemmingen was palatine chamberlain, a privy counsellor and the prince-elector's ambassador to the imperial court. A native of Mannheim, he had founded his own Masonic lodge, To Charity,† in Vienna, with the aid of Ignaz von Born and Thamos, Count of Thebes. Gathering together only a small number of Brothers, it enabled them to experiment with rituals which the mineralogist and the Egyptian had been preparing for several years.

'The Great Magician is approaching the door of the temple,' said Thamos, 'and we must continue to work

* K416a, lost work.
† *Zur Wohltätigkeit*.

without respite. Before then, I should like him to go through a preparatory phase.'

'Why not use the Illuminati of Bavaria's Nursery?' suggested Otto von Gemmingen, who had suggested in Mannheim that Mozart should set to music *Semiramis*, a drama with initiatory resonances.

'Spurred on by Josef von Sonnenfels, the professor of political science, the Illuminati have more and more influence in our lodges,' said von Born, 'but they fear police intervention and hide behind Masonic secrecy. Certain Brothers are attracted by the prospect of conducting a battle against injustice, tyranny and the shackles of religious belief.'

'I have met the leaders of the Illuminati,' revealed Thamos, 'and I am still unsure about their sincerity and their real objectives, all the more so since the summit of their ritual edifice has not yet taken shape. Nevertheless, I do not oppose contact between the Great Magician and those responsible for a Nursery.'

'In order not to run any risk,' advised von Born, 'we must avoid Vienna. Since Baron van Swieten has not obtained any information about the possible secret department which is spying on Freemasons, another city would be better. The best place seems to me to be Salzburg, where several Illuminati are running a lodge which is as yet unknown to the authorities: To Foresight.'*

* *Zur Fürsicht.*

'That is not his favourite city,' Thamos reminded him, 'but he must go there soon in order to see his father and sister again.'

'As soon as we know the date,' promised Otto von Gemmingen, 'we shall do what is necessary.'

'Above all,' advised von Born, 'let us take all possible precautions. Any error would have catastrophic consequences.'

'The Great Magician is less fragile than one might imagine,' said Thamos. 'Many consider him a light, worldly musician, misjudging his true nature. The Nursery will provide him with a framework for reflection and enable him to read many works. He will do his best with it, but it will be only a stage before true initiation.'

'If the Illuminati set out along the road to politics,' ventured Otto von Gemmingen, 'they risk running into serious problems, and the whole of Freemasonry with them.'

'Weishaupt, their founder, seems to pull in one direction, and the writer of the rituals, von Knigge, in another. We shall soon know if this hitherto veiled confrontation will end in recognition or a complete break.'

# 49

*Vienna, 15 February 1783*

The day had started very badly, for Johann Thomas Trattner, printer and bookseller and the husband of one of Mozart's pupils, had asked him for the return of a loan. Suffering slight financial embarrassment because of the cost of copying his three piano concertos, whose subscription had been a failure because of the excessive price, Wolfgang went to see Baroness Waldstätten, who immediately granted him her assistance.

Back home again, he was tackled by Baron Wetzlar, his landlord.

'I need to repossess my apartment and I have found you another place to live, the Angel's Salvation.* It is smaller, but comfortable and well situated. I shall pay your removal expenses and three months' rent.'

* No. 1179 auf dem Kohlmarkt (today no. 7).

In the face of so much goodwill, Wolfgang yielded. He would move the very next day, a day when the Burgtheater was once again to perform *The Abduction from the Seraglio*.

Despite tiredness and the cares relating to this change of domicile, Wolfgang wrote to his father to ask him to return the score of *Thamos, King of Egypt*, which he had been dreaming about all night: '*I am most annoyed not to be able to use the music I wrote for Thamos! That play, because it did not succeed, has been relegated to the ranks of discredited works. It's a real shame!*'

Would the brotherhood of sun-priests and priestesses not soon open a new door to him? As the Egyptian had predicted to him, none of his past works would prove futile. Little by little, the work he had done was taking on its true meaning.

*Weimar, 20 February 1783*

Johann Joachim Christoph Bode was triumphant. Not only had he implanted a small 'colony' of Illuminati in Weimar, but he had also recruited two illustrious followers, Duke Charles-Augustus himself and his minister, the writer Goethe. The former was called Aeschylus and the latter Abaris. Of course, Bode promised them that they would rapidly rise to the higher grades and launched into a speech exalting the greatness of the free man and the need to alter ways of thinking by sweeping away the ossification of the past.

Goethe and Duke Charles-Augustus accepted criticisms of the Church and of an outdated aristocracy. They both saw the need to fight ignorance, corruption and incompetence, provided the battle was won on the field of ideas and not by using violence.

Bode could have wished for nothing more. Fascinated by the personalities of the august pair, he assured them that such was indeed the attitude of Adam Weishaupt, the founder of the Order of Illuminati, who was destined for a brilliant future.

*Munich, 21 February 1783*

Charles of Hesse resolved to make the pilgrimage to Ingolstadt to meet Professor Adam Weishaupt, whom certain Freemasons were praising to the skies. According to his informants, the founder of this new Masonic branch was not opposed to Christianity.

If the Illuminati, who were on the rise, wanted to ally with Strict Observance, Charles of Hesse could envisage making concessions without damaging the mystical path leading to Jesus Christ.

At first, the prince thought that this was the gist of the ritual. Then, when he was sent the 'Little Mysteries', he realized that Weishaupt's true goal was the destruction of the Church!

In fury, he berated the founder of the Illuminati.

'You are a dangerous and perverse man!'

'My Brother—'

'Do not call me such, for we have nothing in common. I am the Lord's disciple and I am leading towards Him an Order which respects His commandments. But you are Satan's henchman! Strict Observance will fight the Illuminati with all its strength.'

Weishaupt did not rejoice at this failure. He would have liked to make Charles of Hesse one of his privileged allies, even his spokesman. Now that the break had occurred, he must accommodate himself to it while he watched the death-agonies of Templar Freemasonry, outdated as it was and undermined by Christian beliefs.


*Vienna, 25 February 1783*


At last Wolfgang had an opportunity for a long conversation with Josef Haydn, who had just had his fiftieth birthday but remained a musician-servant in the service of Prince Esterhazy.

'I congratulate you on your courage, Mozart. Being independent has always seemed impossible to me.'

'You are fortunate to serve a good master who grants you many freedoms. I was the slave of a tyrant. If I had not broken free of my chains, I would have been dead to music.'

'What I have heard of your work gives me infinite pleasure.'

Coming from Haydn, such a compliment made Wolfgang blush.

'Your latest quartets overwhelmed me,' he confessed, 'and I am studying them in order to perfect my skills.'

'You must on no account underestimate yourself, Mozart. Despite your youth, your deep knowledge of many musical forms is completely astonishing. You are preparing a new opera, I hope? The writer of *The Abduction from the Seraglio* absolutely must not stop when things are going so well.'

Wolfgang talked of his plans, with the exception of the six quartets he was planning to dedicate to Haydn. The two musicians ate lunch together, drank some excellent white wine which blended perfectly with smoked Alpine trout, and joked about hypocritical courtiers and limited performers!

A deep friendship was born between them, founded on mutual esteem and the love of music that was capable of lifting the soul. They felt the same creative demands and the same desire to fashion rigorous, precisely sculpted works, like a craftsman who succeeded in uniting the mind and the hand.

*Vienna, 4 March 1783*

The previous evening, Wolfgang had listened to a string quartet playing his burlesque composition for a carnival pantomime,* while he disguised himself as Pantaloon and partnered Aloysia Lange, dressed as Columbine and seduced by Harlequin. As usual, the masked ball held in the great hall at the Redoute brought together all of Vienna, and everyone had unrestrained fun.

That morning, an imperial decree brutally banished all echoes from the celebration: the German Opera in Vienna was dissolved. In other words, there was no further question of composing a *Singspiel* and dealing with a subject in the same way as *The Abduction from the Seraglio*. Wolfgang threw his project into the waste basket, although it was already well advanced.

Greatly saddened, Countess Thun told him the reasons for this decision. The composer Antonio Salieri, who liked only Italian operas, had succeeded in persuading the emperor to dispense with the German trend, which had no future.

Once again, the countess lamented Josef II's lack of character; he was too easy to influence. Why did he pay so much heed to mediocre people and flatterers?

* K446.

# 50

*Vienna, 16 March 1783*

'You are magnificent,' Wolfgang told Constance.

  'I haven't even done my hair yet!'

  'We are almost late.'

  'I shall hurry.'

On the 11th, Wolfgang had taken part in an academy at the Burgtheater involving Aloysia Lange, who sang one of his arias.[*] The programme also featured the *Parisian* symphony[†] and the piano concerto in C[‡]. The delighted audience had forced the pianist to repeat the rondo in D[§] and one of the listeners, the great Gluck himself, had declared himself enchanted, so much so that he had invited the musician, the singer and their spouses to lunch.

[*] K294.
[†] K297.
[‡] K415.
[§] K382.

What a favour from such an illustrious composer!

'Now,' said Wolfgang, 'we are late.'

'There, I'm ready!'

The whirlwind continued. Another fine success at the academy on the 12th at the house of Count Johann Nepomuk Esterhazy, a Freemason whom Thamos had advised to welcome Mozart and observe him. And then the marvellous Sundays at Baron Gottfried van Swieten's house, discovering Handel and Johann Sebastian Bach!

'How do you think I look?' asked Constance.

'More and more beautiful. If you weren't already married, I would want to marry you.'

He could not resist kissing her.

'My hair!'

Fortunately, Aloysia Lange was not known for her timekeeping, and Gluck was familiar with the fantastical nature of divas.


*Frankfurt, 20 March 1783*


The leaders of the Order of Illuminati of Bavaria wanted to meet several Masters of lodges in the city of Frankfurt, which up to now had adhered to English rites and rules.

Accompanied by Imperial Baron Adolph von Knigge, Professor Josef von Sonnenfels and Tribune Bode, Adam Weishaupt presented a future project to the Brothers, one which was vital to the development of Freemasonry. Had a thinker and a politician of the importance of Goethe not just been initiated into the rites of the Illuminati, without whom the lodges were locked away in a bygone past?

The last bastion of submission to English influence, the Frankfurt lodges agreed to found the 'Eclectic Alliance' which preserved their independence and which, nevertheless, enabled them to adopt the secret hierarchy of the Illuminati.

Weishaupt was now at the heart of Freemasonry. How far he had come since the birth of his Order, which had for so long been confined to a few members! No Brother was now unaware of the powerful current of ideas it embodied. But the dead branches had still to be cut off to strengthen the Masonic tree and give it a new dynamism.

Tomorrow, the Illuminati would rule Europe. From the lodges an attempt on power would be prepared, which Weishaupt hoped would not be accompanied by bloodshed. But would the princes and archbishops, who would soon be driven from their palaces, prove capable of abdicating and so averting violence?

*Vienna, 23 March 1783*

In the presence of Emperor Josef II and Gluck, who had become a fervent supporter of Mozart, Wolfgang gave a 'benefit concert' at the Burgtheater, during which he conducted the *Haffner* symphony and played two piano concertos,* before improvising variations on an air by Gluck, an exercise which touched the celebrated composer.

There was no doubt about it: all of Vienna had adopted Mozart.

Wolfgang expected an engagement at the Viennese court, but the emperor merely sent him twenty-five ducats. However, on 30th March Josef II was again present at the academy of singer Theresa Teyber and asked Mozart to play his concerto in C† again.

Surely such manifest interest must presage a brilliant future? On 2nd April, the publisher Artaria brought out six sonatas for piano and violin,‡ which would be played in all the salons.

*Vienna, 20 April 1783*

'Hostilities have been declared!' Geytrand informed Joseph Anton. 'I was wondering how long the Freemasons would continue to do nothing in the face of the Illuminati of Bavaria's conquests. It is the Rose-Cross of Berlin who have launched the offensive, with the support of one of their own, Frederick-William II himself.'

'Is this merely a show of strength or a real attack?'

* K415 and 175.
† K415.
‡ K296 and K376–380.

'The Rose-Cross have denounced the duplicity of the Illuminati and claim to reveal their true goals by publishing circulars which accuse them of upholding the theories of Voltaire and Helvetius, demanding an illusory freedom for all, undermining the foundations of the Christian religion and advocating the coming of a universal Freemasonry whose operational centre would be in Austria. At the end of this process, the Illuminati will proclaim the unity of the German nation, which they will govern as they wish.'

Josef Anton's worst fears were confirmed. The Illuminati were transforming Freemasonry into a war machine, designed to overturn thrones.

'There is one interesting detail,' added Geytrand. 'The leader of the Illuminati is apparently residing in Vienna.'

'His name?'

'Josef von Sonnenfels.'

'The professor of political science at the university?'

'The very same.'

Anton consulted the suspect's file.

'Leading Freemason and legal expert, with the ear of the emperor. Therefore untouchable. He obtained the abolition of torture in 1776, revived the Burgtheater by getting rid of vulgar farces from the stage and, in his publications, he has defended the theses of the philosophy of Lights. He is untouchable and formidable.'

'Perhaps he will not always enjoy such lofty protection,' ventured Geytrand.

'Watch him, but very discreetly. If he were to start a scandal, our department would be dismantled.'

'These Illuminati are going too far. As they are obliged to advance in the open, they will make fatal mistakes.'

'We still have to decode their pseudonyms!'

Geytrand smiled.

'Thanks to our great friend Soliman, we have identified four key individuals: Spartacus is Adam Weishaupt, the Order's founder; Philon is Baron von Knigge; Fabius is von Sonnenfels; and Abaris is Goethe.'

'Spartacus . . . At least the leader of the Illuminati is not hiding his warlike intentions! And now he is emerging at last from the shadows and declaring his intention to overthrow Rome, in other words the established order. You are right, Geytrand, his faithful will be less at ease in the full light of day. But since they cannot eternally play the part of *éminences grises*, they will reveal their true plans, which are sure to shock the emperor.'

'Will he react in time?'

'I shall deliver to him several reports written in a very moderate tone, so that he does not accuse me of excessive suspicion. Little by little, he will come to be wary of these overinfluential intellectuals and of the army they are planning to assemble.'

# 51

While the latest production by Antonio Salieri, *La Scuola dei gelosi,** was enjoying great success and proving the superiority of Italian opera to Viennese audiences, Wolfgang and Constance were moving into a larger apartment, on the first floor of Burgischen Haus 244, Judenplatz.

Constance's pregnancy was progressing without any problems, and the young woman liked this new dwelling very much. Her husband cared tenderly for her health, and the young couple happily walked to the Prater gardens, were they strolled along the great avenue of chestnut trees which led to a semicircle and thence to five, smaller avenues. At the very first sign that the mother-to-be was growing tired, they sat down in a

---

* School for the Jealous.

tavern, and only Wolfgang indulged in a game of darts with other enthusiasts.

Constance loved to see her husband enjoying himself a little, although he continued to compose inside his head, even while he was walking or having fun.

'Will we have enough money to pay the rent and run the kind of household appropriate to your status?' asked the young woman anxiously.

'On the advice of friends, I have written to the Parisian publisher Seiber and offered him my three latest piano concertos for the sum of thirty louis, and my series of six quartets for a minimum of fifty.'

'Are those prices not rather excessive?'

'If I undervalue my works, I shall receive no consideration. And if this publisher does not accept my conditions, I shall find another.'

Constance agreed with her husband. After all, Mozart was not just anyone.


*Vienna, 6 May 1783*


'I have read through a hundred libretti if not more,' Wolfgang admitted to Thamos, 'but I haven't found a single one worthy of interest. I am so desperate that I have asked my father to ask for one from that second-rate hack Varesco. If a miracle occurs, he may perhaps have an idea.'

'We shall arrange for that miracle,' decreed the Egyptian.

'May I remind you that the emperor wants no more *Singspiel*, only an Italian opera! He has fallen under the influence of Antonio Salieri, a perfect courtier and an extremely ordinary composer.'

'I have heard talk of a skilful poet.'

'Who?'

'Father Lorenzo Da Ponte is to be appointed librettist to the imperial theatres. The emperor has been completely won over by him. "A noble face, kindly air, voice that is sweet and smooth, little fuss, simple": that is what the emperor says of him, at the prompting of Salieri.'

'In that case, Da Ponte will refuse to supply me with a libretto.'

'You must try your luck. Tomorrow evening there is to be a dinner at Baron Wetzlar's house. There, you will meet this curious priest, who is capable of casting a spell over the great men of this world. The emperor and Salieri do not know Da Ponte's true nature. Despite his title and his good manners, he is an adventurer, a liar and a womanizer who was almost thrown into prison in Venice because of his escapades and his criticism of the social order. He has no genius but does not lack for talent and he has a feel for musical drama.'

'Assuming we agree on a theme, will he be malleable and accept my demands?'

'Nobody is more adaptable than Father Da Ponte.'

*Vienna, 7 May 1783*

Baron Wetzlar – a wealthy Jew and a great admirer of Mozart – was delighted to welcome this musician with a fine future as well as Da Ponte, the new librettist to the imperial theatres. As the Count of Thebes hoped, would this encounter not favour a fruitful collaboration?

Lorenzo Da Ponte had the face of a rascal and a high-liver. Straight away, he liked Mozart's vivacity and intelligence.

'Your *Abduction from the Seraglio* was a fine success, but opera in the German language has no future. It is up to us poets and musicians to satisfy the tastes of the Viennese public! What are you working on?'

'I am desperately searching for a libretto and I have rejected more than a hundred.'

'Good heavens! You must be extremely demanding.'

'That is why I am happy to meet you. If the emperor has appointed you to his court, you must be the best librettist there is at the moment.'

'Well,' agreed Da Ponte, 'I have had a great deal of experience and I know my art better than anyone . . .'

'Would you be kind enough to suggest an idea to me?'

The priest frowned and seemed vexed.

'I am overburdened with work. Salieri, Martini and others ask me constantly for new projects, and I no longer know where to start. Nevertheless, since I like you I promise I shall think about it.'

An empty promise, thought Wolfgang. The collaboration with Da Ponte had ended before it began.

*Vienna, 21 May 1783*

The publisher Artaria had just brought out two piano sonatas for four hands,* but this small joy did not extinguish the anxiety Mozart felt at the thought of returning to Salzburg. First, he must wait for Constance's confinement, which was now very close; then, as he wrote to his father, he still feared being arrested on the orders of the Grand Mufti Colloredo, for '*a sanctimonious man is capable of anything*'.

It was then that the oafish Josef Leutgeb, at fifty-one a famous horn player and owner of a cheese shop in Vienna, burst into the Mozarts' apartment.

'I say, I have to have an amusing, easy concerto quickly.'

'I have a cold and a cough,' lamented Wolfgang. 'Today, I don't have the heart for the work.'

'Come, don't refuse an old friend! I am sure you can bring a little jewel out of that head of yours, even today. Then we'll go and have a drink to your health. When you're ill, it's most important not to do nothing.'

Knowing that the truculent fellow would not let him be, Wolfgang shut him in his bedroom and told him to wait without moving or making a sound.

---

*K358 and 381.

A few hours later, the horn concerto* was finished. There were heroic accents to make the player sound good, and zest, but also a charming melody line.

Seizing blue, red and green pencils, Mozart wrote the dedication to it: '*Mozart took pity on Leutgeb, donkey, ox and idiot.*'

* K417.

# 52

*Vienna, 17 June 1783*

At two in the morning, Constance felt the first pains of childbirth. At four, Wolfgang sent for his mother-in-law and a midwife.

During the confinement, he composed the minuet for the quartet in D minor,* the second in the series of six he was planning to dedicate to Josef Haydn, in the hope that the magic of the music would enable mother and baby to pass through this difficult ordeal without mishap.

The entire work lived within him: sombre, violent, sometimes feverish, expressing a fierce battle against anxiety and the darkness, it revealed a desire for freedom, without any certainty of attaining it.

Wolfgang spoke to no one, not even his father, about these first two quarters of an ensemble which was

* K421.

perhaps leading him towards the temple. Only Thamos knew of their existence and encouraged him to continue.

'It's a boy!' announced the midwife, at half-past six. 'He is plump and the mother is doing well.'

Filled with emotion, Frau Weber embraced her son-in-law, who went to his wife's bedside. He found her happy and relaxed.

'What shall we call him?' she asked.

'I suggest we pay homage to our ancestor Raimund, to which we shall add Leopold, since my father wishes to be the godfather.'

That same day, Raimund Leopold was taken to the church to be baptized, and the young couple thanked God for granting him His benediction.


*Vienna, 5 July 1783*


Wolfgang's father had just contacted Varesco, who was convinced that a new sung work by Mozart would fail. To him, Wolfgang replied sharply, on 21st June:

> *I find it very offensive that Herr Varesco doubts the success of my opera. I can assure him that his libretto will certainly not succeed if the music is not good. For it is the music that is the essential element of an opera. So he will have to alter and redo things as much and as often as I want. As for little Raimund Leopold, he is perfectly fresh and in good form. He*

*does everything abundantly, drinking, sleeping, crying, salivating, shitting and the rest.*

A recent incident had irritated the composer. Although Aloysia Lange had sung two arias* composed for her and inserted into an opera by Anfossi,† his friend Adamberger, on the other hand, had been unable to perform his‡ because of behind-the-scenes activity by Antonio Salieri. Why had this zealous, wealthy and famous courtier taken against him so much, and why was he proving both petty and jealous?

Wolfgang dreamt of opera, to the point where he fashioned arias to insert into a colleague's work. Whom must he approach to at last obtain an exciting libretto, which would enable him to express himself fully?

'Father Da Ponte would like to speak to you,' his cleaning woman informed him.

Wolfgang was surprised. He had not expected to see the court's official librettist again.

Unctuous and cheerful, Da Ponte seemed as pleased with himself as ever.

'You asked me for an idea, my dear Mozart, and here it is! I had to redirect a little of my precious time, but I have unearthed an agreeable theme: *Lo Sposo deluso. The Disappointed Husband.* I conjure up the rivalry between three women who desire the same lover. Exciting, no?

* K418 and 419.
† *Il curioso indiscreto.*
‡ K420.

This *opera buffa* will enchant the Viennese. Anyway, I am in a hurry. I shall leave you this sketch for you to study, and we shall discuss it. Goodbye for now.'

Neither the story nor the way in which it was handled interested Wolfgang. So this was the extent of Da Ponte's inspiration! Disappointed, he wrote to his father: '*You gave me a piece of advice about opera which I had already given myself. As I am happy to work slowly, and like to have full command of my subject, I did not want to begin too soon. A poet has just brought me a libretto which I may adopt, if he will consent to reshape it to my requirements.*'

*Vienna, 25 July 1783*

'You seem nervous,' observed Constance.

'I am still hesitant.'

'We must leave, Wolfgang! You have confirmed our arrival to your sister, I have placed our son with a wet-nurse, and the luggage is ready.'

The composer felt ill at ease.

'Salzburg ... So many bad memories, so much sadness, and that prince-archbishop who is going to throw me into prison!'

'Has your father not reassured you?'

'He declares that the Grand Mufti will take no action, but is his optimism well founded?'

'I am sure of it.'

'Then let's go.'

# The Son of Enlightenment

On the one side were Wolfgang and Constance, on the other Leopold and Nannerl. The ice was so thick that nobody ventured to break it. Nannerl's hatred and disdain forbade Constance to utter a single word. Leopold's silent reproaches forced his son to remain silent.

The previous day Miss Pimperl, who slept twenty hours a day, had broken the stalemate. Mad with joy, the fox-terrier bitch had jumped into Wolfgang's arms to explore his pockets in search of Spanish tobacco.

At last there were smiles and words of welcome.

'Father,' said Wolfgang in a trembling voice, 'this is my wife. She has been dreaming of embracing you, as well as my very dear sister.'

The atmosphere relaxed a little. Only Nannerl remained cold as marble.

'You will not be bored in Salzburg,' promised Leopold. 'We shall begin by celebrating my daughter's saint's day with a good bowl of punch, then we shall dine with our musician friends, play darts and walk in the countryside.'

At last father and son embraced at length, overjoyed to see one another. Then Leopold agreed to embrace his daughter-in-law, while Nannerl remained distant, determined never to speak a word to this schemer. Was the main culprit in this mismatch, which sullied the name of Mozart, not her own brother?

# 53

Leopold was extremely proud to organize a work reunion with his son and the chaplain Varesco, librettist of *Idomeneo, King of Crete.*

'Wolfgang has become a battle-hardened composer, greatly liked by the Viennese. After the success of *The Abduction from the Seraglio*, he is looking for a good story to set to music.'

'I have one,' declared the Salzburg cleric.

Wolfgang expected the worst, and was not disappointed.

'The title sums up my work,' said Varesco. ' "*The Goose of Cairo*." Astonishing, no?'

Neither Leopold nor his son reacted.

'Here is the drama which, without any doubt, will attract the favours of a large public. The widowed Marquis don Pippo locks away his magnificent daughter,

300

Celidora, who is desired by many, in a tower of his chateau, along with her companion Lavina, whom the aristocrat is planning to marry, and whom he thus shields from temptation. A good start, no?'

'If you like,' conceded Wolfgang.

'Wait, the surprises are not over yet! Don Pippo has signed a contract with Biondello, who is in love with his daughter Celidora. She will only belong to him if he succeeds in getting into the tower within the space of a year. Fabulous, no?'

Leopold's expression remained grim.

'You think that is impossible? Well, you are wrong! Biondello is a friend of Calendrino, who is smitten with Lavina, and he has the support of the two servants who work for the marquis, not forgetting the help of a mysterious Bohemian woman who has come from Egypt and who knows magic like the back of her hand. With such a team, he is convinced he will succeed! In order to add spice, the whole play takes place on the last day before the deadline expires. So the audience will be constantly holding its breath!'

'How many acts?' asked Wolfgang.

'Two,' replied Varesco. 'The first deals with the hero's failed attempt to get into the tower. In the second, there is a dramatic turn of events! Cunning Calendrino constructs an enormous goose inside which Biondello hides. And the Bohemian woman presents it to the marquis, praising the merits of this masterpiece which hails from Cairo! Stunning, no? Generous don Pippo has the goose taken up into the tower to entertain the two prisoners.'

'Biondello emerges, wins his bet and marries the marquis's daughter,' ventured Wolfgang.

'How did you guess?' asked Varesco in astonishment.

'Just a hunch.'

'Another dramatic turn of events: the Bohemian woman reveals her true identity! In reality, she is don Pippo's wife, whom he believed to be dead. Fabulous, no? And all ends well, since Biondello marries Celidora and Calendrino marries Lavina.'

Leopold remained silent.

'Many alterations will be necessary,' said Wolfgang.

'Out of the question! As far as I am concerned, my *libretto* is perfect.'

'From the musical point of view, it demands several adaptations.'

'I refuse!'

'Be reasonable,' advised Leopold. 'A successful opera depends upon the collaboration between the composer and the librettist.'

'We shall perhaps talk of this again,' cut in Varesco, annoyed. 'I shall leave you now.'

Father and son looked at each other in consternation.

'This *Goose of Cairo* . . . How inept! Not a single spectator will believe it!'

'Do not be too intransigent, Wolfgang. By improving the intrigue, you can certainly get something out of it.'

'It's impossible to work with that mediocre fellow!'
'I shall bring you round to a better point of view.'


*Salzburg, 15 August 1783*


The composer Michael Haydn, one of Mozart's good friends in Salzburg, was downcast. White-faced, stooping and feverish, he had lost all enthusiasm for life.

'What has happened to you?' asked Wolfgang anxiously.

'I was supposed to deliver the prince-archbishop six duets for violin and viola. I finished four and then fell ill. Immediately I presented him with my apologies and asked him to grant me extra time.'

'Did the tyrant refuse?'

'He demanded immediate delivery of the last two, but I am incapable of providing him with them. So he has suspended my salary, and I find myself without a penny.'

So, the Grand Mufti had not changed one iota! Cruel, despotic, pitiless, he continued to torture musicians who had neither the courage nor the opportunity to leave Salzburg.

'I am done for, Wolfgang. The prince-archbishop is going to dismiss me.'

'Certainly not, since you will hand over the promised works this very day.'

'I assure you, I have not the strength to compose them!'

'I shall do it.'

'You . . . you would do that?'

'Seeing a friend in distress is unbearable to me.'

Using the language of fugues, touching on the science of Johann Sebastian Bach while keeping to the light style Colloredo liked, Wolfgang wrote the two duets for violin and viola,* which Michael Haydn took to the prince-archbishop's palace.

* K423 and 424.

# 54

*Vienna, 25 August 1783*

'This time, Herr Count, it is a complete rout!' rejoiced Geytrand. 'Strict Templar Observance is on the edge of an abyss. Subscriptions have stopped coming in, the lodges are turning away or becoming openly hostile, and there are no longer even any senior dignitaries to simulate the existence of a hierarchy!'

'Has Ferdinand of Brunswick resigned?'

'Not yet, but he has lapsed into severe depression. His life's work is crumbling before his eyes.'

'And Charles of Hesse?'

'He refuses to give in and still believes all will be saved by the intervention of Jean-Baptise Willermoz and his Charitable Knights of the Holy City.'

'Has the Lyons mystic shown himself?'

'Not to my knowledge. He is evidently working to

produce new rituals which, if they ever see the light of day, will arrive too late.'

'We must not rejoice too soon,' warned Josef Anton. 'The Duke of Brunswick may be gravely wounded, but neither Charles of Hesse nor Willermoz will give up their ambitions.'

'Given their Christian standpoint, which has been clearly declared, and their hostility to the Illuminati of Bavaria, do they represent any real danger?'

'Whatever his philosophical tendencies, any Freemason is dangerous. Strict Observance seems weakened, I agree, but we must not relax our vigilance. It could yet be reborn from its own ashes and retake the offensive.'

*Salzburg, 30 August 1783*

Wolfgang was delighted to meet Professor Josef von Sonnenfels and to have a long discussion with him. They talked first about the Burgtheater, which had become a fine venue for events at which high-quality works were performed, then discussed Emperor Josef II's liberal politics, which they both approved of wholeheartedly.

Since Mozart was staying a while longer in Salzburg, the professor of political sciences introduced him to a few friends, without mentioning to him that they belonged to a Lodge of Illuminati[*].

*The To Foresight Lodge.

'In the greatest secrecy,' he revealed, 'we think together about the problems of our era and discuss important books, such as those of Herder, Wieland and Lessing.'

'Are you also interested in the Egyptian mysteries?'

'Of course. Among our reference works are Father Terrasson's *Sethos* and the little work devoted to the priests of ancient Egypt, *Crata Repoa*, not forgetting Apuleius's *Golden Ass*, which describes initiation into the mysteries of Isis. We call our Gathering the Nursery. Because of your knowledge, Mozart, you are no longer a Novice, but already a Minerval, which we symbolize by means of a bird with a man's head.* In our eyes, the important thing is to emerge from the darkness of ignorance and to propagate the light of knowledge, even if this shocks the established order, the aristocracy, imbued with their privileges, and the Church, attached to its dogmas.'

Wolfgang was making progress across familiar terrain and did not regret this stay in Salzburg. As soon as he had a free moment and could discreetly absent himself, he would come and converse with these thinkers.

Although he did not show himself, Thamos the Egyptian was clearly behind this new stage in his Quest. Indirectly, he was obtaining the intellectual nourishment he needed in order to discover the path to the temple.

---

* One thinks of the *ba* bird of ancient Egypt and of Papageno in *The Magic Flute*.

*Salzburg, 26 October 1783*

That day, St Peter's Church was packed for the performance of Mozart's *Great Mass in C minor*.* It was unlike
anything else hitherto known, and could not have been
performed at the cathedral, which was Colloredo's fief.

Wolfgang had removed certain parts of the traditional
Mass, notably the Credo, whose words no longer corresponded to own his spiritual standpoint†.

Before entering the church, he cast his thoughts back
to his most recent conversation with his new Minerval
friends, who were threatened by police investigations
and would soon be leaving Salzburg. Like him, they were
delighted with Josef II's decisions: to abolish compulsory work on agricultural estates, and to establish civil
marriage in order to facilitate divorces and remarriages.
Moreover, on 3rd September the Treaty of Versailles had
put an end to the War of American Independence. By
recognizing the existence of the United States, England
had validated a movement towards freedom which many
idealists close to the Minerval also shared.

'I'm afraid,' Constance admitted to her husband.

'Don't worry, all will go well. You see, I have kept my
promise: we have got married, and I have written this
Mass for you; and you shall sing the soprano part, here
in Salzburg, my former prison.'

* K427.
† After 1780, Mozart no longer set the Credo to music. He composed
only the beginning of the Credo for this Mass before stopping.

When Constance performed the *Et incarnatus est* with all her heart, Wolfgang trembled. At that moment something took flesh: a fragile moment of happiness, so fragile that every tiny vibration of it must be perceived and never forgotten.

Many listeners, including Nannerl, were shocked by the fact that the work was not very religious in character at all, dissociating itself in an excessive way from the usual rules. Because of this woman Constance, to whom she did not speak, Wolfgang was following a bad path.


*Salzburg, 27 October 1783*


Old Miss Pimperl whimpered with sadness. Why was Wolfgang, her favourite, going away again? During his all-too-brief stay in Salzburg, he had stroked her a great deal and she had even begun to play again!

At half-past nine, Wolfgang and Constance bid farewell to Leopold and Nannerl. The musician took the fox terrier into his arms one last time, fearing that he would never again pet this faithful friend, whose health was failing fast.

He did not know that he would not have another opportunity to see his sister, who was still as icy as ever towards Constance.

'Continue to work hard,' demanded Leopold.

'I promise you I will.'

The young couple reached Linz, where old Count Thun was waiting for them and invited them to stay at his palace. On 30th October, he announced to Mozart that he was organizing a concert for 4th November, with a rehearsal on the evening of the 3rd.

'What will be on the programme?' asked the musician.

'I should very much like a brand-new symphony.'

'In so little time?'

'Are you unable to do it?'

'Let's try.'

Irritated by the sycophants of Salzburg, who were swift to heap praise on any new Viennese idol, Wolfgang wrote to his father, to tell him that he detested flattery in all its forms: '*Sweet words and kisses are not always agreeable. Only stupid people and donkeys can be controlled in that manner. I would rather put up with a rustic who would not blush to relieve himself in front of me than allow myself to be taken in by such false play-acting.*'

After this, he set to work day and night, and created a work which was solemn, meditative and high-minded, although not devoid of optimism, and in which he focused on this strange period which seemed to him like a portal between two worlds. Thus was born the *Linz* symphony,* which lasted almost forty minutes.

To the great satisfaction of Count Thun, it was played on 4th November. How had Mozart succeeded in

* K425.

composing such a long, carefully crafted masterpiece in so little time?

'You are a magician,' he declared. 'We can listen to you, but we cannot understand you. This priceless gift is the light of my old age.'

# 55

*Vienna, 30 November 1783*

The Mozarts left their luggage at their apartment then went to the wet-nurse's home to collect their son.

She was standing on the doorstep.

'We have come to fetch Raimund,' said Constance, impatient to hold him in her arms.

'Frau Mozart, sir . . . I have sad news for you, such sad news.'

'He is not . . .'

'He is dead, sir.'

'Dead . . . But when?'

'The 19th of August. He had violent convulsions, and the doctor was powerless to save him. I decided not to inform you so as not to disturb your journey.'

Constance almost fainted away. Wolfgang held her very tightly in his arms. They sobbed together and went on a very long, silent walk, seeing nothing of what was happening around them.

Despite the violence of the shock, Wolfgang retained a strange serenity, for he knew that death did not mean nothingness. Raimund Leopold had not had the time to experience the joys and sorrows of earthly living; he had returned into the mystery from whence all living beings came.

That same evening, Wolfgang wrote a discreet letter to his father: '*As regards the poor big, fat and dear little man, we are both very, very sad.*'

Prague, 30 November 1783

Ignaz von Born had written a ferocious satire* against official religion, in which he defined obtuse monks as a species midway between monkeys and Man. He had come to Prague for a secret meeting with a few Brothers who wished to found a new research lodge.

The discussions took place in one of the small houses built for alchemists, behind the Hradschin palace, on the orders of Emperor Rudolf II.

Although Baron van Swieten had not obtained any proof of the existence of a secret department whose task was to spy on Freemasons, von Born remained extremely wary. And he asked himself a terrible question: were there informers even within the lodges themselves?

---

* *Specimen monachologiae methodo Linneaeno.*

In any event, Vienna would not escape checks by the police and the emperor. If Josef II kept to the path of liberalism, however, von Born would continue to prepare to welcome the Great Magician there. Nevertheless, it was best to keep Prague as a fall-back position.

The To Truth and Union Lodge* experienced a creation ritual which derived from the *Book of Thoth*. Thamos led the installation ceremony, then handed the Venerable's mallet to Ignaz von Born. The Brothers would devote themselves to the study of symbols and the initiatory tradition which had come down from ancient Egypt.

Now, no matter what happened, Thamos and Ignaz von Born had a safe temple at their disposal.

*Vienna, 4 December 1783*

'A strange fellow is asking for you,' Constance told Wolfgang. 'Apparently it is serious.'

'I shall go and see.'

The little grey man clearly did not smile very often.

'You are Wolfgang Mozart, Kapellmeister?'

'Correct.'

'I represent the banker Ochser.'

'I do not know that gentleman.'

---

* *Zur Wahrheit und Eintracht*, whose name should be placed in parallel with that of the Viennese lodge *Zur Wahren Eintracht*, To True Union.

'But he knows you. During your stay in Paris in October 1778, you contracted, through the intermediary of our bank, a debt of twelve gold louis.'

'I do not remember,' confessed Wolfgang.

'But we remember. It has taken time for me to find you and I demand the immediate reimbursement of that debt, on pain of legal action.'

'So long afterwards . . . What a memory!'

'Your answer, Herr Mozart.'

'As a matter of fact, I was not responsible for that journey. You must therefore address your demands to my father, Leopold Mozart, vice-Kapellmeister to Prince-Archbishop Colloredo, in Salzburg.'

'Is he solvent?'

'Do not insult our family!'

Wolfgang wrote immediately to his father to ask him to intervene and put an end to this ridiculous affair, then returned to his current work on *The Goose of Cairo*. He was not displeased with the three first fragments he had composed,* but he could not go any further with such a libretto. So he demanded numerous changes to which Varesco, despite his sensitivity, would have to agree.

*Vienna, 22 December 1783*

At an academy held for the benefit of the Society of Musicians, Wolfgang played a concerto to a full,

* K422/4–6.

enthusiastic hall. His friend Adamberger finally sang the aria which Salieri had succeeded in banning.

Still tormented by the thought of creating a new opera, Wolfgang wrote Adamberger a tragic aria* evoking the distress of Themistocles, alone and abandoned in the depths of a dungeon. A rebel, he cursed his destiny and could find a little hope only in thinking of the woman he loved. And a second aria,† this time for bass, was even more sombre: remorse tore apart Sebastes because he had betrayed King Xerxes. Even when freed and cleared of all suspicion, he could never forgive himself.

A refusal to show any kind of weakness; a permanent desire to escape from all the prisons in which fate wished to incarcerate him; a determination to see the true Light: the feelings which drove Wolfgang would not let him rest.

'Why are you so tense?' wondered Adamberger. 'Success should make you happy.'

'What if it is only fleeting?'

'You do not realize the extent of your new fame! It is you the public wants to see and hear.'

'At times, I can scarcely believe it.'

'Let us try an experiment: tomorrow evening, same place, same concert, but without you.'

In the absence of Mozart, the hall was almost empty.

* K431.
† K432.

# The Son of Enlightenment

The young couple were recovering from the death of their first child, and Constance was thinking about becoming pregnant again. God gave and took back life; nobody was surprised by the extreme fragility of babies. Only the most resilient got through the harsh ordeal of the first few months.

An echo from the past cheered the Christmas festivities. Count von Sickingen was passing through Vienna and paid a visit to Mozart, congratulating him warmly. The Palatinate Minister in Paris, a Freemason, Brother and friend of Baron Otto von Gemmingen, he had helped the young Wolfgang to bear his difficult stay in the French capital during which his mother had passed away.

Together, Wolfgang and his guest sat down at the piano and played the score of *Idomeneo* which Leopold had just sent his son. But the work that enchanted Constance was a fugue* in which her husband displayed his mastery of the art of counterpoint. This time, he had truly assimilated the teachings of Johann Sebastian Bach. Without detracting from the fluidity of Mozart's style, they brought strength and shape to it.

'I have great news for you, my darling.'

'A commission for an opera?'

'Not yet.'

---

*K426.

'Plans for a big concert?'

'Oh, several! But before anything else, we are going to move home. This time we shall live in a sumptuous residence, which is as conducive to work as it is to family life. Happy days await us there.'

# 56

*Brunswick, 31 December 1783*

Face to face, beside a large, roaring fire, Grand Master Ferdinand of Brunswick and his deputy Charles of Hesse were sitting out the last hours of a horrible year.

'Is the news still just as bad?' asked the Grand Master, who had grown old and tired.

'The lodges are continuing to leave Strict Observance,' nodded Charles of Hesse, whose guardian angel no longer made a sound, 'and very few subscriptions have reached us.'

'We shall soon be ruined, my Brother. Like you, I have devoted a large part of my wealth to the development of our Order, and we have failed.'

'The Templar tradition is dead, I agree, but the support of Willermoz may yet enable us to save Strict Observance.'

'I have the feeling that he is not enjoying his victory very much, and that his Charitable Knights of the Holy

City constitute a very second-rate army! Why do they not hasten to send us some convincing rituals?'

'The task is a long and difficult one, which demands a great deal of thought. Let us continue to hope.'


*Vienna, 27 January 1784*


At seven in the morning, Wolfgang had finished his toilette. In honour of his twenty-eighth birthday, instead of simply powdering his hair he had asked the hairdresser to curl it, draw it back and tie it in a bow.

Through one of the windows of his new apartment, he observed the Graben, Vienna's main square, which was always busy. Four thousand cabs and carriages of various sizes passed through it each day.

Living on the third floor of this vast house* gave him great satisfaction, particularly since the landlord, Thomas von Trattner, a book-seller and printer, had agreed to lower the six-monthly rent from seventy-five to sixty-five florins. Best of all, the building contained a hall where Wolfgang was planning to give private and paying concerts, which would enable him to pay his way without difficulty. And, on his pianoforte built by Anton Walter, he would compose in the evenings and at night, after his lessons and the public performances which his status as an independent musician demanded.

---

*Nos. 591–6 (today 29) am Graben.

Constance gently laid her head on her husband's shoulder.

'Happy birthday, darling. Aren't you going to rest a little today?'

'Alas, today promises to be as full as all the others.'

'Well I shall be obliged to take a siesta and avoid heavy work.'

'You mean . . .'

'I am pregnant.'

They kissed passionately.

'It will be a boy, and he will live to be old!' promised Constance.

Overwhelmed by the joy of this wonderful news, completed by the forthcoming reprise of *The Abduction from the Seraglio* at the Burgtheater, Wolfgang allowed his creative energy to lead him in two different directions.

One took the form of an elegant horn concerto,* whose slow movement was a peaceful romance; the other was the third quartet† of the series of six he wished to dedicate to Josef Haydn.

Despite an atmosphere of profound, almost anxious meditation, the work affirmed a sense of hope, as if the soul, after doubting for a long time, had finally crossed the threshold into a new world. Unlike the first two quartets, this one had a real ending, with stressed chords.

---

*K447.
† String quartet no. 16 in E flat major, K428. When the whole work was published by Artaria in 1785, Mozart placed this quartet fourth, after the quartet in B minor K458, finished on 9th November 1784, which he put in third place.

An agreeable concerto on the one hand, his inner music on the other, searching for the Light . . . But the composer did not feel torn between the two. This diversity vibrated within him, and he knew he was capable of reconciling contraries as long as he never betrayed his sense of what was authentic.

*Vienna, 9 February 1784*

There was no doubt about it: *The Goose of Cairo*, that enormous wooden or papier-mâché creature in the middle of the stage with the hero inside, simply did not inspire him. This was not a theme worthy to follow on from *The Abduction from the Seraglio*, especially in the unbearable form of Varesco's libretto.

Wolfgang turned to other forms of reading, provided by Thamos and the Minerval. He finished the work by Halophilus Irenaeus Oetinger, *Metaphysics in Its Relationship to Chemistry*, whose title concealed its content, i.e. the hermetic philosophy of the Rose-Cross which, notably, dealt with the action of music on the soul. Now he was passionately devouring the research of Giovenale Sacchi, *Of the Number and Measurements of Musical Strings along with Their Correspondences*, and above all, that of Pierre-Joseph Roussier, *Parallel between the System of the Egyptians and That of the Moderns*. The author established equivalences between the notes, musical keys, planets and signs of the zodiac.

That day, Wolfgang put the final touches to a dazzling concerto for piano in E flat major,* which was bursting with energy, although it did not depart from his customary elegance. Written for a small orchestra, the work included incessant modulations, alternating moments of anxiety and tranquil melodies. As for the final rondo, which was extremely fast, he did not forget to unite the soloist's melody and the counterpoint, recalling the beneficial influence of Bach.

Most important of all, Wolfgang attempted a number of experiments using Kabbalistic calculations which he scrawled on one of the pages of the manuscript,† in particular using the geometric figure of the 'long square', which generated multiple harmonies.

It was then that he took a decision as a responsible composer and a serious husband: to keep two notebooks, one devoted to the life of the household, and the other to his works.

In the first, he would note down the income derived from his lessons, his concerts and the sale of his scores, and family expenditure. The second, a hardback notebook with a pink cover,‡ would be the catalogue of his compositions. The first entry was his latest creation: the piano concerto in E flat.

---

* K449, no. 14.

† See Philippe A. Autexier, *La Lyre maçonne*, p. 153. *et seq*.

‡ This document is a mine of information, but Mozart did not note all of his creations in it and, several times, registered on the same day several works whose composition was spread out over time, hence the need for a critical study.

How eager he was when evening came and he could return to his inkwell, his pen and his manuscript paper! In order to reassure Leopold, who was still worried about his son's professional future and what was to follow *The Abduction from the Seraglio*, he was swift to reveal his convictions: '*The music I have made sleeps and rests in peace. In all the operas of our age which may be staged before mine is finished, not a single idea will resemble one of mine, I am quite calm about that.*'

*Vienna, 11 February 1784*

At a reception given by Prince Dimitri Galitzin, Thamos had an opportunity to speak to Gottfried van Swieten.

'I have carried out still more investigations,' revealed the baron. 'With no result. True, the police are discreetly watching certain Freemasons, but also agitators with ideas that have no connection with the Order. According to recent information, the emperor is rather inclined to view Freemasonry favourably, as long as the Viennese lodges agree with his reforms.'

'Is he not suspicious of the Illuminati of Bavaria?'

'He believes them neither formidable nor opposed to his policies. So why entrust surveillance of the lodges to a secret department?'

'Because Josef II, as a good head of State, always has several irons in the fire.'

'So you believe there is a shadowy figure, in direct contact with the emperor . . . and who would never do anything incautious, almost as if he never emerged from his office!'

'If he has created a network of informants, he will maintain his files, remain hidden in the shadows and take action only when he is certain of success.'

'Informants . . . inside the lodges as well as outside?'

'I fear so.'

Count Johann Esterhazy greeted the head of censorship and his Brother, the Count of Thebes.

'May I join in your deliberations?'

'We were waiting for you,' said Thamos. 'From this evening on, with a view to the next carnival, let us join forces with Prince Galitzin in launching Mozart's career and establishing him once and for all in Vienna.'

The four men planned a titanic programme. Despite his phenomenal energy, would frail Wolfgang manage to fulfil it?

# 57

*Vienna, 22 March 1784*

Wolfgang wondered how much longer he could maintain the infernal pace he had adopted since the beginning of Lent. On 1st, 5th, 8th, 12th and 15th March, there had been concerts at Count Esterhazy's palace; on the 4th, 11th, 18th and 19th, more concerts at Prince Galitzin's, not forgetting his first academy by subscription on 17th March, at the Trattner hall! Each time there had been an enthusiastic audience and good takings. 'In this way,' he confided to Constance, 'I shall not get out of practice.'

Despite this intense performing activity, Wolfgang composed constantly, for his listeners always demanded something new. And so on 15 March he had played a concerto* that demanded so much virtuosity that it 'brought me out in a muck sweat'. Proud and all-conquering, the soloist proved a vigorous match for a full orchestra.

* Concerto for piano no. 15, K450.

This evening, at Count Esterhazy's house, he created a concerto in D major,* which also unleashed a tide of perspiration. It possessed the same all-conquering joy as in the preceding work, and just as much ardour. The composer and the player won hearts, and Wolfgang was intoxicated by his success.

'Why don't you play even faster?' asked one of those world-weary, disdainful critics who were never astonished by anything.

'Acrobats believe that speed gives a performance fire. Well, when there is no fire in a composition, you don't play it at the gallop! It is much easier to play quickly than slowly. In the difficult passages, you can leave out a few notes without anybody noticing. But is that fine music?'

'Too cutting an opinion, Mozart!'

'Is it not the equal of yours?'

'I am accustomed to judging musicians!'

'Oh? And what have you composed?'

The critic turned away in fury. Wolfgang had made himself a new friend.

*Vienna, 23 March 1784*

There was no rest in sight, quite the contrary! Not a single empty evening until the beginning of April. That

---

*No. 16, K451.

evening, at the Burgtheater, a new joy gave Wolfgang energy: a reunion with his close friend Anton Stadler, now a full-time clarinettist at the Viennese court.

'May I speak with you, O illustrious Mozart?'

'Stop poking fun at me!'

'We were right to leave Salzburg, you and I. As I have never doubted your genius, your success does not surprise me, though I am beginning to wonder if you will emerge from this carnival alive!'

'To be honest, so am I! But how can I refuse invitations from Esterhazy and Galitzin? Baron van Swieten encourages me too, and I have received numerous responses to my proposal for subscription concerts.'

'In short, you will keep going until you are completely exhausted!'

'You know, music regenerates a person.'

'Yours does, that is for sure! I cannot tell you how happy I am to play your serenade in B flat major.* The Viennese are purring with pleasure over it. When you have a spare moment, we shall talk about the clarinet again.'

'Would you like to change instruments?'

'Absolutely not, but its capacity for expression needs to be improved. You alone can perceive its immense potential, which has been scarcely exploited. It is so close to the human voice that it touches the deepest parts of one's being. Unfortunately, I already have several

*K361.

children to feed and I lack the financial means necessary for real research. Will you help me?'

'Rely on me.'

*Vienna, 1 April 1784*

On 24th March, Wolfgang had given his second academy by subscription with, as a highlight, the concerto in D,* on the 25th, there was a concert at Galitzin's palace; on the 26th, at Esterhazy's; on the 27th, at the Trattner hall, he took part in the pianist Richter's academy; on the 29th, a concert at Esterhazy's house; on the 31st, the third and last subscription concert; and this evening, an enormous programme at the Burgtheater, where he was to conduct the *Haffner* and *Linz* symphonies, and play the concerto in D major, not forgetting several arias and a quintet for piano, oboe, clarinet, horn and bassoon,† which he had created the previous day.

'I regard it as the best thing I have done in my life,' he confided to Constance.

The art of marrying different timbres and instrumental combinations had reached its height.

Never again would Wolfgang return to such an ensemble, for this miracle could not be reproduced. Was it an end-point, or a false limit to be exceeded?

---

*K451.
†K452.

The musician had dreamt of success and glory, above all to ensure his independence. Having attained this goal, he was not content with it, since this success had not opened the door of the temple to him.

At last, this crazy period ended. One last concert at Count Palffy's house, on 9th April, and the composer could get his breath back.

*Vienna, 12 April 1784*

The first two movements of the concerto in G major* were finished when Wolfgang walked past a bird-seller's shop and heard a goldfinch† sing a melody which he memorized, exclaiming: 'How beautiful that is!'

As soon as he got back home, he noted down the first five bars of a very enthusiastic rondo with variations, in which gaiety alternated with passages that were almost melancholic.

And yet, as popular wisdom would have it, he surely had everything to make him happy. Even a bird had offered something to feed his inspiration – he, the fashionable musician Vienna simply could not do without!

But popular wisdom was wrong, for he lacked the vital ingredient: the knowledge of the mysteries into which the sun-priests were initiated.

---

* Concerto for piano no. 17, K453.
† Or possibly a starling.

# 58

*Vienna, 15 April 1784*

The meeting did not take place either at Schönbrunn or in the building housing Josef Anton's secret department, but inside a barracks frequented by many members of the Viennese nobility who were destined for military careers.

The Count of Pergen was not a happy man. Why did Josef II want to speak with him?

According to the latest rumours, he was becoming more and more favourable towards Freemasonry, an unshakeable foundation of his policies. Although a Papal bull of 1731 had condemned it, it had not been published in Austria. In his *Constitutions* of 1717, the pastor Anderson had written: '*If the Freemason understands the Art properly, he will never be a stupid atheist or an irreligious libertine.*'

'The Church today is incapable of defending the spiritual and moral values our society needs,' declared the emperor. 'That is why Freemasonry is useful to us, as long as it is closely controlled. So your patient toil merits my gratitude.'

Had he not been in the presence of Josef II, Anton would have let out an enormous sigh of relief.

'What has become of mystical and Templar Freemasonry in Vienna?'

'Majesty, I regard it as eradicated. The Rose-Cross confine themselves to Berlin and, very recently, Paris. As for Strict Observance, it is dying and no longer has any representative.'

'Excellent news. So only Freemasonry which is adept at reason and humanism remains within our walls.'

'I beg Your Majesty to permit me to put you on your guard against the expansion of the Illuminati of Bavaria, who now number more than two thousand five hundred members.'

'Prominent figures such as Herder, Goethe and von Sonnenfels belong to this movement, do they not?'

'Indeed they do, Majesty. I shall shortly procure you a complete list of the intellectuals hidden behind their strange pseudonyms. I have discovered that Greece stands for Bavaria, Athens for Munich, and Eleusis for Ingolstadt, the city of the founder, Adam Weishaupt. As for Egypt, that is the code name for Austria.'

'What do you fear?'

'That these intellectuals are using Freemasonry as a mask to prepare for a revolution.'

'I strongly doubt it, Count Pergen. And if such were the case, we would prevent them succeeding. Provide me with detailed reports on the activity of the Viennese lodges and the tenor of the speeches made there.'

'You shall have them, Majesty.'

'So you have zealous informants, including some false Brothers?'

'In view of the difficulty of my task, Majesty, all methods are acceptable.'

'I appreciate your discretion and your efficiency. Continue as you are.'

Josef Anton bowed.

He did not despair of persuading the emperor of the harmfulness of Freemasonry in general, and of the Illuminati of Bavaria in particular.


*Vienna, 22 April 1784*


Following final conversations with certain high-ranking Brothers, the emperor proclaimed the birth of a Grand Lodge of Austria, and entrusted the position of Grand Master to an inoffensive fifty-six-year-old dignitary, Count Johann Carl von Dietrichstein-Proskau, and that of Grand Secretary to Ignaz von Born. These two individuals had honourable reputations, and would be able to peacefully run this new institution, which was made up of seven provinces. Austria had seventeen lodges, eight of them in Vienna; Bohemia, seven; Galicia, four;

Austrian Lombardy, two; Transylvania, three; Hungary, twelve; and the Austrian Netherlands, seventeen.

'A good move,' said Josef Anton, 'a very good move. Now we have the Brothers under control within the "Royal Order of Freemasonry". This official recognition is a real straitjacket, though they will not realise that immediately. And the emperor is sure to have other surprises in store for them.'

'We no longer serve any purpose,' moaned Geytrand.

'On the contrary, my fine friend, on the contrary! When the most dangerous Brothers realize that they no longer have any freedom to manoeuvre, they will attempt to form dissident lodges. So we must be even more vigilant.'

*Vienna, 22 April 1784*

Thamos and Ignaz von Born were awaiting explanations from their Brother Tobias Philippe von Gebler.

The vice-chancellor sat down heavily in an armchair, emphasizing the weight of his fifty-eight years.

'I confess I had a good deal of influence on the emperor. The creation of this Grand Lodge of Austria seemed essential to me.'

'For what reasons?' asked von Born.

'We were heading for catastrophe,' explained the author of *Thamos, King of Egypt*. 'The Archbishop of Vienna, Anton Migazzi, a sworn enemy of Freemasonry,

has infiltrated several spies into the lodges. The emula-
tors of the Rose-Cross dream of bringing us back to
Christianity, and those who are nostalgic for Strict
Observance would like to reawaken the Templar spirit.
In short, Freemasonry is in complete disarray! Thanks to
this new institution, we shall be able to see things more
clearly. The Grand Master is a man of straw who will be
content with his fine-sounding title. In the eyes of everyone, the real leader of our Order will be our Brother von
Born, whose appointment I secured without difficulty.'

'What are the emperor's demands?' asked Thamos.

'Strict respect for the founding charter of the Grand
Lodge of Austria and the drawing up of an internal
system of rules pertaining to all lodges. Of course, it will
be brought to his attention.'

'The real Grand Master,' von Born corrected him, 'is
Josef II.'

'At least the situation is improving now, and we can
follow our path in safety, far from mystical and occult
influences. We shall examine this charter this very
evening, during the Gathering of Venerables.'

Ignaz von Born did not hide his scepticism.

'The emperor wants to control everything,' he
concluded. 'He will no longer leave us in peace and will
take other measures which will reduce our freedom to
the point of annihilating it.'

'Let us continue to prepare for the initiation of the
Great Magician,' advised Thamos. 'Fortunately, that
moment is drawing near.'

# 59

The emperor's charter recognized the sovereignty of the Grand Lodge of Austria and of each lodge belonging to this new structure.

Everyone could celebrate their own rituals, full of the Order's signs, hieroglyphs and symbols, on condition that they had no goal and no activity but charity in its widest sense.

The official phrasing hid Josef II's determination to control the leaders, or even get rid of candidates and dismiss those elected in order to replace them with men who were loyal to the established power.

The discussion of general principles, which each lodge must include in its own particular regulations, was the subject of controversy.

'Before all else,' von Gebler recalled, 'we must proclaim the need for charity, that virtue which the emperor is so fond of. It alone will give us the ability to fight the evils which oppress humanity.'

'That implies freeing us from all forms of belief and tyranny,' added von Born. 'Charity also consists of doing good, acting properly, and therefore celebrating precise and correctly constructed rituals.'

'What will be our criteria for admission?' asked one dignitary.

'All Brothers must take part in the works in an active way,' replied von Gebler, 'and therefore possess one of the following qualities: either they should enjoy sufficient consideration in the outside world, by birth or by status, to protect oppressed virtue and the general good; or they should possess material goods within a framework of order and family life, so as to be able to provide assistance if necessary; or they should possess knowledge and talents vital in order to correct erroneous ideas, to combat harmful prejudices and to spread the true light.'

'Will we go as far as admitting a manual worker?' asked a count anxiously.

'In former times, the lodges of cathedral builders were made up of craftsmen,' von Born reminded him. 'No reason exists to refuse entrance to the temple to anyone, as long as the postulant can meet his own needs, is not a burden to his Brothers and feels a true desire to see the Light.'

No one protested.

'On the other hand,' went on the Grand Secretary, 'we must be wary of nobles who are full of themselves and their privileges. We must try to impose a lengthy trial period upon them, and reject them if they show too much pride or vanity to participate in our brotherhood. Those who look down upon the decent, simple middle-class man because he has no titled ancestors do not deserve to pass through the door of the temple. Nor do aristocrats who mistreat their servants or their subjects, show harshness and cruelty towards them or increase their own wealth in an ignoble way and behave in a vile manner. For a Freemason, virtue and righteousness must be more than just words.'

'All these precepts were contained in the Rule of the temples of ancient Egypt,' recalled Thamos. 'Putting them into practice is a daily necessity, without which initiation would be just a mirage.'

'And so we come back to true charity,' insisted von Born. 'It is not just a case of financial support, but of assistance of another kind, spiritual help and the gift of knowledge which makes it possible to pass through the successive doors that are placed along the path to initiation.'

'Must we still admit men of the Church?' asked a Brother.

'As long as they are basically tolerant,' replied von Born, 'and do not seek to spread their beliefs within the Lodge.'

Nobody challenged the Grand Secretary's opinions, which did not displease von Gebler. So the vice-chancellor could reassure the emperor and guarantee that the lodges would adhere to his policy.


*Vienna, 29 April 1784*

The concert given at the Gate of Carinthia Theatre, in the presence of Josef II, was taking on the appearance of a particularly perilous exercise. During it, Wolfgang would create a sonata for piano and violin,* along with the Italian Regina Strinasacchi.

There was just one small problem: the piano score was almost blank, for he had not had time to note down the music. He would therefore have to play from memory and without any rehearsal.

The work began with a largo, a slow movement during which a dialogue was played out between woman and man, sensitivity and the determination to conquer. How could these apparent contraries be reconciled, if not through the fervour of an allegro that went beyond their mutual opposition? The andante brought the work back to a sense of meditation and almost painful doubt, which was dispelled by the final rondo, a celebration of the joy of living.

Having heard the astonishing rumours, the emperor checked for himself. Dumbfounded, he realized that Mozart was playing from blank pages!

* K454, in B flat major.

As for the Dutch pianist Richter, who was watching the player's fingers, he could not contain his bitterness.

'My God, I have to work until I sweat and still have no success! And you, my friend, make a game of it!'

'Oh!' exclaimed Wolfgang, 'I have also had to work hard so that now, I have no more left to give.'


*Vienna, 26 May 1784*


After the academy he had organized himself on 8th May at the home of the Trattners, his landlords, Wolfgang finally got his breath back. Nevertheless, he continued to rise between five and six, and kept to his pace of work while granting himself a delicious walk with Constance each morning, in the Augarten park.

Her pregnancy was going well, and their tender, intimate love flourished as the days went on.

'There is a serious difficulty poisoning our life,' she declared.

'Our good woman from Salzburg, Liser Schwemmer, I'll wager?'

'She doesn't even know how to lay a fire or to make coffee. Her only skills consist of putting the food on the dining-room table. When she helps me to iron a dress or take it up, she complains that she is overworked! Her salary serves her only to buy wine and beer. Yesterday, I found her dead drunk on her bed. She had vomited so much that I had to replace the sheets and the mattress. This cannot go on! We must dismiss her and replace her.'

'You are right, darling, but . . .'

'But?'

'If I was the kind of man to make people unhappy, I would dismiss her instantly. Let us be charitable and keep her as long as possible.'


*Vienna, 27 May 1784*


The more he thought about it, the more Wolfgang felt he had been ungrateful and regretted it. So he went to the bird-seller's shop in the hope that the creator of the first bars of his concerto in G major* had not found a buyer.

The goldfinch was still there!

As soon as it saw Mozart, it launched into its favourite song.

'How much do you want for it?' the musician asked the bird-seller.

'Thirty-four kreutzers.'

Wolfgang did not haggle.

'We shall be good friends,' he promised his new companion. 'What name shall I give you . . . Ah! I have it: Star. For are you not a star that lights up our days with your remarkable talent?'

Star hailed his christening by singing *forte* and *allegro*.

* K453.

# 60

*Vienna, 13 June 1784*

Wolfgang did not note down in his *Catalogue* the eight 'Like a lamb' variations* which he had just composed on an air from the *Decent Man* by Sarti, who was visiting Vienna. Instead, he headed for Döbling, in the Viennese countryside. At an academy there, he played his quintet for piano and wind instruments† while his host, the dazzling Barbara Ployer, played the concerto in G.‡ This performance was well paid and increased his already substantial income.

This financial success reassured Wolfgang and gave him wings. What a joy to give Constance a comfortable life, without material cares! Never could he have imagined such prosperity when he was ruining his talent as a

---

* K460. He nevertheless remembered to make them one of the themes of the banquet offered by Don Juan to the commander.
† K452.
‡ K453.

musician-servant in the service of the Grand Mufti Colloredo. Audacity had been a success for him, and he would never go back, even if he still dreamed of a stable post at the Viennese court, provided it was accompanied by an excellent remuneration and a maximum of creative freedom.

Artaria published three piano sonatas[*] and another publisher, Torricella, brought out three other works[†] which consolidated his reputation as a fashionable Viennese musician.

At the end of the concert, he had a conversation with old Count Thun.

A friend and Brother of Ignaz von Born, the Freemason spoke of the language of symbols, the importance of the initiatory tradition, and the presence of the spirits who dwelt within all forms of life, from stars to minerals.

These prospects prevented Wolfgang from allowing himself to become drunk with his success. Beyond material satisfactions, was there not the door of the temple, at once close and far away?

Only Thamos the Egyptian could open it. When would he at last consent to do so?

*Berlin, 15 June 1784*

'Why are you so angry, my Brother?' asked Bischoffswerder, one of the leaders of the Golden Rose-Cross, who were so

[*] K330, 331, 332.
[†] K284, 333, 454.

highly regarded at court that they influenced the highest authorities.

'The Illuminati of Bavaria, to whom I belong, want to destroy the established powers and society,' replied Utzschneider. 'They must be prevented from doing harm.'

The traitor omitted to mention that he wanted revenge because he had just been refused a promotion.

'Do you have proof of what you are saying?'

'I took discreet notes,' revealed Utzschneider. 'I shall give you an explosive file which contains declarations by several dignitaries and reveals the true intentions of the Illuminati. It is up to you to strike quickly and decisively.'

'Rely upon me, my very dear Brother.'

The Golden Rose-Cross of Berlin had not dared hope for such a gift! The document was sent immediately to their principal supporter, Frederick-William II. Refusing to intervene on their territory or to act openly, he entrusted the dirty work to the Prince-Elector of Bavaria, Karl Theodor.

*Munich, 22 June 1784*

The Jesuit Frank, Karl Theodor's political adviser and confessor, rubbed his hands with glee. With the aid of Utzschneider's dossier and additional material from the Rose-Cross in Berlin, he had convinced his illustrious patron to take a decision that was as radical as it was explosive.

Karl Theodor's edict formally banned all secret societies in the states under his jurisdiction. Regarding himself as being on a sacred mission to save the Church, the prince-elector wished to put an end to the activities of subversive and formidable sects – principal among them being the Illuminati of Bavaria and the Masonic lodges – but did not actually name them.

Frank was hoping for a violent reaction, especially from the Illuminati. This would oblige Karl Theodor to use force and incline the courts to hand down sentences of imprisonment.

Whatever the case, this decree broke them and halted their growth in its tracks. The Church could congratulate itself on this success, which would be followed by many others if Josef II, in his turn, perceived the danger and adopted the necessary measures.


*Munich, 23 June 1784*


The leader of the Illuminati of Bavaria, Adam Weishaupt, and his right-hand man, Baron Adolph von Knigge, reread the decree word by word.

'Although we are not specifically named,' observed Weishaupt, 'we are the principal target for Karl Theodor and his accursed confessor!'

'Given the imprecise way in which the decree is written,' commented von Knigge, 'no court will convict us.'

'We must on no account take any risks! We would be accused of rampant subversion and conspiracy against the prince-elector, who would be delighted to make examples of us.'

'In that case, what do you suggest?'

'We must know how far Karl Theodor and his allies want to go. So let us pretend to obey him by pronouncing the apparent dissolution of our Order and asking all our members to keep silent. Perhaps this attitude will show the prince-elector that he has won a great victory.'

'Just a bad moment that will pass, do you suppose . . . ? I scarcely think so!' objected von Knigge. 'This declaration of war is bound to have consequences. Religious obscurantism would like to destroy our movement by using the stupidity and cowardice of princes who wish to keep their thrones at any price. But I refuse to give in. I will agree to more or less putting the Order to sleep, if the lodges continue to meet in secret. Moreover, we shall set up reading societies, open to all, where we can spread our ideas. Even Karl Theodor cannot claim they are secret.'

'Interesting,' agreed Weishaupt.


*Vienna, 30 June 1784*


'My friend Frank has manoeuvred magnificently,' said Geytrand. 'The Illuminati have been struck right at the heart of their kingdom, Bavaria!'

'Alas,' lamented Josef Anton, 'Prince-Elector Karl Theodor's decree is much too vague. It does not explicitly name the Illuminati and the Freemasons.'

'No one can be mistaken!'

'Highly placed individuals, including magistrates who belong to the Order, will delay or block the application of this law by claiming that Freemasonry does not perform any illegal actions and does not threaten any throne.'

'Since it is certainly a secret society, the courts will ban it!'

'That would be too simple, my dear Geytrand. The Freemasons will find a thousand and one ways in which to escape punishment.'

'Frank wants to bring them down and Karl Theodor follows his directions blindly.'

'The Illuminati are on the rise and will not give up attempting to establish themselves. Doubtless they will pretend to comply, the better to counter-attack. The war has only just begun.'

# 61

After his horse ride, around seven in the morning, Wolfgang divided his time between composition and lessons. In order to rest, he liked to play billiards while chatting to Constance. He had bought a fine table covered with superb green baize, twelve cues and five balls. A lantern and five chandeliers lit up the playing surface.

That evening, the Mozarts played host to several singers, including Michael O'Kelly and the nineteen-year-old soprano Nancy Storace, accompanied by her suitor Stephen, a jealous and impetuous violinist. They asked Constance for news of her health before singing the praises of England and playing a game of billiards while emptying quite a few bottles of wine.

Star the bird accompanied these diversions by singing a pretty melody which Nancy Storace repeated.

'Your voice is splendid,' said Wolfgang.

'Will you choose me to perform in your next opera?'

'If I manage to unearth a good libretto, certainly.'

'Is that so difficult?'

'I have read nothing but stupid stories devoid of interest. But I have not yet lost hope.'


*Vienna, 4 July 1784*


Geytrand laid a piece of sheet music on Josef Anton's desk. It was the Torricella edition of two piano sonatas[*] and a sonata for piano and violin by Mozart.[†]

'Have you become a lover of fashionable music?'

'Look closely at the title page, Herr Count.'

Anton's scrutiny was revealing.

'Several Masonic emblems . . . What does this signify?'

'Either Mozart is declaring himself to be a Freemason, or the publisher is declaring his own convictions and sympathies.'

Josef Anton consulted his lists.

Mozart was not on them. So the second hypothesis was the correct one.

'Bizarre,' commented Geytrand. 'Can the publisher have permitted himself this audacity without the author's explicit agreement?'

---

[*] K284 and 333.
[†] K454.

'Of course, since he can even alter the score.'

'In other words, nothing proves that Mozart is linked in any way to Freemasonry.'

'Nothing,' concluded Anton. 'However, his name keeps coming up a little too often. So I shall take a closer interest in him.'

*Vienna, 5 July 1784*

In Brazil, an archaeologist discovered the traces of the realm of the Amazons. While a meteorologist continued his research, a distracted lover thought only of his beautiful love.

On the rather slender basis of this libretto by Petrosellini, Wolfgang began an opera.*

Swiftly becoming bored with writing music devoid of meaning, he soon stopped.

'Father Da Ponte wishes to see you,' Constance informed him.

Wolfgang was not expecting this visit. Appointed official poet to the court with a salary of six hundred florins, thanks to the help of his protector Salieri, the librettist had probably come to explain to him that he was overwhelmed with work.

'Dear Mozart, I have given my idea more depth! And I like this *Disappointed Husband* a great deal! Emilia,

---

* K434 (fragments of *Realm of the Amazons*).

a young and noble Roman, loves Hannibal. Learning of his death, she listens to her tutor, who advises her to marry an old greybeard. Dramatic moment: Hannibal reappears, very much alive, but coveted by two other women who are madly in love with him, one of them a singer! One man exposed to the rivalry of three female suitors: you can imagine the complications and the repercussions. Everything ends well, and Hannibal marries Emilia. So work on it, Mozart.'

Da Ponte was in a hurry, and rushed off.

Wolfgang scanned the libretto and felt no enthusiasm. If he said yes to Da Ponte, that would mean an assurance that the work would be staged. But accepting the story the way it was . . . He had to think.

*Ingolstadt, 15 July 1784*

Baron Adolph von Knigge exploded.

'I am not accustomed to being summoned like a common valet,' he told Adam Weishaupt, 'and I will not tolerate your behaviour. Must I remind you that I am responsible for writing the rituals for the Order of Illuminati?'

'It was I who entrusted you with that task and it is I alone who will assess the results.'

'While constantly hindering me at every turn!' protested von Knigge. 'Your sectarianism and blind criticism of religion are the product of a limited mind, incapable of perceiving the importance of rites and esotericism. Only the Egyptian mysteries will lead us to knowledge, and you do not grant them any consideration.'

'You remain an old-fashioned mystic, Baron, and I cannot tolerate that type of individual in my organization.'

'Is that why you are spreading such calumnies about my private life?'

'Do you consider it beyond reproach?'

'That does not concern you!'

'Everything the Illuminati do concerns me. Criticizing their leader, opposing him, insulting his sovereignty, daring to denigrate him to other Brothers: these are unforgivable faults. You have committed them, Baron, and are no longer worthy of belonging to the Order.'

'Do you intend to throw me out?'

'I have drawn up a deed of accusation, signed by myself and several senior dignitaries, which accuses you of opportunism. If you contest it, we shall go further. Much further. I therefore advise you to resign, taking three formal oaths: to maintain secrecy, to leave your offices and to withdraw all your grievances with regard to me.'

The violence in Adam Weishaupt's eyes terrified Baron von Knigge. The tyrant was not joking and was threatening him with death.

'You are a sad leader and a formidable manipulator. May heaven ensure that your contemptible adventure ends badly.'

'Do you accept my conditions, Baron?'

'You will hear no more of me, Weishaupt. But your edifice of lies will soon crumble.'

The leader of the Illuminati had finally got rid of that spiritualist, who had become a hindrance. True, he did not possess the rituals of the Great Mysteries. But the result of his efforts, a political and social revolution, would make him forget that inconvenience.


*Vienna, 2 August 1784*

The husband was not the only disappointed one! After composing an overture, two ensembles and two arias for *Lo Sposo deluso*,* Wolfgang halted in irritation.

It was a pitiful libretto! How could such a theme be handled in the *buffa* style and how could a scorned and unhappy heroine be made amusing? Blackening the nature of women like this displeased him to the highest degree. And none of them had sufficient character.

Since his contacts with the Illuminati of Salzburg and his reading of esoteric works, Wolfgang needed depth, not Father Da Ponte's derisory little amusements. So he abandoned this poor project, convinced that he would never again spend time with that playboy courtier, who was far too close to the mediocre Salieri.

This disappointment was exacerbated by some very sad news from Salzburg: Miss Pimperl, the fox-terrier

* K430.

bitch, had just died. How he would have loved to hold her to the very last moment, thinking of the thousand and one memories they had shared! Wolfgang was her favourite; he could detect every tiny emotion in Miss Pimperl, and their closeness had provided them with some wonderfully happy times.

After the death of this dog he had loved so much, the last of Mozart's youth faded away.

# 62

Wolfgang wrote to his sister Nannerl to congratulate her on her marriage, which was planned for the 23rd. The happy groom was called Johann Baptist von Berchtold zu Sonnenburg. A magistrate and legal administrator of his city, he was no spring chicken but a fifty-year-old widower and the father of five children. At thirty-three, the severe Nannerl was to move with this old husband into the house where his mother was born, in Saint-Gilgen.

Wolfgang had no desire to be present at this sinister ceremony, and contented himself with this polite but distant letter. An insurmountable gulf had opened up between him and his sister, and neither he nor she wished to overcome it.

He thought of his father, now alone in his large Salzburg apartment. Determined not to remarry, Leopold had lost his son, and now his confidante, Nannerl, was leaving him. Fortunately he still had his post as deputy Kapellmeister and his pupils, to whom he dedicated himself with patience and a much-appreciated sense of his duty as a teacher. Would God grant him the opportunity to spoil one or several grandchildren?

*Vienna, 23 August 1784*

As he watched the performance, at the Burgtheater, of Paisiello's opera *King Theodore in Venice*, Wolfgang sweated profusely. Back home, he shivered. Overcome with stomach pains, he vomited and thought he was done for.

Fortunately, young Doctor Barisani, whose praises were sung by the whole of Vienna, agreed to come to his bedside and lavish his skills upon him. Because it was such a serious chill, he predicted that his patient was going to have several difficult weeks and asked him to take proper care of himself.

However, as early as the 25th, Wolfgang spruced up an improvisation on an air by Gluck, which had been played on 23rd March 1783 in the presence of the emperor, and extracted two variations for piano.[*] The text was an extract from the *Pilgrims of Mecca*, and amused the convalescent greatly: a sort of dervish

[*] K455.

passed for a holy man of exemplary austerity in the eyes of a credulous population, while he was in fact leading a dissolute existence and enjoying the inexhaustible pleasures of high living!

Star the bird's joyous arpeggios echoed his master's good humour, and Constance was reassured to see her husband so quickly regaining his taste for life. Nevertheless, he must follow a strict regime and not overwork. Because of his insane timetable during the musical season, Wolfgang had exceeded his own limits and had gravely compromised his health.

As good old Liser Schwemmer from Salzburg was still just as lazy and ineffectual as ever, Constance – who was only a month from her confinement – engaged another servant. Each day, the mistress of the house divided up the tasks in order to avoid conflicts. The young woman proved remarkably skilful in this difficult exercise.

*Vienna, 29 September 1784*

Constance could not believe her eyes.

What a sumptuous, spacious apartment! Just behind the cathedral, Camesina House* was one of the most famous in Vienna. Josef, a celebrated interior decorator and father to the landlords, the brothers Camesina,

---

* No. 846, Schulerstrasse, formerly no. 5, Domgasse.

had ornamented part of the vast dwelling with rococo stuccos.

Four main rooms on the first floor, one hundred and seventy square metres, every comfort ... Constance rubbed her eyes.

'How much is the rent?'

'Two hundred and thirty florins per half-year,' revealed Wolfgang.

'That's enormous!'

'Don't worry, we have sufficient means. And doesn't this little fellow deserve a good start in life?'

In his arms, Wolfgang was delicately cradling Karl Thomas, born on 21st September and baptized at St Peter's Church. Both mother and child were doing extremely well.

'May God grant him a long and beautiful life,' murmured the musician, kissing the infant, who rewarded him with a broad smile.

'We shall have to buy furniture,' commented Constance.

'My harpsichord will be moved in this very evening,' said Wolfgang. 'Here, I shall have a thousand ideas and be able to work in complete peace.'


*Vienna, 30 September 1784*


The first work Wolfgang finished in his new and prestigious residence was a concerto in B flat for piano and orchestra,* designed for a blind virtuoso, Maria-Theresia von Paradies.

The two fast movements, the first and the third, highlighted the player's skill by providing her with a score that was light-hearted, voluble and cheerful with a few moments of tenderness and reverie. In contrast, the andante with variations in G minor was a long meditation by Wolfgang on the meaning of his own existence. Attempting to overcome impatience and rebellion, he demonstrated apparent calm without concealing the profound doubt that haunted him: would he one day walk the path that led to the Light?

A cry rang out in the orchestra; a brutal question was asked: what do you really want? He would never give up fighting! So he rediscovered the tranquillity linked to this certainty, and yet he ended these painful variations by returning to his initial doubt.

Every Sunday, Wolfgang went with Constance to Baron van Swieten's house, in the hope of discovering new works by Johann Sebastian Bach.

The previous day, the baron thought he had at last identified a serious clue leading to the man hunting down the Freemasons. But after making checks, he had established that it was just a police officer whose job was to keep files concerning those courtiers who had links to the Minister of War.

---

*No. 18, K456.

Next to the harpsichord stood Thamos, looking even more impressive than usual. Van Swieten introduced Constance to some other guests, leaving the Egyptian alone with the musician.

'Are you pleased with your new apartment?'

'It is a marvel! Josef Haydn and some colleagues are coming soon to play some chamber music there. Of course, you have a permanent invitation to visit.'

'I have another invitation to pass on to you.'

The solemnity of his tone made the composer shiver.

'After all these years of research, successes and failures, after your contacts with Freemasons of various different tendencies, after your wide-ranging reading, do you wish to continue your path alone, or attempt to pass through the door of the temple?'

For a second, Wolfgang closed his eyes.

'I have been hoping for that question for so long!'

'What is your answer?'

'It is my dearest desire to pass through that door.'

'Before that happens, you must face one final, probationary ordeal. If you fail, we shall never see each other again.'

# 63

*Vienna, 14 October 1784*

Incapable of resuming work on *The Goose of Cairo*, Wolfgang returned to a musical genre he had not practised for six years: the piano sonata.* He dedicated this work to his pupil Theresa von Trattner and chose the tragic key of C minor in order to express his anxiety that he might fail and the violence of his spiritual desire. The music was breathless, jerky, effervescent. Would this fire burn him or bring him illumination?

As Thamos had not specified the nature of the ordeal he was to undergo, he did not know how to prepare himself for it.

This wait was a time of hope and anguish. The hope of discovering a new universe and of at last seeing the Light, and the anguish of being rejected for ever. For he would have no second chance.

*K457.

Waiting with no precise date ... What torture! But that was perhaps the beginning of the ordeal.

*Lyons, 15 October 1784*

The Charitable Knights of the Holy City greatly admired their leader, Jean-Baptiste Willermoz, victor of the Wilhelmsbad Assembly. As for the few Grand Professionals who celebrated mystical ceremonies, they were awaiting the creation of rituals that were destined for the whole of Freemasonry, as Grand Master Ferdinand of Brunswick had been promised.

Willermoz held all the cards. All he had to do was play them in order to win the game.

Only one Brother had doubts about this triumph: Willermoz himself. On reading the first attempts by close colleagues he had entrusted with writing the new rituals, he was cruelly disappointed.

Why not face facts? The Lyons brotherhood would never succeed in keeping their promises. Their victory at Wilhelmsbad was proving to be pointless and sterile, since they were incapable of exploiting their advantage. Hunting on the Germans' own territory would bring only trouble. It was better to keep to one's own domain.

Willermoz decided to forget the promise he had made to Ferdinand of Brunswick. The Grand Master would get by without him.

'Count Phoenix wishes to see you,' one of his disciples informed him. 'He resides at the Hôtel de la Reine, on the quai Saint-Clair, and claims to possess vital information.'

Intrigued, Jean-Baptiste Willermoz headed for the address he had been given.

The other man revealed his true identity straight away.

'I, Cagliostro, am going to found a lodge here, according to my Egyptian Rite. Help me to recruit followers, and I shall pass on my secrets to you.'

'What are they?'

'What are yours, distinguished Brother?'

'You tell me first.'

'Out of the question, since I am the Great Cophte, the Superior of all Freemasons! If you know the Great Mysteries, you may speak without fear.'

'My disciples recognize only my authority,' Willermoz reminded him. 'If you wish to gain a foothold in Lyons, you will have to submit to me and entrust me with your rituals, so that I may pronounce upon your legitimacy.'

'I understand your demands, my Brother, but accept mine! Our good understanding assumes trust and mutual gifts.'

'First, let us be sure that we are talking the same language. Do you believe in the divine nature of Jesus Christ?'

Cagliostro thought.

'Christ is the son of God, a philosopher, an initiate, but not God himself.'

Willermoz's affable face grew stern.

'That thought is heretical and reprehensible.'

'You are a Freemason, my Brother! So exercise some critical sense.'

'You are sinking deeper into error, Cagliostro, and so proving that you are an impostor. In reality, you possess no secrets and you misdirect minds by distancing them from Our Lord Jesus Christ.'

'You are wrong to laugh at my knowledge, Willermoz. You are the impostor! You deceive your Brothers by making them the slaves of a narrow-minded religion.'

'That miserable speech highlights your mediocrity. You should know, sir, that I can speak conjurations against the depraved, to which you belong. You will pay dearly for your ignoble words, I promise you that.'

Cagliostro's anger flared.

'I am indifferent to your threats. Do not under any circumstances try to use your black magic against me, for it will swiftly rebound upon you!'

'We shall soon see which of us is the stronger.'

Henceforth enemies, the two men glared at each other.

*Vienna, 31 October 1784*

To celebrate their teacher's saint's day, Mozart's pupils had arranged a little concert in the large Domgasse apartment. Star the bird much appreciated the performers' talents, except those of one Parisian guest, Baron

Bagge, who made himself look ridiculous by attempting to play a violin concerto which exceeded his abilities.

Although he took part in the general hilarity, Wolfgang's mind was elsewhere, and he was thinking about the worrying ordeal Thamos had spoken of. What was going to be demanded of him? What qualities must he display? He had difficulty sleeping, for he doubted his abilities and wondered if he would really be capable of working with people whose knowledge extended so much further than his own!

And if he failed, what despair he would feel! However, there was no question of giving up. He would confront his judges, whoever they might be, and would conceal nothing of his personality, ideas and feelings.

Wolfgang's guests had just bade him farewell, and he was closing the inner shutters of his apartment when he glanced down into the street below and spotted the familiar silhouette of Thamos the Egyptian.

He immediately ran out to join him.

'Have you thought about it, Wolfgang?'

'I do nothing else, and I don't even compose any more!'

'Are you still determined to attempt the adventure?'

'Still!'

'In that case, try to rest a little. The decisive test will take place tomorrow evening.'

# 64

*Vienna, 1 November 1784*

An old man Wolfgang did not know blindfolded him, took him by the hand, led him into a room which he could tell was very large, and helped him to sit down on a chair.

'Outsider,' said a stern voice, 'a temple greets you. Here are gathered Brothers who are in search of light and knowledge. They intend to sound out your heart and your mind, to find out if you really wish to share their Quest. I would ask you therefore to answer them honestly. At the end of this trial, we shall take a unanimous decision. Either our roads will separate, or you will be admitted among us, and this judgement will be without appeal. Here is the first question: what is initiation?'

Wolfgang had the impression that he was getting hopelessly muddled. He could not find the right words, got his ideas mixed up and did not express himself as he

would have wished. Nevertheless, thanks to the blindfold he was able to look within himself and maintain his
concentration.

Despite the intensity of these moments, despite the
fear of failure and the need to respond to the many and
varied questions on his thoughts, his existence, his tastes,
his concept of music, his good qualities, his defects and
so many other subjects, he felt a kind of detachment, as
if all of this did not really concern him.

Around him he felt no negative energy, only people
who listened to him attentively and, far from judging him,
attempted to understand him and to determine whether
he could succeed in following the path of initiation.

'We thank you for having agreed to speak in a straight-
forward manner,' concluded a solemn voice. 'You will
be taken back outside. In a little while from now, we will
inform you of the result of our vote.'

Wolfgang was helped to stand up and leave the room.
Then the same elderly man removed the blindfold and,
without saying a word, opened the door of the dwelling
to which he had been summoned.

It was raining.

Wolfgang did not go straight back home, for he felt a
need to wander through the streets of Vienna.

Now his destiny was sealed. If the lodge rejected
him, he would not cross the threshold of the temple
and would never again see Thamos the Egyptian. If the
Brothers welcomed him among them, a new life would
begin, a life which would give a meaning to all his past

experiences and reveal to him new horizons, whose presence he could perceive but which he could not make out clearly.

His destiny was sealed, yet he did not know the decision. How, under such conditions, could he possibly get to sleep?

*Vienna, 2 November 1784*

'Your eyes are red, but your face is all pale!' remarked Constance worriedly. 'Are you ill?'

'No, I didn't sleep well.'

'Because of your strange evening?'

'You cannot imagine the weight of uncertainty! Being the last to know – what an ordeal!'

Wolfgang improvised on the harpsichord. Charmed by a melody, Star repeated it.

Was this a good sign?

'I'm going for a walk.'

Unable to concentrate or stay in one place, the composer planned to walk until he was exhausted.

Before St Stephen's Cathedral stood Thamos.

'It is a beautiful day,' said the Egyptian. 'A generous sun and a suitable temperature.'

Wolfgang was unable to hold back the question that burnt his lips.

'Do you have . . . the verdict?'

'Of course, since I was present.'

'Are you willing . . . to give it to me?'

'Willing is not the correct term.'

'Then which should I use?'

'In reality, Wolfgang, my Brothers have entrusted me with the duty of informing you of the result of their deliberations.'

As Thamos's face remained inscrutable, the composer feared the worst.

No, it was impossible . . . His dream wasn't going to crumble like this, in one brief second!

Thamos laid a hand on the Great Magician's shoulder.

'The To Charity Lodge has decided to initiate you.'

Wolfgang was incapable of expressing what he felt. It was an unknown joy, so powerful that it gave him the impression that he was soaring above mountains.

'This is the start of an immense journey, and not its end,' said Thamos.

'If you knew . . .'

'I know, Wolfgang. I too have experienced this moment. Never forget how it feels. Initiates may often be disappointing, but initiation will never disappoint you. Now, there is one formality left to carry out: your letter of application.'

'When am I to be initiated?'

'The lodge will choose the date.'

'I won't have to wait too long, will I?'

Thamos smiled.

'I hope that you will be able to celebrate your most wonderful Christmas ever.'

# Christian Jacq

Leopold-Aloys Hoffmann, known as Sulpicius to the Illuminati, was a teacher of German language and literature, and Secretary of the To Charity Lodge. As such he sent out notices to attend to the Brothers, kept a record of the names of those present and absent at each gathering, wrote the administrative reports which were sent to the Grand Lodge of Austria and received letters of application.

That morning, it was an application from Wolfgang Mozart, an independent musician. Hoffmann had heard of the author of *The Abduction from the Seraglio*, who had not a drop of noble blood and did not feature among the influential people at court. In short, he was a recruit of little interest to the small To Charity Lodge, whose chosen direction displeased Hoffmann.

At the instigation of the Venerable, who was in turn influenced by Ignaz von Born, the lodge paid too much interest to the study of symbols.

For his part, Hoffmann was searching for friends in high places. Moreover, he could not bear criticism of institutions and the questioning of certain values. This Masonic movement was taking a bad turn, which he would denounce by confiding in a former Brother, Geytrand.

True, Hoffmann was betraying his oath to reveal nothing of what he saw and heard in lodge. But a word was only a word, and since he disapproved of To Charity's ideas, his conscience was clear.

According to custom, he should pass on Mozart's application to the other lodges in Vienna, in order to obtain their approval. From time to time, a Brother would manifest his opposition. He was then asked to set out his arguments, whose veracity was checked.

But this task bored him. His successor would soon be appointed, and he could deal with the Mozart file.

# 65

Wolfgang composed the fourth* of the six quartets he was planning to dedicate to Haydn, while awaiting the date for his initiation. Declaring his desire for conquest and discovery in the initial movement, he devoted the adagio to a meditation on the profound transformation of his existence. For was this not a kind of beneficial death, the passage from a world of darkness to a universe whose light was inaccessible to the eyes of an outsider? Using a dance rhythm, the finale expressed the intense joy of a man who would soon pass through the door of the temple, after fearing that it would close once and for all.

On 17th November, *The Abduction from the Seraglio* was to be performed in Salzburg for the first time.

---

* K458, which, on publication in 1785, became the third.

Wolfgang felt that this event was like an exorcism, a definitive victory over Colloredo and the tyranny whose chains he had shattered. The composer believed not in chance but in the organization of reality by a divine architect, and he linked this small additional pleasure to the immense happiness he was shortly to experience.

*Paris, 13 November 1784*

Following the failure of the Wilhelmsbad Assembly, the Marquis de Chefdebien and the other Brothers from the Philalethes Lodge decided not to abdicate. If the Freemasons did not extricate themselves from this impasse, the Order was in danger of disappearing.

As several vital questions had yet to be resolved, the Philalethes opened their own Assembly, up to 26th May, in the hope of attracting large numbers of delegates from all the European lodges.

They put the questions clearly: what is the fundamental nature of Freemasonry? What origin should reasonably be attributed to it? An oral or written tradition? Who is the current repository of that tradition? To which secret sciences is Freemasonry linked? Of the current rites, which will enable the Order to make progress?

Unfortunately, the audience was a sparse one, and participation by Brothers was extremely limited.

To the great despair of those who had initiated this meeting, few clear answers were given. Interested as they were in alchemy, magic and theosophy, the Philalethes would have liked to take the leadership of a great philosophical movement and set up an initiatory Order which was capable of profoundly altering people's ways of thinking.

As this allegedly eccentric lodge noted, French society was shot through with other schools of thought besides esoteric research. The criticism of power, of the nobility, of the Church and of their privileges was growing, and many Freemasons were more interested in this than in the world of symbols.

Despite the crushing failure of the Paris Gathering, several Brothers called for renewed discussions.

*Vienna, 20 November 1784*

'The Illuminati's situation has not resolved itself,' commented Geytrand. 'According to my latest information, Berlin is squaring up to Munich and declaring war on them. The Rosicrucians accuse them of scorning princes and attacking religion. Because of their philosophical and political positions, the whole of Freemasonry is at risk of being considered as a revolutionary and particularly dangerous sect.'

'How have the leaders reacted?'

'With complete silence.'

'Very worrying! I would have preferred open war, passionate disputes and losers on both sides.'

'The Rosicrucians are less harmful than the Illuminati,' opined Geytrand. 'Their Christian mysticism is undermining the foundations of Freemasonry.'

'Let us hope so! In any event, the Illuminati are returning to their lairs. The hotheads will abandon neither their opinions nor their plans. They will simply become more pernicious.'

*Vienna, 1 December 1784*

At the end of a meeting of the To Charity Lodge, Thamos questioned the new Secretary, Schwanckhardt.

'Did your predecessor, Hoffmann, process the application by the composer Wolfgang Mozart?'

Schwanckhardt examined the files he had inherited.

'He seems to have forgotten,' he lamented. 'As you must have noticed, Brother, he had little interest in his duties. Mozart's letter has not been circulated to the other lodges in Vienna. I shall deal with it immediately.'

Irritated, he did not conceal the truth as he wrote his missive: '*Proposal relating to Kapellmeister Mozart. Our former Secretary, Hoffmann, neglected to register this outsider and to inform the sister lodges of this proposal. However, notification was given to the district lodge four weeks ago. On account of this, we therefore hope to proceed to his admission, if no sister lodge has any objections to this.*'

*Vienna, 11 December 1784*

Wolfgang was working on a piano concerto[*] whose first movement Star the bird liked very much. Filled with determination, the music was both joyous and supremely elegant. It aroused a desire to rediscover the world, to believe in Man, to forget one's baser qualities and to think that tomorrow would be better.

During his morning walk, Wolfgang encountered Thamos.

'The administrative procedure is at an end,' he revealed. 'No Viennese lodge has opposed your admission.'

'Do you know the date of my initiation?'

'The 14th of December, at half-past six in the evening. You must be punctual at all costs.'

'How am I to prepare myself?'

'Do not worry about anything. I shall see you again soon, Wolfgang.'

The man who was walking calmly away had changed his life. Without him, he would have remained as an ordinary musician, immersed in the petty quarrels of a second-rate working environment where there was little room for idealism.

Wolfgang ran to his office to compose the end of his concerto. Instead of the usual slow movement between the two fast ones, he wrote an allegretto which was both poetic and profound, expressing the depth of his emotion.

[*] No. 19, K459.

Constance, the baby, Star and the servants listened to this melody of incredible purity.

The final allegro came back to a very tangible reality, fed by a dynamism which swept away everything in its path.

At that moment, Constance knew that she had not merely married a talented man, but a genius capable of perceiving the mystery of life. Did she have the ability to understand and love him as he deserved to be?

# 66

*Vienna, 14 December 1784, 6.30 p.m.*

The little To Charity Lodge worked in the premises belonging to its bigger sister, To True Union, which was itself a daughter of the important and influential lodge, To Crowned Hope. Ignaz von Born controlled all of them. Thamos had chosen Charity so that Mozart would be received into a sort of cocoon before discovering the complexity of the Masonic world.

As custom decreed, the musician – entered in the register as number twenty – was to be initiated with a 'twin', who as it happened was a religious, Wenzel Summer, chaplain at Erdberg. It was hoped that this symbolic alliance would keep the evils of destiny away from both men.

Thamos the Egyptian greeted Wolfgang. In accordance with the demands of Abbot Hermes, he had brought the Great Magician to the threshold of this temple where, thanks to Ignaz von Born's research and ritual training, based on the *Book of Thoth*, Mozart would receive an authentic initiation.

However, the Egyptian's mission was not at an end. After he had been received into the lodge, many trials awaited Wolfgang. Would he succeed in mastering the tools placed at his disposal, translate the initiatory tradition into music and create a sacred language accessible to all, beyond himself and his own era?

'I am your godfather and I lead you to the centre of the Earth, where you will meditate.'

Thomas took Wolfgang into a small room whose walls were covered with black hangings. The only light came from a single candle.

The Novice had the impression that he was in the middle of a cave. He sat down on a cube-shaped stone, facing an altar on which featured various symbols.

Close to the candle lay a skull. Light and death, light or death . . . The 'old man', whatever his age might be, must disappear and make room for a new being.

The crossed hourglass and scythe referred to the inexorable measurement of time and to the action of Saturn, which separated what was essential from what was useless. Had Wolfgang not wandered down a hundred side-roads? Had he not yielded to the temptation of superficiality?

The piece of bread and carafe of water provided him with the food vital to his Quest. As for the three bowls containing salt, sulphur and mercury, the elements fundamental to the alchemical process, they offered him the chance to begin preparations for the Great Work, in which he would serve both as the craftsman and the raw material.

On the walls, phrases were written: 'Know yourself', 'If curiosity brings you here, begone', and the alchemical term V.I.T.R.I.O.L.*, each letter of which was the start of a Latin word. The whole phrase translated as: 'Visit the interior of the Earth, rectify yourself, and you will find the hidden stone.'

Within this matrix, shielded . from Mother Earth, Wolfgang felt perfectly safe. Although motionless, he travelled. How was he to rectify himself? Introspection was not enough. He needed a kind of initiatory teaching which did not lead to individual improvement but to the hidden stone.

It lay at the heart of the Word, the spoken words passed on through the spirit and through truth.

Above a cockerel, whose song hailed the rebirth of the sun after its victory over the darkness, stretched a banner bearing two words: 'Vigilance' and 'Perseverance'.

Vigilance, the state of awakening to knowledge. Perseverance, the determination to continue, whatever the obstacles.

Wolfgang passed through time and space. Was he not living at the centre of the hidden stone, of which he was becoming one of the elements? Absorbed by the flame,

---

* Visita Interiora Terrae Rectificandoque Invenies Occultum Lapidem.

he found himself at the origin of creation, at that moment when divine thought was embodied as light-filled air, capable of rendering all matter fertile.

Here, the eternal and the immutable were expressed. Nothing could sully them, not even the presence of an outsider.

The door opened.


How brief that meditation had been! Wolfgang would have liked to spend long hours in that place and become still more imbued with this Earth-matrix in which one prepared for rebirth.

'Novice,' asked Thamos, 'do you wish to continue on the path?'

'I do.'

'You must confront formidable trials. In full consciousness of the danger, do you still wish to continue?'

'I do!'

'Weigh your decision carefully, Novice. You may still withdraw.'

'I accept the trials.'

'Since it is so, we shall strip you of your metals and render you ritually in a state to receive other purifications.'

Wolfgang realized that his 'metals' were not limited to a watch, a tobacco tin, some jewellery or other metallic objects. They were also removing his rigid attitudes, his preconceptions and his shackles in order to recreate a brand new human being, freed from everything that was weighing him down. But this absence of armour rendered him fragile, exposing him to outside attacks. Would he have the strength to resist them?

The fine suit was removed, the elegant garments that hid both body and soul so well, enabling him to disguise himself and parade in society where hypocrisy and conventions reigned.

Thamos left him his shirt, but pulled it down so as to reveal the heart. He also bared the right knee, thus revealing the angle of Pythagoras, and the left foot, then shackled his leg to oblige him to limp. Finally, he passed a rope around his neck and blindfolded him.

There was nothing left of the proud Mozart, only a deformed, blind individual.

Thamos took his hand.

'Alone, you cannot go forward. If your heart is pure, if you wish to act and not react, place your trust in your guide. Through this blindfold, learn to see beyond what is visible. Shall we go further?'

Wolfgang nodded.

# 67

Someone knocked three times on a door, which opened noisily.

Holding Thamos's hand very tightly, Wolfgang was forced to go forward. Suddenly, the point of a metallic object touched his chest.

'Withdraw that sword!' ordered the Egyptian. 'This Novice does not threaten the existence of this respectable lodge.'

'Do you undertake to guide him?' asked a stern voice.

'I stand as guarantor for Wolfgang Mozart.'

'What does he desire?'

'To see the Light, to be initiated into our mysteries and to take part in our works.'

'Is he free and of good morals?'

'I am!' declared Wolfgang.

He had won his own freedom. And he could swear before God that his conduct was irreproachable.

'If you betray our brotherhood,' went on the stern voice, 'the sword will pierce your chest. Do you truly ask for initiation in all freedom and of your own free will?'

'In all freedom and of my own free will!'

'Think carefully about the seriousness of what you are doing. It demands courage and determination from you. Will you be capable of that?'

'I will.'

'May the Sovereign Architect of the worlds support you and give you his help during your journeys. He is One, but is revealed in all things. May he deign to protect the Brothers gathered in this temple and may he open the way to this Novice who wishes to know the Mysteries. Here, we have only duties: to work constantly in search of wisdom, to fight ignorance and prejudices, to practise brotherhood and to keep silent about our works. Novice, do you undertake to fulfil these duties?'

'I do.'

'You are still free to withdraw. Soon, you will no longer be able to do so. Do you persist?'

'I persist.'

'Let the first journey take place, during which the Novice will undergo the trial of the air.'

A great tumult was unleashed. To the musician's ear, it sounded like an abominable cacophony, from which the power of the wind eventually emerged. This hurricane doubtless evoked the inner tumults which must be overcome every day.

A veil was torn asunder, and the celestial gates opened. A gust of wind carried Wolfgang's thoughts away to the four cardinal points, and he breathed new air, the principal one of the changes which an initiate experienced. With its aid, creative energy became conscious.

The path was long and difficult. With the aid of his guide, the neophyte managed to circumvent many obstacles. And when the torment grew calmer, he had the feeling that he now possessed a new strength.

A second journey followed, corresponding to the trial of the water. There was no more storm and no more violence, but there were strange sounds which slid over the waves and freed the soul from all its burdens as an outsider. The way was less difficult, despite the traps which the traveller managed to escape, thanks to his guide's vigilance.

The Novice was no longer the slave of a fixed world. He was moving within – deep, swirling undercurrents, swimming in a limitless ocean, at the origin of all forms of life.

Wolfgang perceived the moment when the Light was born at the heart of the primordial waters, creating life in all its forms.

One final journey remained, corresponding to the ordeal of the fire. Although the way was devoid of obstacles, Wolfgang sensed the danger. Dancing on the pathways of the wind, a flame consumed the air and the water, filling the space with its thoughts. It brought the Novice to the gates of the region of Light, where the initiates who had passed into the eternal East dwelt with the gods.

This flame devoured the curious and the unworthy, but increased the desire for initiation. Wolfgang knew that he was about to take a decisive step. Either he would be consumed, or he would attempt to cross a river of fire, in order to perceive the source of creation.

Gripping Thamos's hand even more tightly, he passed through the purifying flames.

The gates of the East opened.

'Soon we are going to demand from you the oath which will unite you with the sacred Order of Freemasonry,' announced a firm voice. 'From that moment on, you will no longer belong to yourself. Perhaps one day it will be necessary for you to spill the last drop of your blood to defend this Order. Would you have the courage, if that sacrifice was necessary?'

Wolfgang could not promise lightly. If he consented, he entered into a family of spirits, an initiated brotherhood whose continuance he must, in his own way, ensure.

'I will have that courage,' he declared, 'fully aware of the scope of his promise.'

'Since that is so, speak the words of the oath.'

Thamos led the Great Magician to the Eastern altar. He made him rest his left knee on the ground and his right hand on the Three Great Lights of initiatory Freemasonry, the Rule, the Set Square and the Compass.

Then the Egyptian placed an open compass in the Novice's left hand, pressing one of the points against his heart.

And, phrase after phrase, Wolfgang uttered the solemn oath: 'I, Mozart, of my own free will, in the presence of the Great Architect of the Universe and this respectable lodge of Freemasons, swear never to reveal the Mysteries which are passed on to me. I promise to love my Brothers and to help them if necessary. I would rather have my throat cut than betray this oath. May the Great Architect of the Universe come to my aid and save me from perjury.'

'Since the Novice is judged worthy of being admitted among us,' ordered the stern voice, 'remove the blindfold so that he may see and meditate.'

# 68

*Vienna, 14 December 1784, To Charity Lodge*

Thamos removed the blindfold.

There was no blinding light, only half-light; no benevolent Brothers, but menacing weapons.

And the worrying spectacle of death.

Did the long and difficult path of initiation lead only to this disaster?

'Discern the Light in the darkness,' advised Thamos. 'Know, from this moment, that treason is an integral part of the Tradition. Aware of the ordeals imposed on the initiate in his quest for knowledge, do you confirm your oath?'

'I . . . I confirm it.'

Overwhelmed by this sight, which would remain engraved in the deepest part of his being, Wolfgang listened to the words of the Venerable, who revealed to him the significance of this extraordinary moment. He gave him the keys to the accomplishment of the alchemical Great Work, the springing forth of life beyond nothingness.

And then the temple was lit up, and Thamos proceeded to the ritual dressing of the new Freemason, the main part of which was an apron, emphasizing his nature and duties as a builder.

Wolfgang recognized the Venerable Master who was preparing to consecrate him as a Brother: it was Baron Otto von Gemmingen, whom he had met in Mannheim.

He received the Light making him an Apprentice, worthy of participating in the chain uniting past, present and future initiates.

Then Wolfgang was entrusted to the Second Overseer, charged with revealing the secrets of his grade, consisting of a sign, an action and a sacred word which he could not utter alone. With the aid of a Brother, he was able to assemble the shattered word and to 'make the symbol'.

Throughout the ritual and the instruction given to the Apprentice, Wolfgang noticed the presence of the Three, the ternary thought which went beyond contradictions and oppositions in order to accomplish the union of spirit, soul and body.

In this year of true light 5784, dated as such in Freemasonry because its origins went back into early antiquity, the initiation of Wolfgang Mozart was registered in the lodge's Book of Architecture.

Before the banquet, the extremely emotional new Apprentice received the brotherly embrace from Thamos.

'How can I thank you for giving me such a treasure?'

'This is only the beginning of the path, my Brother Wolfgang. Now, we can build better together.'

The musician met the members of the To Charity Lodge and visitors who had come from other lodges. There was no shortage of surprises: Count Johann Baptist Esterhazy, nicknamed Red-haired John, imperial chamberlain, oboist and Mozart's great protector, having organized several concerts for his benefit; his musical adviser, orchestral leader and violinist Paul Wranisky; Prince Karl Lichnowsky, friend of Countess Thun; and Count Thun, who congratulated the composer warmly.

'You see, Wolfgang, the spirits favour you! Our lodges are not reserved for great lords. Here, you will encounter senior officials, scientists, soldiers, men of the Church, writers, merchants, servants and many others! Without Freemasonry, these very different people would never have met. By spending time together, do they not surely become more tolerant, and therefore more intelligent?'

Amused by Count Thun's frankness, Adamberger (who had sung the role of the hero Belmonte in *The Abduction*) and Fischer (who had portrayed the appalling Osmin) congratulated Mozart, whose head was spinning. They were followed by the librettist Stephanie the Young, a member of the Three Eagles Lodge, and the musician's publishers, Torricella and the Artaria brothers!

'You too, Josef!' he exclaimed as he came face to face with his brother-in-law Lange, Aloysia's husband.

'As our oath demands, I remained silent. And I wanted at all costs to avoid influencing you. On the other hand, I did support your application to join!'

'As did I,' nodded Thomas von Trattner, husband of one of Mozart's pupils and godfather to his son. A member of the Palm Tree Lodge and a book-seller and printer, he had at one point provided the musician with accommodation.

So, all these men whom he had so often encountered and whom he thought he knew well belonged to Freemasonry!

A question passed through his mind.

'How long have you been preparing me for admission?' he asked Thamos.

'Since for ever, my Brother, for you are predestined.'

Despite his far-from-impressive behaviour, the former Secretary of the To Charity Lodge was also keen to congratulate Mozart. A great friend of the Venerable von Gemmingen, Leopold-Aloys Hoffmann considered himself untouchable.

Wolfgang did not like the look in his eyes, but he made an effort to forget this bad impression, which was doubtless the result of emotion and tiredness. Were not all Brothers by definition men of worth?

During the banquet, Brother Friedrich Hegrad spoke to Mozart's 'twin', the chaplain Wenzel Summer, and recalled the position of his lodge with regard to the Church:

'What may we not expect from you, my Brother, as an educator of the people and an apostle of the Truth? With what ardent zeal, what rare modesty, what prudence and what intelligence I see you working for the good of your brothers, mankind! And I see you also confounding those who ignore their mission, like Archbishop Migazzi and the bad monks, those who dishonour their respective Orders and are concerned only with their own personal interest. It is priests who exert the greatest power over men, more even than monarchs, for he who holds the heart achieves more than he who enslaves the body. You will make use of this power for the honour of humanity, and you will teach the principal virtue, brotherly love. In this way, you will prove that you are not a slave of your priestly title, but concerned to make men better by teaching them that the only and true service of God consists of a pure and noble heart, kindness, gentleness of nature, tolerance and charity.'

Since Archbishop Migazzi was no better than the Grand Mufti Colloredo, Wolfgang approved of this speech. On the other hand, the words of the Venerable Otto von Gemmingen left him perplexed.

'Freemasonry aims to improve social wellbeing. In a word, it must be entirely practical. Any speculation which pursues ideas without finality, loses itself in overspiritual abstractions, exhausts itself in the domain of knowledge which is devoid of applications, would be basically contrary to the goal of Freemasonry. It does not transform us into new men, does not make us acquire any mystical nature. We hope to raise ourselves above our own inadequacy and our weakness, in order to improve ourselves as human beings. Freemasonry purifies the sentiments, stirs up a love of humanity, runs to the aid of oppressed innocence, and offers assistance and consolation to the unfortunate. In this way, it implements innumerable means and procedures in order to act and prove useful to the human race.'*

---

*For these declarations, see the documentation gathered by Philippe A. Autexier (cf. Bibliography).

# 69

Since it was impossible for him to sleep after such an event, Wolfgang invited Thamos for a glass of punch and immediately began questioning him.

'Why does the Venerable minimize the role of spirituality? The initiation ritual says the exact opposite!'

'You are already applying the first piece of advice: vigilance. Otto von Gemmingen resembles the majority of the Brothers, who see Freemasonry as merely a humanist movement. Nothing contemptible, that is true, but the goal of initiation resides well beyond it. Born in the eternal East, the royal art of the Freemasons is too often brought down by human beings to their own mediocre level. Only the stone is open and free from faults, not the individual.'

'Is he not worthy of initiation?'

'The Ancients asked us to act as the gods act, to walk in their footsteps and celebrate the rites so that the creative power might remain upon the earth. Beliefs enslave consciousness by imposing revealed truths which distance us from knowledge. By passing through the door of a lodge, even one that is imperfect and made up of limited human beings, you link yourself to the initiatory Tradition, to the very essence of life, beyond our brief temporal existences. A man is but the shadow of Man, the male and female Being on the cosmic scale. In order to perceive the reality, follow the alchemical path of transmutations, whose first elements were taught to you in the primordial cave.'

The two Brothers talked all night. Wolfgang still had a thousand questions to ask, eager to learn the language of symbols and to familiarize himself with the temple, which was both open to the cosmos and as closed as an alchemical athanor.

*Vienna, 16 December 1784*

Josef Anton was very worried. And yet, the vigorous crusade waged against Freemasonry by Anton Migazzi, Archbishop of Vienna, ought to have filled him with joy. At last, the Church was becoming aware of the danger! The spies infiltrated by the prelate into the lodges were informing him about the Freemasons' violent criticisms of him, but also of priests, narrow-minded monks and blind beliefs.

Unfortunately, Migazzi had come up against the emperor's liberal and progressive policy. And Josef II had not forgiven the archbishop for bringing the Pope to Vienna in order to attempt to make the sovereign more kindly disposed towards the Catholic Church.

The emperor and the Holy Father, who had obtained nothing, had cordially detested each other, and Josef II was continuing to close monasteries, transforming them into charitable institutions.

Furious, Archbishop Migazzi did not hesitate to inspire and finance brochures stigmatizing the attitude of the sovereign, who was extremely displeased by these criticisms. So the prelate had provoked the reaction Josef Anton had feared: the emperor was relying on the Freemasons to counter the Church, to highlight its reactionary ideas, its refusal to educate the population and its obstinate insistence on propagating ignorance.

By openly fighting Josef II and Freemasonry, the prelate had made himself some allies. The first made use of the second, while Freemasonry began to take on an official appearance.

It was a veritable catastrophe.

Was the emperor not creating a monster, which would soon be uncontrollable, despite the foundation of the apparently loyal and obedient Grand Lodge of Austria? If they felt encouraged, would the Brothers not enter the political arena more frequently, in order to spread their devastating ideas?

Geytrand was looking even more sinister than usual.

'Bad news, Herr Count. Here is the publication I managed to procure.'

He handed Josef Anton the *Freemasons' Newspaper*, which was reserved for the Brothers but whose influence extended beyond the lodges.

'Who is responsible for this initiative?'

'Ignaz von Born, assisted by Professor Josef von Sonnenfels. He has entrusted the management of the newspaper to a poet, Blumauer. There is a print run of a thousand copies. The themes dealt with derive from the work carried out in the Masters' Lodge, which is run by the mineralogist.'

'Von Born, it is always von Born!'

'Untouchable,' lamented Geytrand.

'Nobody is untouchable for ever,' murmured Anton, leafing through the publication, which dealt with the importance of the oath, with faith and fanaticism, and the necessity for rituals.

He lingered over a long study signed by Ignaz von Born and devoted to the Egyptian mysteries. In it, the author stated that Freemasonry's origins were Egyptian and, summarizing elements from the *Book of Thoth* which Thamos had given him, he dealt with the knowledge and duties of the ancient initiates who had inscribed their wisdom in monuments such as the pyramids.

'We are a long way from politics and humanism here,' commented Geytrand.

'On the contrary, my friend, on the contrary! The true spiritual master of Viennese Freemasonry has committed himself to the battlefield of essential ideas, in order to awaken his Brothers by dragging them out of their torpor. This reference to Egypt is decisive. It directs Freemasonry towards the knowledge of the Mysteries and highlights the poverty of our ideologies.'

Geytrand shared his superior's analysis and felt even more regret at having left Freemasonry now that such prospects were emerging. Well, if he could not possess it, he would destroy it.

'The newspaper's director, Blumauer,' he said, 'is a friend of Mozart.'

'The musician on whom I opened the file?'

'It will grow full, Herr Count, for Wolfgang Mozart has just been received as an Apprentice Freemason in the small To Charity Lodge.'

# 70

*Vienna, 24 December 1784*

Thamos took his Brother Wolfgang to the Assembly of the large Viennese lodge To True Union which, that evening, was receiving Anton Apponyi. So little time after his own initiation, the new Apprentice had the immense good fortune to relive the ritual without a blindfold covering his eyes. Instead of undergoing it as a Novice, he saw it as a Brother, and could thus savour each moment.

First, he saw the lodge, a vast rectangular hall lit by a chandelier suspended by a rope, candelabra on the walls and candlesticks to the East, where the sun in the north and the Moon in the south flanked the Delta. The first embodied the brightness at the heart of the darkness, the start of the alchemical work, the second the right action at the right time, and the third, ternary thought, a tool used by the Great Architect to fashion the Universe.

Ignaz von Born, the Venerable,* impressed Wolfgang. With his long face, wide forehead and dark eyes, the Master of the lodge had more presence and authority than the emperor himself. On his tray lay the illuminating sword with which he created the initiates, and the builder's mallet which enclosed the thunder.

The other 'officers' of the lodge made up a body of functions, symbols of the creative forces perpetually at work. Each fulfilled a precise task in the service of the whole.

Wolfgang paid particular attention to the 'mosaic pavement', an oblong made up of alternate black and white squares. Did it not reveal the rectangle of Genesis, the constant metamorphosis, the very game of life?

Day and night, speech and silence, and all the other oppositions . . . Was the duty of the initiate not to overcome duality and to reconcile contraries?

Proud to wear an apron which recalled the operational nature of Freemasonry and one of its major roles, the building of the temple, Wolfgang had also received the emblem of his lodge, a small set-square suspended on a blue ribbon.

For the first time, the musician experienced an Opening of the Works, evoking the birth of the Light and the creation of the world, and was then present at the reception of Anton Apponyi, gazing wide-eyed at the stages he too had passed through.

* Often called in Germany *Meister von Stuhl*, Master in the Chair.

Brother Franz Saurau welcomed the new Apprentice, advising him to take no interest in the advantages of birth, not to congratulate himself upon wealth and titles, which were due to circumstances and not to merit, and not to allow himself to be impressed by the threats and intrigues of outsiders who were powerful but whose thoughts were not elevated.

Johann Baptist Alxinger, a poet and secretary to the court theatre, rejoiced at meeting the composer of *The Abduction from the Seraglio*, and hoped that he would very soon write an opera in which Brothers would participate, either as singers or musicians.

Then came Angelo Soliman, who boasted of having presented Ignaz von Born's application to the lodge of which he had become the Venerable. Wolfgang did not much like the way in which this Brother thrust himself forward. He preferred to exchange a few words with Johann Michael Puchberg, a fabric merchant. A member of the Palm Tree Lodge, he had been appointed Treasurer of To True Union.

'My business activities do not prevent me from loving music,' revealed the jovial forty-three-year-old. 'I hope you like silks, velvets and ribbons!'

'My wife will ask your advice for decorating our home.'

'I also sell the most beautiful gloves in Vienna,' added Puchberg, 'and I am certain that she will find them to her taste. Ah, my dear Mozart, life is not always a laughing matter! I was content with my job, working for an excellent boss, but he died in 1777. In order to save his shop, I became the manager, and destiny determined that I was to marry his widow. And now here I am, the owner of a business and laden with troubles of all kinds! Fortunately, in the lodge I meet agreeable people and forget my heavy responsibilities. It will be the same for you, you will see! Freemasonry is a marvellous institution which should exist in every country in the world. Thanks to it, men become less egotistical and learn to help each other. In any event, if you have problems one day, do not hesitate to ask me for help. Since wealth is a gift from God, it must be given back by helping one's Brothers.'

'I hope I shall not need to importune you.'

'With your increasing fame, all Vienna will soon be at your feet!'

Wolfgang met a variety of Brothers, all very different from one another, and this diversity excited him.

At the end of the Works, Thamos introduced him to the Venerable Ignaz von Born.

'I am relying upon your assiduity, Brother Mozart.'

'You may be certain of it, Venerable Master.'

Thamos handed the musician the copy of the *Freemasons' Newspaper* in which the study on the Egyptian mysteries had been published.

'As you read this, you will rediscover many things that have already helped you and which you will use again.'

'*Thamos, King of Egypt* . . . That sketch of an opera continues to haunt me!'

402

'You have much still to discover, my Brother,' said von Born. 'Gaining access to the Great Mysteries demands a considerable effort, and very few people are capable of it.'

# 71

Constance and Star had noticed Wolfgang's transformation. There was a new light in his eyes.

'The door of the temple has opened,' he revealed to his wife, 'and I have begun to walk along a very long path.'

Wolfgang wrote to his father[*] to tell him about the event which had just changed his life so profoundly. He talked to him of the ideals of Freemasonry and the countless riches offered by initiation.

Many important people and great lords were Freemasons, he revealed. In lodge, they forgot their titles and privileges and became Brothers. And he, the simple musician, was their equal. Each man had his place, according to his Masonic age and his symbolic grade.

---

[*] All Mozart's letters mentioning Freemasonry have disappeared and were probably destroyed.

Would Leopold perceive the importance of such discoveries? If so, Wolfgang would continue to open his heart to him.

*Vienna, 26 December 1784*

During a brief stay by Josef Haydn in Vienna, Wolfgang could not resist talking to him about the thing that mattered most.

'I have just had a most extraordinary experience.'

'You do indeed look overwhelmed. Nothing serious, I hope?'

'On the contrary, something that makes me fabulously happy!'

'Let me guess: has the emperor commissioned a German opera from you?'

'Even better!'

Haydn sought the answer in vain.

'I am an Apprentice Freemason,' declared Mozart.

The master was intrigued.

'There is much talk of this secret society in Vienna. According to various rumours, the emperor approves of its existence because it is favourable to his liberal policy and does not veil its criticisms of a Church which is opposed to all progress.'

'Initiation goes well beyond these temporal problems,' said Wolfgang. 'It leads to light and to knowledge, and opens the mind to undreamed-off realities.'

'The world you describe seems too wondrous to me.'

'It becomes so, if one stops being blind and gazes upon the universe of symbols and speaks the language of brotherhood.'

'Brotherhood . . . is that not an unrealistic dream?'

'Without initiation, certainly. Even with it, it is a difficult ideal to attain! But the lodge strips us of our artifices and pretences. Is a musician not also a builder in the service of the Great Architect of the Universe?'

'Does this initiation really enable you to deepen your knowledge of your craft?'

'I am convinced of it. And I would be happy to number you among my Brothers.'

The direct aspect of the invitation, characteristic as it was of Mozart, did not shock Josef Haydn, who also detested circumlocution and vague hints.

'If I understand correctly, you will plead in my favour!'

'That will be an easy task, for everyone holds you in esteem and admires you. All you need to do is make an application.'

'And submit to certain rites?'

'It is not a submission, but an elevation. Instead of chaining us in the way of prejudices, beliefs and conventions, the rites liberate us.'

'For a servant-musician, as I have been all my life, what satisfaction that would be! Have you met any of the great of this world?'

'Nobles of all ranks!' exclaimed Wolfgang.

'And are they still just as pretentious?'

'Princes, barons and counts learn to become Brothers.'

'And what about the men of the Church?'

'There are few of them and they seek an approach to the divine which broadens the soul.'

'Surely a lodge cannot be made up entirely of perfect individuals?'

'On the contrary, since they are aware of their imperfections and meet together precisely to combat them together. But all of this remains inconsequential in the face of initiation and the immense prospects it opens to us.'

'Mozart, you intrigue me.'

'I have been fortunate enough to meet exceptional individuals and, now, to work with them in complete brotherhood. This year has brought me so many happy things! Sometimes, it makes me dizzy.'

'You deserve your happiness, and destiny will grant you much more.'

Suddenly, Josef Haydn's expression darkened.

'My place of work is far from Vienna . . . Are the meetings frequent?'

'It is up to each lodge to fix its own calendar of meetings.'

'Which would you recommend to me?'

'To True Union. It includes a large number of musicians, and you will enjoy yourself there.'

'I must think! Thank you for your trust and your friendship, Mozart. They go straight to my heart.'

His father and Josef Haydn: Wolfgang did not regret opening himself up to these two people he cherished so much.

## 72

*Strasbourg, 30 December 1784*

Despite his comfortable carriage, Prince Charles of Hesse, who had become the brains behind Strict Observance, felt a little weary. He had experienced great disappointment at seeing the immortal Count of Saint-Germain die in his arms. A false alchemist, the opportunistic adventurer had not possessed a single secret.

And the publication of an anonymous pamphlet, *Saint Nicaise or a Collection of Remarkable Masonic Letters Used by Freemasons and by Those Who Are Not*, had dealt another very hard blow to the Templar Order. This tract attacked the principal dignitaries and their French allies, who were accused of having fixed the Wilhelmsbad Gathering.

Baron de Hund, founder of the Order, saw himself treated as a crook and a liar. What did these Freemasons want, these people who were stupid enough to believe in a chivalrous legend? To get back the Templars' lands and reconstitute their vast fortune! Indeed, naïve Brothers had paid enormous sums to their leaders without receiving anything in return, and they found themselves duped and disappointed.

The secrets? A monumental hoax! And who was Ferdinand of Brunswick, the Grand Master? A second-rate soldier severely beaten in 1760, during the Seven Years' War, and a despot clinging to his high-sounding titles, with no vision of the future.

Faced with this storm, Charles of Hesse's guardian angel had advised him to go to Strasbourg in order to ask for the help of Willermoz's disciples, initiates into the rites of the Lyons mystic, and to rally them to his cause.

The German prince was well received, but the local dignitary's declarations stunned him.

'Our Master Willermoz has revealed to us that a young girl, Marion Blanchet, who was closely observed for ten days and ten nights, has described to him the existence after death of her mother, her three sisters and her uncles. All are expiating their sins in Purgatory! She told him the precise number of Masses and prayers necessary to soften their punishment. Consequently, in accordance with Willermoz's instructions, we are seeking sleepwalkers who can put us in contact with the spirits.'

Charles of Hesse was speechless. This was not the place to obtain active support for Strict Observance.

*Vienna, 31 December 1784*

Just as Geytrand was about to enter the building where Josef Anton worked, he noticed, for the second time, a middle-aged man gazing at the door.

Geytrand did not believe in coincidences.

They were being spied on.

Jaws clenched, indifferent to the snow and the cold, he hid behind a barouche and watched the watcher.

Half an hour later, the spy left his post and walked slowly away.

Geytrand followed him.

Thanks to the thickly falling snow, there was no risk of his being spotted. Was this curious individual a Freemason, instructed by his lodge to identify those who were tailing members of his Order? In that case, he would go and make his report to a senior dignitary, perhaps Ignaz von Born himself, whom the Count of Pergen could then accuse of harming State security.

Geytrand was disappointed and surprised.

The spy crossed the threshold of an official building he knew well: police headquarters.

*Vienna, 31 December 1784*

Josef Anton was not celebrating. He loathed compulsory festivities and being forced to be nice to people, and preferred to classify his files and keep his records

410

up to date. Only this constant work enabled him to exploit effectively the information he had accumulated on Freemasonry.

Shortly before midnight, he was surprised by a visit from Geytrand.

'Aren't you celebrating either?'

'Herr Count, I believe our department may be under threat.'

'By the Freemasons?'

'No, the emperor.'

'How can you be sure of that?'

'A spy was watching us. I followed him to police headquarters, where he went to report on his mission. Should we not move premises immediately? If we do so tonight, nobody will notice us.'

The two men transported the archives to one of the Count of Pergen's private residences which he had left unoccupied with a view to this kind of incident.

All they encountered were two drunks who wished them a Happy New Year. By the time dawn broke, after several comings and goings, the main records were safe.

'Prepare us some very strong coffee,' Anton ordered his right-hand man. 'Then we shall have a drop of excellent plum brandy to warm ourselves up.'

'Is this the end of our mission?'

'I do not know.'

'It seems the emperor is disowning us!'

'Perhaps it is a question of competing circumstances, or a routine enquiry.'

'You do not believe that, any more than I do! Power bows down before the Freemasons, and they want our hides.'

'First thing in the morning, I shall know the truth.'

# 73

*Vienna, 1 January 1784*

Contrary to the majority of the Viennese, Emperor Josef II had not drunk himself unconscious and was already back at work. Austria must show herself to be the model of a healthy, well-managed economy where not a single florin was unwisely spent.

The monarch's private secretary announced the arrival of the Count of Pergen.

An official who pays visits so early in the morning deserves respect, thought Josef II.

'What is so urgent, Count?'

'My mission appears severely compromised, Majesty.'

'For what reason?'

'I fear arrest by the police.'

'The police? But you are one of them!'

'That is not their chief's opinion.'

Josef Anton calmly set out the facts, to the emperor's amazement.

'Someone is acting without my authorization,' he declared, irritated. 'Wait for a moment, and I shall clarify the situation.'

The matter was swiftly settled.

'A simple administrative misunderstanding,' concluded the monarch. 'This misplaced zeal will not be repeated. Continue to provide me with detailed reports.'

'In order to avoid serious unpleasantness, Majesty, I moved out my files.'

'An excellent initiative.'

'If my name has been spoken, or indeed written down, I am no longer safe. My entourage and my relatives are beginning to wonder about my real activities. They need to be reassured, as do the police.'

'In what way?'

'Give me a sufficiently visible post, with clear duties. Suspicious minds will be taken in, and any unhealthy curiosity will be kept away.'


*Vienna, 2 January 1785*

Constance, Wolfgang and Star the bird had slept late. Each night, the musician relived his initiation ceremony and identified himself with the four elements. He travelled the cosmos of the lodge and was transformed as he gazed upon the splendid landscapes.

414

The goldfinch struck up a sweet melody to waken the household. Constance kissed the adorable Karl Thomas, who smiled angelically.

The substantial breakfast was accompanied by Leopold's response to his son's surprising letter. Wolfgang tore open the missive anxiously.

'Is he angry that you have become a Freemason?' asked Constance worriedly.

'On the contrary, he congratulates me! He thinks it is excellent that I should spend time among great lords, since they will help me to consolidate my reputation in Vienna.'

'That is not your goal,' objected the young woman.

'You must understand my father: the only thing that interests him is my professional success. Well no . . . not the only thing! He does not dislike the Masonic philosophy. As he detests bigotry and is interested in all forms of progress, he would like to know more about my lodge.'

'Do you think . . . that he might join?'

'A son initiating his father . . . What a fine dream! We are not quite at that stage yet. I shall answer his questions in detail.'

'Will Nannerl read your letter?'

'I don't think so.'

'Be careful, Wolfgang. She hates me and doesn't like you very much.'

'I agree that she has a rather bad nature, but she is still my big sister. We travelled Europe together.'

'She is jealous of you. Because of your genius, her mediocre talent as a pianist was extinguished. Sooner or later, she will make you pay for that humiliation.'

'Do you really believe she would bear a grudge for so long?'

'Even longer!'

A little sad, Wolfgang went to the window and gazed at the sky.

'The clouds are receding. A walk will do us good.'

*Vienna, 2 January 1785*

The celebratory meal had visibly increased Baron Gottfried van Swieten's corpulence, and he would soon have to diet. While preparing for Mozart's initiation, he had congratulated himself on the long work carried out by Thamos and von Born to lead the Great Magician to the temple, where he would find the keys to a new enlightenment.

The baron continued to wonder about the emperor's real intentions. If his hostility to the Archbishop of Vienna, to the hide-bound Church and to the pointless monasteries still stood firm, his position with regard to Freemasonry remained ambiguous. Was he really favourable to it, or was he merely content to use it as one of the instruments of his policy, which he would get rid of after he had used it?

During the lunch with a senior official, van Swieten received some unexpected information.

'The chief of police has just had his knuckles rapped.'

'Why?'

'Because of a badly judged investigation which the emperor did not like. A count was suspected of heading a sort of secret, more or less official department, whose task was to spy on our honest Freemasons. Ridiculous, isn't it?'

'Completely grotesque.'

'If it were true, you can imagine the scandal! Eminent individuals belong to this honourable society and would not appreciate being suspected of goodness knows what misdeeds in this way.'

'Did the police chief believe that this secret department actually existed?'

'A routine investigation aroused his attention.'

'And whom did it accuse?'

'The Count of Pergen, an aristocrat of undeniable probity who enjoys an excellent reputation. After faithfully serving the late empress, he now displays absolute loyalty towards the emperor and in no way fits the profile of a spy with a twisted mind!'

'Was anyone else called into question?' asked Baron van Swieten.

'Fortunately not! As I told you, the chief of police has been called to order and told to end these ridiculous investigations. The Freemasons unreservedly approve of Josef II's policies and are helping him to fight all forms of obscurantism. To persecute them would be a tragic mistake!'

Van Swieten was careful to pass on to other subjects, as though he had little interest in this incident.

As soon as lunch ended, he went to the court to obtain as much information as he could on this man Pergen.

Had the baron just identified the man who was hiding in the shadows, spying on Freemasonry and dreaming of its destruction?

# 74

Geytrand detested the Freemason Angelo Soliman, but he paid him sufficiently highly to obtain first-hand information.

The two men met in a small house on the outskirts of Vienna, which was rented by the Count of Pergen under a false name.

'You were not followed were you, Soliman?'

'Do not worry, nobody suspects me! Am I not one of the principal friends and supporters of Ignaz von Born, our great patron? I receive a thousand confidences and am considered the best of Brothers.'

Geytrand had arrived two hours earlier, and checked that nobody was watching the building.

'Is the birth of the Austrian Grand Lodge of Austria approved of by the majority of Freemasons?'

'I am not convinced,' replied Soliman. 'Many consider

this administrative structure too rigid, in the hands of power.'

'What does von Born think?'

'To all appearances, he is playing the game. But only in appearance! So as not to arouse the suspicions of the archbishop's spies, he does not place all his eggs in the same basket.'

'Be clearer.'

'No lodge seems really secure to him, so he has shared out his faithful supporters and launched several subjects of work. He is observing the development of the different workshops before choosing one which will be at the forefront of the research. The creation of this Grand Lodge conflicts with his plans, since the emperor must be kept permanently informed about Masonic activities.'

'Nothing more specific?'

'The Grand Secretary is a cold and private man. If I asked him direct questions, he would be suspicious and I would lose all credibility.'

'I want to know what he is planning.'

'Have you read his article on the Egyptian mysteries? A remarkable piece of work! That is certainly the direction he is planning to take: to forget the humanistic nonsense and the apologia of charity in order to set out resolutely along the path to esotericism, symbolism and initiation.'

'Who will follow him?'

'A small number of Brothers determined to emerge from the torpor and cosiness of official Freemasonry.'

'That would be subversion!'

'Von Born belongs to the Illuminati, as do several influential Brothers. While they approve of Josef II's policies, they are planning to go further, much further.'

'Are they planning a revolution?'

'Certainly not! These people have a horror of blood and violence. They want to emphasize individual merit and a person's intrinsic value, forgetting the privileges given by birth and wealth. Does this programme not sound just as formidable as an armed insurrection? Altering current ideas and received opinions amounts to changing the world.'

'Would a few Freemasons really be capable of this?'

'Does your work not consist of taking this kind of hypothesis seriously?'

Geytrand scowled.

'Do not give me advice, Soliman! I pay you, and you give me information.'

'According to rumours, you yourself were a Freemason, in line for the highest office. But certain Brothers detected your all-consuming ambition, so you threw down your apron on the floor of the temple and resigned, swearing to make Freemasonry pay dearly for this lack of respect.'

Geytrand longed to strangle his informant.

'I despise you, Soliman!'

'As I do you.'

'It matters little, you need money.'

'It is pointless for us to insult each other, for we are as alike as twin brothers. Only the colour of our skin differentiates us. Ah, one detail: as of today, my fee has increased.'


*Vienna, 3 January 1785*

Baron Gottfried van Swieten must make no mistakes. First, he scoured all the publications submitted to the censor's office in the hope of finding an anti-Masonic text signed by the Count of Pergen.

It was a waste of time.

Next, he went to see Countess Thun.

'Pergen? That name is vaguely familiar . . . A senior official without much personality, who was close to the late empress. Since Maria Theresa's death, he has disappeared from view.'

'Was he linked to the police?'

'I do not know, Baron.'

Van Swieten was making progress. Maria Theresa loathed Freemasons and undoubtedly employed shadowy men to inform her about this growing danger. Without occupying any official post, this Count Pergen was probably continuing his shadowy task in the service of the emperor.

Questioning the chief of police directly was too risky. Countess Thun advised van Swieten to consult an old court chamberlain, who prided himself on knowing absolutely everything about the Viennese aristocracy. The fellow sometimes came up with spicy snippets of information.

The chamberlain greeted the baron warmly and offered him some excellent coffee. They talked about the weather, traffic problems in the capital, vital economic measures and a few eminent figures of State.

'It is a long time since I saw the dear Count of Pergen,' ventured Gottfried van Swieten. 'It seems he no longer has any official duties.'

'Do not be mistaken, Baron! After a long time in the wilderness, he has just been appointed president of the government of Lower Austria. So we shall see him back at court when his heavy administrative burden allows him the time. He is a perfect senior official, who will obey the emperor's commands to the letter, enjoy a peaceful existence and appreciable material benefits, then retire to his estates, satisfied that he has done his duty.'

The trail followed by van Swieten had come to a sudden end. Such a visible individual could not be running a secret department operating in the shadows. Basically, the emperor was manipulating Freemasonry with great skill and his police procured the information he desired.

Relaxed, the baron could reassure Ignaz von Born and Thamos the Egyptian. There were no demons hidden in the shadows, eager to destroy Freemasonry.

# 75

*Vienna, 4 January 1785*

During a modest and inexpensive reception held at the Schönbrunn Castle, the emperor congratulated several senior officials, including the Count of Pergen, on devoting themselves to the public cause and advised them to tighten their budgets still further by avoiding any unnecessary expenditure.

The unassuming Josef Anton exchanged a few pleasantries with devoted courtiers before being approached by Professor Leopold-Aloys Hoffmann, former Secretary of the To Charity Lodge which had just welcomed in Mozart.

'I hope this year will not be unfavourable to our country.'

'What do you fear?' asked the count in astonishment.

'Despite our beloved emperor's firmness, morality is crumbling and hypocrisy continues to increase.'

424

'Your pessimism worries me. Have you any specific examples?'

'Take Freemasonry,' murmured Hoffmann. 'People think it is a society which respects the laws and religion, but they are severely mistaken.'

'Are you certain of that?'

'Do you know anything of this secret society?'

'Nothing at all,' declared the count.

'Well, I know it well! It publishes a newspaper officially intended for its members, but which spreads its ideas on the outside. Now, the director of this periodical, Blumauer, is an atheist! Behind the word "God", Freemasons put nothing but emptiness. An emptiness into which our entire society will fall if we tolerate such attitudes.'

Knowing that Hoffmann was a Freemason himself, Josef Anton was amused by this attack on his own Brothers.

'Worrying revelations, Herr Professor! But are they not somewhat . . . exaggerated?'

'I am well informed.'

'I had no idea such turpitudes were going on. And then . . . are you not unwise in revealing them?'

'I have attempted in vain to alert the authorities, but nobody believes me! Sooner or later, they will realize that I am right.'

Hoffmann walked away and approached another courtier, whom he pestered as he had the previous ones. A traitor and a loudmouth, he hoped to demonstrate his own importance, but was not convincing anyone. Conscientiously, Josef Anton took a note of what he had said and added the words 'to be checked'.

*Vienna, 4 January 1785*

'Whatever the disadvantages of the ultra-official Grand Lodge of Austria may be,' said Gottfried Van Swieten to Thamos and von Born, 'one thing is certain: there is no secret department charged with spying on Freemasons.'

'The police are not idle,' Thamos reminded him.

'Their investigations are still limited, since the emperor looks favourably upon the development of the Viennese lodges. Are they not separate from the mystical and Templar tendencies?'

'I do not share this optimism,' cut in Ignaz von Born. 'Our links with the Illuminati are well known, and they have just been condemned by Prince-Elector Karl Theodor.'

'An entirely theoretical condemnation,' pointed out van Swieten. 'They continue to meet and have even formed reading societies, open to all. Nobody will destroy such an expansive movement.'

'Since the break between Weishaupt and von Knigge, it is cracking from the inside out,' Thamos reminded him. 'The leader of the Illuminati is an intellectual and a politician, not an initiate. By cutting himself off from all spirituality, he will dry up and become subject to the thunderbolts of power.'

This prediction shook Baron van Swieten.

'Do you fear that Josef II will change his position with regard to Freemasonry?'

'As he does not know it from the inside,' replied von Born, 'he could not have a correct view of it. I fear intervention by opportunistic Brothers whose only goal is to achieve a higher grade and exercise their miserable authority.'

'Let us not forget the loudmouths and the traitors,' advised Thamos. 'In every age and every place, the ambitious, the embittered and the disappointed attempt to destroy what they used to adore. The internal dangers are no less formidable than attacks that come from outside. However, there is no question of interrupting the process concerning the Great Magician.'

'How did he fare in his initiation?' asked the baron.

'He showed extraordinary composure and intensity. His perceptive abilities are such that he has already successfully travelled a path without being aware of it.'

'Only our Brothers recognize us as such,' von Born reminded him. 'Given Mozart's situation and personality, we shall soon pass on to the first stage.'

*Vienna, 4 January 1785*

Josef Anton felt reassured.

Furnished with a high-sounding title and an official mission, he now enjoyed the perfect cover. Devoted colleagues were carrying out the administrative tasks he supervised while pursuing his anti-Masonic crusade.

There was one tiny disadvantage: the increase in his working hours. But knowing that he was fighting a secret society that was leading the world into chaos, and working to safeguard the empire, Josef Anton forgot his tiredness.

In the silence of a snowy night, he went back to his main files and lingered over a few of them.

Ignaz von Born, Grand Secretary of the Grand Lodge of Austria and Venerable of the To True Union. Renowned mineralogist, favourable to the Illuminati of Bavaria, a true leader and the most dangerous of all the Freemasons. A perfect reputation, an exemplary life, morality in the face of every ordeal . . . A sombre picture!

Von Born must have some blameworthy aspect. Either Josef Anton would discover it, or he would invent one.

Despite his titles of palatine chamberlain and councillor, Otto von Gemmingen lacked stature. Imbued with humanism, believing in universal goodness and the improvement of society, he was the very embodiment of the naïve Freemason, the cheapjack philosopher.

Baron Tobias von Gebler appeared more complex. Passionate about the Egyptian mysteries, he had wagered on Freemasonry before detaching himself from it then coming back, wishing to make it subject to the superior authority of Josef II, in order to ensure that it endured. Worn-out and sceptical, did he himself believe that what he was doing was useful? There was nothing to fear from this old warhorse.

Wolfgang Mozart, an independent musician, one of the fashionable entertainers, a mere Apprentice . . . Why linger over such a slender file? An ordinary Freemason, in search of highly placed contacts who could help him to build a career.

Josef Anton almost classified him among the second-rate, but his instinct held him back.

Why such hesitation, since this minor artiste did not feature among the thinkers who governed Freemasonry?

His name had already appeared several times, and Anton never ignored his intuition.

Mozart therefore featured prominently among the agitators who were to be closely watched.

# 76

*Vienna, 5 January 1785*

With eyes and ears wide open, Apprentice Mozart revelled in the solemn Gathering. Seated between Ignaz de Luca, the future biographer of Josef Haydn, and the writer Johann Caspar Riesback, who criticized the poverty prevailing in Hungary, he experienced the lodge's Opening of the Works as though it were a new birth.

Above the Brothers stretched the celestial vault with its geometry of constellations, where the music of the spheres was played. However, they worked 'under cover', for the temple was hermetically sealed after the metals had been stripped away and purified. No longer dwelling in the outside world, the initiates became the crew of a communal boat, voyaging beyond the visible world.

Along the tops of the walls ran a rope, which in several places formed knots called 'lakes of love'. Focusing the celestial energy, they represented the surveying of a land rendered sacred by practising the rites, and the eternal unity of the words of light. This rope did not shackle, it liberated.

As he gazed at these symbols, Wolfgang realized that their wealth was inexhaustible.

With the other Apprentices, Wolfgang sat on the Northern column. The North, the region of the sacred space which was least well lit. Was it not necessary to search there for the secret light, the base and primary material for the Great Alchemical Work?

To the East, the Delta brought life to the lodge by making the thoughts of the Great Architect of the Universe shine forth.

For the musician, this was a vital discovery. Building a work was not about divulging one's own limited passions, but attempting to carry on the creative work of the builder of worlds, who was active at every moment. Concentrating on oneself, putting oneself constantly at the forefront and caring only about one's own personal improvement were tantamount to betraying initiation and were sure to end in an impasse.

Ritually dressed, Wolfgang was no longer just a man and an individual, but also a Brother, a unique and irreplaceable being assimilated into one of the living stones of the temple which was in a perpetual state of construction.

At the Gathering, each Brother must conduct himself in an impeccable manner. The apron reminded him of his duties as a worker, the belt kept him in a state of rectitude, and the distinctive signs of the lodge attached him to a great body, one of whose functions he became.

To the East, on the Venerable's dais, shone an eternal star.

'Brother First Overseer,' said the Venerable, 'what is the first duty of an Overseer in Lodge?'

'Venerable Master, it is to ensure that it is covered, both outside and inside.'

The External Coverer guarded the door of the temple, at risk of his own life, in order to prevent outsiders from entering. It was his task to warn his Brothers in the event of danger. As for the Internal Coverer, he checked the quality of each initiate and his ability to take part in the works.

These precautions still did not satisfy the Venerable.

'Brother Second Overseer, what is the second duty of an Overseer in Lodge?'

'Venerable Master, it is to ensure that all those who make up the assembly are Freemasons.'

'Ensure that this is so, Brothers First and Second Overseer, each on your column, and report back to me. Stand up in ranks, facing the East!'

At a blow from the Venerable's mallet, the Brothers stood up and, as the Overseers passed by, they adopted the correct posture. There were no more counts, barons or commoners, no outside age, wealth or titles, only Brothers.

With each man in his correct place, it was possible to light up the three pillars then to draw up the 'table of the lodge', featuring the elements necessary for an initiatory construction.

Thamos had insisted that, in accordance with the Egyptian tradition, they should be drawn on a pure white floor. Too many lodges were content to unroll a carpet covered with fixed signs, which removed all significance from this major moment in the Opening of the Works.

Taking part in a ritual generated such powerful energy that it banished all tiredness and cares. After the banquet, Thamos and Wolfgang went for a stroll. The sky was clear and the temperature icy cold.

'Why was I initiated so late?'

'Because you had to be ready on your side as we did on ours. Your musical precociousness was both an advantage and a handicap. You proceed so quickly that it was right to train you slowly. As for European Freemasonry, it is a fragile edifice. Many mistakes have already been made.'

'Could initiation disappear?'

'It is a radiant, transfigured form of life, which gives birth to itself constantly. A man capable of initiation is a very threatened species, without doubt on the path to extinction. Compared to the world created by the ancient Egyptians, ours, in both the East and the West, appears very mediocre to me. But we must think only of the next stage of your journey.'

Wolfgang halted. He dared not understand.

'After the Apprenticeship come the grades of Companion and Master,' explained Thamos. 'One of the major faults of present-day Freemasonry consists of rushing the progress from grade to grade. In an old lodge, you would have remained as an Apprentice for at least seven years. But your path is unique. That is why you will soon be a Companion. The teaching given at this grade will play a vital role in the way you conceive and express music.'

'Will you continue to help me?' asked Wolfgang anxiously.

'You have my word,' promised the Egyptian, embracing his young Brother.

# BIBLIOGRAPHY

Partially preserved, the letters of Wolfgang and Leopold Mozart are a mine of information which we have used widely, notably by putting words from these writings into the musician's mouth.

Several partial editions of this correspondence exist, along with one complete edition, *Mozart: Briefe und Aufzeichnungen* (ed. W. A. Bauer, O. E. Deutsch and J. H. Eibl), most of which has been translated into French by G. Geffray and published in seven volumes by Éditions Flammarion, Paris. For this second novel, see *Correspondance III, 1778–1781*; *Correspondance IV, 1782–1785*.

We have also consulted the following works:

ABERT, Hermann, *Mozart* (2 volumes), Leipzig, 1919.
ANGERMÜLLER, Rudolph, *Les Opéras de Mozart*, Milan, 1991.
AUTEXIER, Philippe A., *Mozart et Liszt sub rosa*, Poitiers, 1984.
AUTEXIER, Philippe A., *Mozart*, Paris, 1987.

AUTEXIER, Philippe A., *La Colonne d'harmonie*, Paris, 1995.

AUTEXIER, Philippe A., *La Lyre maçonne. Mozart, Haydn, Spohr, Liszt*, Paris, 1997.

*Dictionnaire Mozart*, ed. H. C. ROBBINS LANDON, Paris, 1990.

EINSTEIN, Alfred, *Mozart, son caractère, son œuvre*, Paris, 1954.

*Encyclopédie de la Franc-Maçonnerie*, Paris, 2000.

FAIVRE, Antoine, *L'Ésotérisme au xviii$^e$ siècle*, Paris, 1973.

GALTIER, Gérard, *Maçonnerie égyptienne, Rose-Croix et Néo-chevalerie*, Monaco, 1989.

GUY, Roland, *Goethe Franc-Maçon*, Paris, 1794.

HAVEN, Marc, *Rituel de la Maçonnerie égyptienne*, Paris, 1948.

HENRY, Jacques, *Mozart, Frère Maçon*, Paris, 1997.

HILDESHEIMER, Wolfgang, *Mozart*, Paris, 1979.

HOCQUARD, Jean-Victor, *Mozart*, Paris, 1994.

HOCQUARD, Jean-Victor, *Mozart, l'amour, la mort*, Paris, 1994.

LE FORESTIER, René, *La Franc-Maçonnerie templière et occultiste aux xviii$^e$ et xix$^e$ siècles*, Paris, 2000.

MASSIN, Jean and Brigitte, *Mozart*, Paris, 1970.

*Mozart*, coll. Génies et Réalités, Paris, 1985.

NETTL, P., *Mozart and Masonry*, New York, 1957.

PAHLEN, Kurt, *Das Mozart Buch*, Zurich, 1985.

ROBBINS LANDON, H. C., *Mozart, l'âge d'or de la musique à Vienne, 1781–1791*, Paris, 1989.

ROBBINS LANDON, H. C., *Mozart et les Francs-Maçons*, London and Paris, 1991.

SADIE, Stanley, *Mozart*, London, 1980.

WYZEWA, Théodore de, and SAINT-FOIX, Georges de, *W. A. Mozart. Sa vie musicale et son œuvre*, Paris, 1986.

Concerning Freemasonry we consulted the following collection: *Les Symboles maçonniques* (Maison de Vie Éditeur), published volumes:

1. *Le Grand Architecte de l'Univers.*
2. *Le Pavé mosaïque.*

**Christian Jacq**
# THE GREAT MAGICIAN

*"After 1500 years of waiting, Osiris has permitted the
Great Magician to be reborn . . . Find the Great
Magician, Thamos, protect him and enable him to
create the work which will give the world hope."*

Thamos, Count of Thebes, is one of the last
members of a spiritual brotherhood, keeping alive
the secrets of the pharaohs. Now he has been
entrusted with a vital mission. He must leave
Egypt for the cold lands of Europe to find and
protect the 'Great Magician', a genius whose
works will save humanity.

When he encounters a child prodigy, a six-year-
old composer lauded throughout Prague, Vienna
and Frankfurt, Thamos senses that he's found the
one. Is this young musician really the 'Great
Magician' foretold by Osiris, the one who can pass
on the light of the East to mankind? And if he is,
can Thamos succeed in saving the boy from the
traps that lie in wait for him?

'An author who artfully combines story with
truth' *Good Book Guide*

**ISBN 978-1-41652-661-2**

All these titles by Christian Jacq are available from your local bookshop or can be ordered direct from the publisher.

**Free post and packing within the UK**
Overseas customers please add £2 per paperback
Telephone Simon & Schuster Cash Sales at Bookpost
on 01624 677237 with your credit or debit card number
or send a cheque payable to Simon & Schuster Cash Sales to
PO Box 29, Douglas Isle of Man, IM99 1BQ
Fax: 01624 670923
E-mail: bookshop@enterprise.net
www.bookpost.co.uk

Please allow 14 days for delivery. Prices and availability are subject to
change without notice.